Among the Living

AMONG
the
LIVING

Jonathan Rabb

Other Press
New York

First softcover printing 2018
ISBN 978-1-59051-924-0

Production editor: Yvonne E. Cárdenas
Text designer: Julie Fry
This book was set in Fairfield and Bernhard Modern
by Alpha Design & Composition of Pittsfield, NH

1 3 5 7 9 10 8 6 4 2

LIBRARY OF CONGRESS CATALOGING-IN-PUBLICATION DATA

Names: Rabb, Jonathan, author.
Title: Among the living / Jonathan Rabb.
Description: New York : Other Press, [2016]
Identifiers: LCCN 2016008314 (print) | LCCN 2016014056 (ebook) |
ISBN 9781590518038 (hardcover) | ISBN 9781590518045 (ebook)
Subjects: LCSH: Jewish families—United States—Fiction. |
Man-woman relationships—Fiction. | Georgia—Social life and
customs—19th century—Fiction. | Jewish fiction. | BISAC: FICTION
/ Historical. | FICTION / Jewish. | FICTION / Literary. | GSAFD:
Historical fiction.
Classification: LCC PS3568.A215 A83 2016 (print) | LCC PS3568.A215
(ebook) | DDC 813/.54--dc23
LC record available at http://lccn.loc.gov/2016008314

For Marta, Jodi, and Edi

We said to each other things that are not said among the living.

—PRIMO LEVI, "THE JOURNEY"

PART ONE

I

YITZHAK GOLDAH pressed his sallow brow to the glass and stared out at the slowing platform. It was late summer and he felt the beads of his sweat gather like warm rain on his skin. Down a ways a small black boy walked alongside the train. He was carrying a stack of newspapers and barked out the headlines in a voice that was far too low for his frame. Goldah had read the papers in New York. He had read them in Washington, in Richmond, in Raleigh. He would read them here. They all spoke of America and of confidence, and he marveled at their certainty.

Standing there, Goldah looked perfectly human. His suit hung crisply on his frame and lent it a heft that wasn't his. He was like a sail still holding its shape even after the wind has died away. He braced himself for the train's final heave, then took his suitcase and hat and followed the line of passengers to the door. Down on the platform the smell quickly turned to coal dust and scorched metal. The cement and well-washed marble reminded him of distant places from before the war, the iron beams thick and vaulted. Goldah walked and peered ahead and waited for the first glimpse of his future.

It was there, just beyond the single chain between stanchion and gate. A man, early fifties, stood in a suit that was

3

far more forgiving of the heat than Goldah's own. The wife was younger, thicker, and with a netted hat to match the floral print of her dress. They stood without moving, like two potatoes, upright, full, misshapen, and solid.

Goldah handed the guard his ticket and nodded as if only now he had seen them. The woman raised her hands with too much enthusiasm, scurried over, and they met, all three, as Goldah placed his suitcase on the ground.

"Yitzhak?" the man said. "Yitzhak Goldah?"

"Yitzhak Goldah, yes." Goldah had learned to repeat when he could.

"Good. I'm Abe. Abe Jesler. And this is my wife, Pearl."

The man's tone was low and smooth, and his words came in a lumbering ease: This was the voice of America's South. The woman's, when she spoke, carried more breath, as if her words were meant to float atop the heat.

"We're so delighted to meet you," she said.

"You made it, then—no difficulties?"

"No difficulties. Yes."

"Good, that's good," said the man. "Not much of an accent there. I was expecting—well, we were expecting more of an accent, weren't we, Pearl? That'll serve you well."

"Yes," said Goldah.

"Well..." This seemed the perfect moment for a hand-shake or embrace but instead, the man took the suitcase. "Okay then." They began to walk. "Are there still Jeslers in Brno? My family was from Brno."

It was a moment too long before the man realized the carelessness in the question. He had spent the drive to the station telling himself to avoid such things, history and families and place. The man often spent drives talking to himself. It was instinct and careless.

4

"You're far more handsome than in your photograph," the woman said. "And younger. I wouldn't have you a day past twenty-five."

"Thirty-one," Goldah said. "This past April."

"That's right. Thirty-one in April."

They moved into the station, where an amplified voice cut through the hum of scattered conversations.

"No trouble in Richmond?" the man said. "You can have trouble in Richmond changing to the Seaboard Air Line. The tracks can be confusing."

"No. No trouble."

"Good, good. Glad to hear it."

They stopped at the door to the street. Goldah thought the woman might speak again but the man said, "It's quite a thing, isn't it, having you here."

Goldah was struck by this first breach of sentiment, cautious sentiment, and he took the woman's hand and held it. He knew it was for him to console for his past.

"Thank you," he said, "for letting me come. It's a great kindness."

The woman stared up at him before she began to cry. She quickly embraced him. Her head reached only as high as his chest, and Goldah awkwardly wrapped his long arms across her shoulders. The man, uneasy behind a smile, patted a soft hand on her back.

"Okay, Pearl honey. We're still in the train station."

Outside the air was damp with salt. Goldah had smelled the sea before but the air here was nothing so bracing. It was the smell of sodden land and untamed growth and, he thought, were he to toss a seed in the air, it might sprout even before touching the ground.

5

Up ahead, the sun caught the windscreen of a sedan, whitewall tires and an aerial for the radio, and they stopped.

"Brand new," Jesler said. "Forty-seven Ambassador with the unitized body. You know your cars, Yitzhak?" Jesler opened the trunk and placed Goldah's suitcase inside. "Twenty-eight cubic feet without the spare—that's something, isn't it?" Jesler shut the trunk and stepped around. "You come sit up front with us. Pearl'll squeeze in between. You don't mind, Pearl honey, do you?"

There was no reason to squeeze. The bench seat was plush and wide, with room enough for Jesler to point out awnings and street signs as they drove. He detailed the weather for the next week: rain with some cooling off before the mercury would shoot back up, but that was okay because it meant the gnats would be keeping out of sight, too. Jesler laughed. He liked the sound of the word "okay" and said it as if it were some kind of code, the way GIs had said it to make you feel better: "You're okay, buddy. You'll be okay."

"Johnny Becker's," Jesler continued, nodding toward a dry goods store. "And that's Levin's—everybody's worked at Levin's."

The buildings were tightly packed two- and four-story affairs with ragtag fronts and stalls that spilled out onto the paved sidewalk. Goldah noticed one that was sporting shoes, tied at the laces on long sticks and selling two pair for a dollar.

"You don't go into business in Savannah without first working for Joe Levin," said Jesler. "I had overalls then ladies' hats before the shoes. Levin taught you how to make a living. Pearl worked there weekends before we were married. You remember that, honey?"

Pearl smoothed out the lap of her dress. "I remember."

"I was going with a working girl, Yitzhak, can you imagine?" Jesler laughed and Pearl's cheeks grew red, and Goldah smiled without knowing why.

"And that's Yachum and Yachum. Funny story there, Yitzhak. You wouldn't know it, but Yachum's not the family name. The Perlman brothers own it—Hymie and Morris—but the two of them used to yak so much that everyone just started calling it Yachum and Yachum, and now there's a big sign on the door. That's pretty funny, don't you think?"

Goldah nodded and said, yes, it was a good story, he had heard stories like it before—"Who hasn't"—and the string of names continued: Lang and Max Gordon, Blumenthal and Odrezin, which was National Tailors where the *schwartzes* went for their box-back suits, but still, they do very good work, and aren't the *schwartzes* entitled to a suit the same as anyone? This was the second code, the second assurance that Goldah belonged, because here there were Jews—vital Jews—who made the city what it was, and wasn't that a comfort to know given everything else.

"You missed the turn," said Pearl.

"I didn't miss it."

"You missed the turn for the house. You're going to the store."

Jesler seemed to grip the wheel a bit tighter. "I'm just driving past."

"Yitzhak will be tired, and you're driving past the store?"

"Yes, just driving past the store. Yitzhak," he said, "I was thinking of driving past the store, but if you're not feeling up to it—"

"I'd love to see the store," said Goldah.

"He'd love to see the store. Well imagine that. Okay then."

Jesler took the turn onto a wide avenue. This had the feel of all those photographs from American magazines, the kind Yitzhak had peeled through while sitting in a white-walled sanatorium somewhere west of London, with nurses who smelled of rose water and bleach, and who never once

7

showed an excess of pity for all those dreadful things that had happened but instead very kindly—very sternly—said it was time to be on the mend, time to push on, which wasn't much good thinking about anyway, and weren't the photographs of America quite lovely? There was a Sears and a Kress and a Kaybee and streetlamps along the paved walk, where a few lines of bulbs hung high across the street. Windows showed furniture and mannequins, an entire car glistening in light blue, and Goldah watched Jesler's eyes wander to it as they drove by. Men strode with newspapers or packages tucked under an elbow while women sauntered arm in arm. Up ahead a crowd had gathered outside a store, where free neckties were being promised with the purchase of any $49 suit. Goldah noticed one woman, slender and with a child in tow, who was stepping away from the crowd, the silk of her dress brushing against her calves. He watched her and thought how the past here was young and untried, and how the world made sense only in the grasp of such promise and abundance.

"It's up here," Jesler said as he slowed the car. "Friedman Jewelers, Harris the Hub, and us, with the big blue awning."

The *h* of Jesler Shoes had gone slightly askew on the sign above the door, and an older black man stood at the base of a ladder, while a younger one was perched at the top trying to realign it.

"I don't want to stop, Abe," Pearl said. "Just nod to the boys and let's keep driving."

Jesler had been planning on more but knew it was best to keep them moving along. He slowed and leaned his head out the window.

"Looks like we're making good progress there, Calvin. We need it by tonight."

The older man, gray hair and overalls, quickly took off his soft cap and started toward the car. When he realized it wasn't going to stop, he nodded and raised a hand. "Yes, suh, Mr. Jesler. Have it done by tonight."

Jesler waved back. "They're good boys there, Yitzhak."

He took the next turn, where the stores and shops quickly gave way to a street lined with houses. Staircases and railed balconies huddled under a dense canopy of tree limbs and hanging moss. The heat remained, but it seemed somehow tamed here, as if the air could breathe more fully hidden away like this.

Jesler drove them around a square with a small park at its center, benches and hedges along the sides, and the ease of the afternoon written in the drowsy gait of the few who were walking through. If Goldah had forgotten the depths of his own exhaustion, he imagined this might be the gentlest reminder of it.

"We do mostly American," said Jesler, "but I also sell the Ferragamos. That's Italian. Very high-end. They're doing something with a sandal this year. Invisible they call it. Been in all the magazines. You ask me, it looks like a heel with a suspension bridge made out of nylon on the top, but I display it so we'll have people coming by and taking a look." He glanced over at Pearl. "You want some invisible shoes, honey?"

"If I can pay for them with my invisible money, why not?"

Jesler laughed and Pearl laughed and Jesler cleared his throat. It was only a moment but Goldah saw Jesler sharpen his gaze. Pearl's smile also disappeared as if she knew full well what her husband was going to say.

"We were thinking," Jesler said with a newfound weight in his voice, "and of course this would be entirely up to you, Yitzhak—what with everything that folks are beginning to

9

know about what was going on during the war, you know, all of that can be difficult to understand, painful even...more so for you—naturally for you—I wouldn't mean to imply or make light of...You understand what I'm saying. It's just that we don't want you to feel outside of things, or for folks not to know how to make it easier to invite you in, make you feel a part of the community."

"What Abe is saying," Pearl piped up, "is that it's such a different kind of name—Yitzhak. We just don't hear it all that often, even in shul. Hardly ever, really. You see it's Isaac there and we were thinking maybe it would be better if you had something more familiar, something that would be more inviting—"

"Easier," said Jesler.

"Yes, I said that, Abe."

"I know you did. I just think Yitzhak needed to understand that it's not that we don't care for the name."

"No, of course not, that's not the case at all."

"Or that we'd be forcing him to do this in any way."

"No. Nothing like that. He understands that, Abe. You understand that, Yitzhak."

Jesler said, "It's just more about...protecting—"

"*Yes*," said Pearl with no small amount of relief. "Protecting. That's a *very* good way of thinking about it. As Abe said, Yitzhak, it's a way of protecting."

"And making things easier."

"Easier," said Goldah. It was such a simple, desperate word. "I can see that, yes."

"Of course you can," said Jesler. "Good man. You'll see it'll make a world of difference. Especially when you'll be wanting to make a name for yourself."

Goldah noticed a group of children in a park with sticks and a small rubber ball that was cut in two. They were laughing.

"What did you have in mind?" he said as he continued to watch the children. "Isaac then?"

"Well…" Jesler rubbed the back of his hand along the soft flesh of his throat and Goldah was drawn by the sound of the stubble against Jesler's rough knuckles. "It's a possibility, certainly a possibility."

"We thought about Izzy or Iz," Pearl said, "but Isadore Rabinowicz—that's the treasurer of the shul—he goes by Izzy, and Isher Laski is Iz as well."

"'Is Iz,'" Jesler repeated with a quiet laugh. "That's always been funny to me: Is Iz. 'Is Iz coming to the store?' 'Is Iz at home, Mrs. Laski?' Is Iz. What do you do with that?"

"He went to Chapel Hill on a music scholarship," said Pearl, "so I'm thinking it worked out just fine for him. Now, we were thinking of something—"

"Ike," said Jesler. "Ike Goldah. That's good and strong."

Goldah realized the name had been in the car with them all along. "Ike," he said.

"Yes," said Pearl. "Ike Goldah." She was masking her disappointment at having had her husband say it first. "Like the general. That has a *very* good sound to it, don't you think?"

"Strong," said Jesler.

"Very strong," said Pearl.

"And familiar," said Jesler.

Goldah said, "Like the general."

"*Yes*," said Pearl. "Like the general."

Goldah thought he might wait until they arrived at the house to agree, but Jesler and his wife seemed so eager to have it all taken care of. "Squared away," a GI had put it. "Get things squared away."

"Well," said Goldah, "Ike it is."

Jesler tapped his hand on Pearl's knee, and Pearl smiled and took hold of Goldah's hand. "That's just fine, then," she said. "Just fine."

Jesler held out his hand across his wife, and tried to keep his eyes on the road. "Well, glad to meet you, Ike Goldah."

Goldah let go of Pearl's hand and took Jesler's. They shook firmly.

"Yes," said Goldah. "Glad to meet you."

———

Pearl insisted on a short detour. She had forgotten flowers — it simply couldn't be helped. She said her boys could wait in the car. It was an uncomfortable few minutes until Jesler remembered the scrap of paper in his pocket. With all the preparations for Goldah's arrival, he'd let it slip his mind completely. Jesler checked his watch. It was nearly two. He'd told Jimmy he'd get back to him no later than one thirty.

"I've got to make a quick call," Jesler said as he took his hat. "Just a few minutes. You don't mind do you?"

He was already out the door and heading across the street before Goldah could answer. Inside the Texaco station, Jesler found the booth free, pulled out the scrap, and dialed the number. A woman picked up. She sounded tired, irritated. Half a minute later, a man came on the line: "Jimmy, here."

"It's Jesler."

"Hey, Abe. I was just about to give up on you."

"You said by two," said Jesler. "It's not even quarter of." He tried not to breathe through the silence.

"Sure . . . I was just thinking you might be having second thoughts this time around."

"Hardly," said Jesler.

"Good. New shipment comes in tonight."

"I thought it was tomorrow."

"Well, one a.m. *is* technically tomorrow but I call it tonight. Either way, that's when it's docking. If you're coming, you'll need two boys with you."

"I know the drill."

"'Know the drill.'" Jesler heard the snort before Jimmy said, "It's funny but you don't sound like a Jew."

"And that's good?"

The snort became a full-fledged laugh. "So how much of a markup you getting on all this?"

Jesler heard another voice in the background. It became muffled: Jimmy was holding the receiver to his chest. It gave Jesler time to think, but thinking was the problem, wasn't it? Thinking left you staring up in the middle of the night at added shelf space and distribution fees and exclusivity agreements and a wife who insisted that this was how one was meant to live. So why not just cut to it? Why not fill those shelves when the opportunity presented itself? The Italians were getting their money; he was getting his shoes. And Jimmy—Jimmy just needed him there tonight.

"You come in the back gate," Jimmy said. "Like last time. Two envelopes, two boys. One a.m. Don't be late this time."

"No," said Jesler. "I won't."

————

Jesler pulled up to the curb rather than into the drive. He and Pearl had discussed this earlier: better to have Yitzhak see the house from a distance this first time. A sign was strung across the portico in papered letters that read, "Welcome! Welcome! Welcome!" Beneath it, a wraparound porch sported two rocking chairs and a swing that hung idly from a chain. The lawn spread out in a wide swath of deep green grass—peppered by a few mounds of dirt and sand—and was cut in two by a stone walk that sprouted small tufts of weeds and dandelions on either side.

Goldah stepped from the car and offered his hand to Pearl. She had told Jesler not to say a word so that Yitzhak could take it all in for himself.

"Three thousand square feet," said Jesler. "Not bad on Thirty-Sixth Street."

Pearl took hold of Goldah's arm and walked with him along the path. She seemed to breathe more deeply as she stared up at the old Victorian, sky-blue and white trim. It was a far cry from the shack they had lived in when they were first married, down by the river, with the Greeks and the blacks and the smell of human smallness buried in the bleached clothes and too-sweet wine of a Friday night. Abe had made her a promise back then—a house on Thirty-Sixth. There had been other promises but those hadn't been his to make.

She mounted the steps and, on the porch, she laughed and cried and, in a flourish, reached for Goldah's arms and pressed her head to his chest.

"Such a joy," she said. She pulled a handkerchief from her purse and looked down at Jesler, who was nearing the steps. "Look who's here, Abe. Look who's standing on our porch."

She laughed and her eyes filled. There was a moment when all three thought she might grab for Goldah again, but instead she lifted both her hands into the air and turned to the door. "Such a joy."

Jesler joined Goldah on the porch. "Always a lot of emotion with a woman. She'll be all right."

Pearl's voice echoed from the front hall. "Mary Royal! We're back from the station. Mr. Ike is in from the station."

Jesler said, "Don't feel you have to give in to it. We're here to get you on your feet, so don't think we're expecting anything more of you."

Goldah had no idea what Jesler was talking about except that maybe Jesler needed to hear this for himself.

Inside Goldah smelled something familiar, a roast, but it was sharper in the nose with a sweetness that seemed out of place. He couldn't recall the last time he had eaten a meal prepared just for him.

Jesler led him into the front parlor—settee, chairs, lamps, and some cushioning by the window. Goldah noticed small silver cups filled with nuts and raisins perched about. Jesler pawed a fistful from one and popped a few into his mouth.

"Don't eat the nuts, Abe!" Pearl shouted from another room. "They're for the company. If Yitzhak—if Ike wants some, tell him he's more than welcome."

Jesler popped a few more into his mouth. "Like a drink?"

Pearl shouted, "Offer him a drink, Abe. Mary Royal's made a nice lemonade and we have tea. Don't start in on the hard liquor. Ask him if he drinks hard liquor."

Abe shouted back, "He's right here, Pearl. He's hearing everything you're saying."

"Just ask him if he wants something. I'll be right out. Don't make such a to-do."

Jesler tried a smile. "I guess there's lemonade or tea if you want some. She'll be right in."

"Could I use the toilet?"

Jesler's smile faded. He looked as if he had made a terrible mistake, as if somehow he had missed the most obvious question.

"The toilet," he said. "Of course. Yes . . . of course. It's right through here. We've got two more upstairs if that'd be better. Would you be needing anything from your bag?"

Evidently Jesler and his wife had been told about Goldah's recent medical trouble: the requisite letters exchanged between government offices, health departments, all the warnings about "mental and physical difficulties" to be expected.

Goldah's kidneys had been in fine working order for the past three months but why tell the Jeslers that? No need for a follow-up letter, especially when the news was good. Let them prepare for the worst.

"No, I don't need anything," Goldah said. "Thank you. Just through here?"

Inside the bathroom, Goldah turned on the light and shut the door. He heard Jesler move quickly past, whispering, "He's gone into the bathroom. He's using the *bathroom*."

The sink sat in front of a mirror and Goldah turned on the water. He brought two palmfuls up to his face and felt the roughness of his cheeks, the heat still in them. He let the water drip through his fingers as the tap ran, unsure if he was meant to take the soap—a light pink in the shape of a small flower—but brought it up to his nose nonetheless. Roses. Working it in his hands he barely mustered a lather. He washed it off and rinsed the little plate it sat on before setting it back down. All the while he kept his eyes from the mirror. He knew the face, knew the expression. Why bother with that? Instead he looked at his nails. He was finding them strangely compelling these days. They were cut and white and seemed even more foreign to him than the face. He turned out the light and opened the door.

"We're in here," Pearl said from the parlor. "Was everything all right? Do you need something from your bag?"

Jesler was sitting with Pearl on the settee. A young black woman stood by the window in a calf-length dress and maid's apron.

"No, thank you," said Goldah. "Everything is fine."

"Mary Royal," Pearl said, "this is Mr. Ike Goldah. Ike, this is Mary Royal. She's been with us nearly three years."

"Afternoon, Mr. Ike."

Mary Royal had soft features with slim fingers that held a pitcher of dark, dark liquid.

"She's brought in the tea, and we have some pie I thought would be nice for you. People won't be coming until after eight, but that's still a few hours off and I want you to have an appetite. I thought pie would be good to tide you over."

Jesler and Pearl already had their plates on their laps. There was a third on the coffee table and Goldah stepped across to a chair.

"Mary Royal makes an excellent tea," said Pearl. "Would you care for some?"

"Thank you. Yes."

"She makes it with a little mint. That's the secret."

Jesler said, "Not a secret now." He was eager to get to his pie but was doing what he had been told.

Pearl said, "I said he was a handsome man, Mary Royal. Isn't he handsome?"

"He's a grown man," Jesler said with more edge than perhaps he intended.

"Yes, Miss Pearl. A handsome man."

Goldah took a sip from his glass. He did his best not to wince. He wondered why they called this tea. "It's very nice," he said and set the glass down.

"The bathroom was all right?" Jesler said. If he couldn't have his pie, he wanted information.

Goldah said, "Your soap looks like a rose."

"Specialty company in Atlanta," said Jesler. "They also do cars, stars, and shells, if that's what you like. They know how to run a business, I can tell you that."

"I tried the shells," said Pearl, "but I think I prefer the rosebuds."

Goldah realized they were waiting for him. He picked up his fork and sliced into the pie. "They're very pretty." He ate.

Jesler spoke through a mouthful. "She won't let you in on the secret, but let me just say we go through a lot of honey this time of year."

"Abe!" said Pearl.

Mary Royal stayed by the window and Goldah found it remarkable that she could stand so still with the pitcher and show almost nothing in her face. It seemed effortless, unconsidered, yet perfectly in control, and he envied her for it. He imagined she was no more than twenty.

"It's the crust," said Jesler. "Even I don't know what makes it this good."

"And you won't—will he, Mary Royal?"

"That's our secret, Mr. Abe."

Jesler took another healthy forkful. "You stick to that. You like apple pie, Ike?"

To his surprise, Goldah did. He had worked his way back to food, real food, with taste and texture and heat, and while his stomach had learned to reaccommodate it, the rest of him was having more difficulty. There were any number of reasons for it—obvious reasons such as memory and shame—but the simplest was that to savor a plate was to recognize his own worth and that was something not so easily restored.

"It's very nice."

"You probably grew up on strudel," said Pearl. "I thought about making you one, but this seemed more...I don't know...welcoming. Does it feel more welcoming?"

"Much more welcoming," said Goldah.

"Good. That's good." She took Jesler's empty plate and handed him hers, still with her untouched piece on it. "When you're done, I'll show you to your room and you can have a little lie-down before the company comes. That's all right that we asked a few people over tonight, isn't it? Everyone was just so eager to meet you."

Goldah wondered if there was a word in English to describe the exhaustion he now felt.

"Of course," he said.

"Good. Good. Would you like some more tea? Mary Royal, leave the pitcher in case Mr. Ike wants some more tea." She stood. "Don't you get up. Just enjoy that pie and drink your tea, and when you're ready you shout for me and I'll come and show you to your room. And don't you give Abe your piece. If you want another, you call for Mary Royal. We'll be in the kitchen."

Jesler was focused on his plate as Pearl moved toward the door. She stopped at Goldah's chair and kissed him on the top of his head.

"Eat your pie," she said and headed out. Mary Royal set the pitcher on the table and followed, while Jesler was busy running the back of his fork over what was left of his crust.

"She'll do that," he said, "dote on you, like you were a little boy." He stopped the fork and his eyes grew narrower as if he had just felt a small pain at the back of his head. "You don't tell Pearl I said that. It wouldn't do her good to hear it. Okay?"

———

Upstairs, Jesler set the suitcase inside the door while Pearl turned on a lamp and moved to the drapes at the window.

"Best to keep them closed when you can," she said. "This room gets far too much sun and just bakes you like an oven if you're not careful."

Goldah watched as her entire body seemed to stiffen. Her face grew paler.

"Oh my God," she whispered. Tears formed in her eyes. "I didn't mean to say that. I didn't mean that. That's a terrible thing. I'm so sorry."

Goldah answered gently, "You said nothing." He wondered how many ways he had learned to numb himself to this. "This is a hot room. I leave the drapes closed when I'm not here. Very simple."

Jesler seemed momentarily at a loss.

Goldah added, "And you've given me a blotter and pen on the desk. How very kind."

The silence was worse than the heat until Jesler said, "A Montblanc. If you want to do some writing. And that's another lamp." He turned it on. "Plenty of light even if you keep the curtains closed." He pointed to the bureau where a porcelain basin sat with a cloth draped across it. "A damp towel at night can do wonders. Mary Royal changes the water every day." He tried to find something else in the room to talk about but found only Pearl. Her eyes had glazed over.

"Well," said Jesler, "we'll leave you to it then. Have a little lie-down or just take it easy." He gently took Pearl by the arm. "Come on, honey. I'll help you with the..." He lost the thought. "Got to have something they need me for in that kitchen, don't they, Yitzhak?" He caught himself. "Ike. I mean Ike. Ike Goldah. I'm the one who came up with it, and here I am...Anyway. Okay then."

Jesler moved Pearl to the door. As they passed, she placed a hand on Goldah's arm and Jesler let her stand there.

"She'll be fine," said Jesler. "It just comes over her sometimes. I'll call you when it's time to come down. Maybe we'll have a little talk." He turned to Pearl and said quietly, "All right, honey. Ike's here and we couldn't be happier."

Jesler led her out of the room and pulled the door closed behind them.

Goldah waited until he heard them on the steps and then turned off the lamps. He pressed his palms down onto the bed. The mattress was thick and gave with the springs. He sat down and placed his hand on the pillow. It was cool and crisp, and he leaned his shoulder down until his cheek was resting on it. The cloth creased against his skin and, keeping his shoes on, he brought his feet up, drew his knees into his chest and placed his hands under the pillow. He stared across at the fan and tried to feel its air blow over him.

He would lie like this, he thought, with a solitude he could barely recall, and know it would ask more of him than he could ever give.

———

Goldah dreams, the same dream he has had for the past three years.

It never varies, the sound of a train whistle, then another, then the first again, and his brother is sitting across from him. They are at a table under a tree, water nearby, and a small glade where Goldah remembers holding a girl by the arms for the first time. A kiss, the redness in her face, the heat in his. Others sit beyond them, eating and laughing and listening to him tell of the hunger and the filth and the beatings from the Kapos. A wonderful feeling to be at home at last, with so many he knows and with so much to tell. And Goldah speaks and they listen until they are no longer listening because they have turned away to talk among themselves—words he cannot fully hear, things he cannot understand—and his brother looks at him as if he does not know him. His brother stands to go and Goldah is left to sit and to watch and to feel the heat through the leaves, and he wonders if he has ever left the camp except in this dream.

He remembers the first time he recounted it to Pasco, an Italian Jew, small, who shared the wooden bunk with him and who spoke German. Pasco who taught him the most important thing—that shoes are life, that shoes are food, that swollen feet are only for the dead—and who explained that they all have this dream. All? Yes all. The exact same? Exact—what is exact? There is family and friends and listening and then no more listening, and grief because they have forgotten you or never knew you at all. That is enough. And when Goldah asks how it is that so many different minds can find this one dream, Pasco says it is a kind of gift, something owned and hidden away in the night where not even a Kapo can find it and take it. This is mine, he says, this is ours, this is what we share, but Goldah, even then, finds it strange to cling to such despair, even hidden despair, as the only promise of life. What gift is that? For him they share it only so that they can know its truth; they share it so that they can each recount it … one day, one day, one day.

———

Jesler sat with a whiskey held just below the lip of his desk. The light behind him had slipped in through the blinds, almost by accident.

The study was an affectation, but Pearl said men of a certain standing required one. The real paperwork was down at the store. Even so, Jesler kept a few outdated files scattered across the desk, just enough to have her think he was putting the place to good use. He heard her in the hall and set the half-full glass in the bottom drawer.

She said, "He's asleep."

She was leaning her shoulder against the jamb and, for a moment, Jesler recalled something almost carefree in her face.

"Feeling better?" he asked.

"Ike's asleep."

"Is he?"

"I looked in. With his shoes on, poor dear."

"I'm not sure you should be looking in on him when he's sleeping, do you, honey?"

Her head tilted against the jamb. "He has a funny sort of walk, did you notice that?"

"I hadn't," said Jesler, "no."

"In the station and out to the car. Long strides with a little hitch."

"He's a tall fellow."

"You don't think—"

"No, Pearl, I think he's just fine."

She gave a weak smile. "We need to look after him, Abe."

"We are."

"I mean really look after him."

"He's a grown man."

"You keep saying that."

He heard the accusation. "Did you take a Bayer? Headache all gone?"

"The house feels full, doesn't it? Already. As if it was meant to be, him coming."

Jesler knew to tread lightly. "I'm not sure he'd see it that way, honey."

Pearl's eyes wandered, her voice with them. "It was a terrible thing I said, wasn't it? I should never have even thought it."

"We're all thinking it," said Jesler, drawing her back in. "Can't be helped at the start. We'll get better. Oh, by the way,

I was thinking, if Ike doesn't want to come and work with me down at the store—"

Pearl straightened herself up. "What does that mean?" she said sharply. "You said he'd be working with you."

"I know."

"You said it. I thought we agreed on this."

"We did. Don't get so het up. He'll come work at the store, but if it's not what he wants—"

"How can he know what he wants? We talked about this, Abe. That's for us to help him with. And especially with the expansion."

Jesler said slowly, "Pearl, honey, I don't want to talk about that."

"But you said it's all set out."

"I said—" Jesler stopped himself. "That's not for you to worry about, okay? How's your head?"

"Fine, Abe, fine. But you know I wanted to have a party for it. Your announcement—and then Ike here. What a chance it would have been for tonight—introducing Ike and telling everyone how he's going to be a big part of the store's expansion. Don't you see how nice that would have been for me? The whole day would have been different."

"I do—I do see that."

"You weren't always like this, you know, keeping everything so close to the chest, and taking me along with you."

"I know. I'm a mean and terrible man."

"Oh, stop. But joys don't come along all that often, and you know it."

"I do—except sometimes it's best to wait on them, don't you think?"

He saw the sudden coldness in her expression and thought she might lash out—buried pain has such a refined capacity

24

for cruelty—but instead she said, "Well anyway, it'll give us a chance to celebrate twice. Once for Ike tonight. And once when you let me tell the whole world about the expansion. So there." She flipped her wrist with too much youth and Jesler gave her a bright fake smile.

He said, "And there you are."

"Yes, there I am. Mary Royal!" she shouted. "The meatballs should be done." She pointed a finger at him. "So. There."

Pearl blew him a kiss and moved along. Jesler retrieved his glass from the drawer and toasted to his latest reprieve.

———

"Ike?"

Goldah heard the knocking. It grew stronger and he checked for his shoes. He pushed himself up and dropped his feet to the floor. Beyond the knocking was the low hum of voices, laughter, glasses tinkling. There was a sudden swell of light that passed across the wall and he stood and pulled back the drape to see a line of cars along the street. He tasted the sleep in his mouth and ran his hand across his face.

The door creaked open and Jesler's head emerged into the room.

"Ike?"

The light from the hallway angled across his bed. "I'm here," said Goldah.

"Oh, yes. There you are. Good. Pearl thought it'd be best if we let you sleep. She's set everything out for you in the bathroom. Tooth cream, toothbrush, razor, comb, towels, that sort of thing. If you need a shirt, there's one of mine laid out. Shouldn't be too bad under the jacket. There's a tie or two as well."

"Thank you."

25

"Take your time. People are still arriving. You'll get to make a grand entrance. How about that?"

"Yes. Thank you."

Jesler looked as if he might go; instead, he stepped farther into the room.

"Just so you know"—Jesler spoke to explain or to apologize, Goldah couldn't tell which—"most of the folks coming tonight are in business like me. They'll probably want to talk to you about the kind of work they do, maybe the kind of work you were doing. You were in newspapers before the war, weren't you?"

"I was, yes."

"Well there, you see . . . that's something they'll be interested in. And they're going to want to help you fit in, maybe talk about opportunities, I don't know, so if it gets too much and you're feeling out of sorts, you just come and find me. Pearl's not too good at knowing when things can get a bit much. Then again if something *does* interest you, well that's okay, too. That'd be great. So you just let me know. Okay?"

Goldah nodded and Jesler nodded, perhaps expecting more. Jesler said, "All right, then. I'll see you down there."

He closed the door behind him and Goldah waited for his eyes to find the lamp. He stepped over and turned it on and winced at the light. The room was still so hot and all he felt was that he had never known sleep, only this exhaustion. Why not give him this first night, he thought. Why not that? It was the first and only self-pity he had allowed.

Five minutes later Goldah noticed how the shirt was too big in the chest. Pulled back, it was still better than the wrinkles and stench of his own. The tie was wide and he put some water in his hair to give it a shine. His face smelled of mint from shaving.

He tried to empty his mind as he stood at the top of the stairs. It was always best to come at these things without something to say: so much anticipated of him, as if he were only waiting for the opportunity to unburden himself. To see them all thinking, "I understand what it is you've lived through"—if only there wasn't such a desperate longing in each of them to run. What a bind to put themselves in, the moral weight of it all, to be brave and consoling even as they felt nothing but pity and revulsion. Was it wrong to be revolted by a man like this? Did his story forgive them that? Wouldn't he forgive them that? Didn't they deserve to be forgiven?

A few words of conversation rose up and Goldah followed them down the stairs. He smelled the cigarettes and the sour breath of whiskey in the air. A phonograph played something jaunty, and he heard the rough laughter of men who needed their laughter to be heard, the sound of women underneath.

He reached the last step and at once saw Pearl making her way toward him.

"At last!" she said maneuvering through and raising her hands. "Here he is everyone! Here he is." She drew up next to him and placed her arm around his waist. "Everyone! Everyone! Arthur Goldberg, if I have to raise my voice one more decibel just because you can't hush up...Thank you. Now." She gathered herself. "Here he is. This is Abe's cousin, Mr. Ike Goldah. *Our* Ike Goldah. He goes by Ike. That's what he likes, and he's had a very long day, but he's been kind enough to let us fete him for the night—his first night with us here in Savannah—so we'll have something to eat, you all will get a chance to make your introductions, and then you will have to go because I can't imagine how tired the poor boy must be. Did you get all that Arthur Goldberg? Good."

Goldah passed through the first brave nods and hand-shakes and realized that Pearl would be keeping her arm around his waist for the remainder of the evening. They were conjoined, hers to parade, his to be protected.

Jesler appeared with a glass—"Lemonade, Ike. Liquor won't do you too well tonight, I don't think"—and then he was gone.

Goldah drank and followed and listened. There was a pair of women, seemingly indistinguishable, who told him that he reminded them of their late husbands—much younger, of course—both in the clothing business, *still* in the clothing business, and they'd make sure he had some nice new sports jackets, suits, things like that. Another introduced her daughter on three separate occasions, the girl slim and sleeveless in white gloves, a teal blue variation on the greens and blacks that hugged or swayed just below the knees with shoes that seemed almost too painful to wear. "This is the King Cole Trio," a woman with crimson lips told him. Nat King Cole, a Negro, and, yes, she preferred him, "better than Sinatra and Como, and there I've said it!" The lemonade became water then lemonade again, everyone else high on bourbon, rye, and gin, while Goldah, returning from the bathroom, settled into a conversation with a man named Champ who said Goldah needed a car—a man *had* to have a car—and Champ, gen-erous to a fault, said he'd give him one, not a new one, of course, but something down on the lot because that's just what we do in Savannah. And on his last go-round with the girl in teal, Goldah asked if she had a cigarette and discovered she was sixteen.

Through it all, Mary Royal moved in and out of the kitchen. She was joined by three other servers, two young women and a boy no more than thirteen. The boy looked surprisingly at ease in his white waiter's coat, and Goldah smelled a cigarette on him when he returned from the carport with another few bottles of something. A cigarette would have been nice, he thought.

"I've got them right here," said the mother of the teal dress, searching her purse. "I know I do."

"No, it's fine," said Goldah. "I don't really want one."

"Right in here, unless you don't smoke Dunhills?"

"I'm all right. Thank you."

Pearl said, "He said he's all right, Ethel."

"They say it's a lady's cigarette," the woman went on, "but I don't see what the difference is, except maybe the shape."

"*Ethel*," said Pearl, "this boy needs some more meatballs," and without waiting for an answer, she started him toward the dining room and the hors d'oeuvres. Out of earshot she said, "I'm not sure I'd let my sixteen-year-old daughter dress quite so enchantingly as that." Hands raised, smiles, "Yes, hi there, Jeannie...No he's starving and we've got to get some food inside him...Yes, Champ was wonderful...Yes...We'll bring him by this week," and through the door.

An ancient man was moving off from the chopped liver while another stood in the corner examining a spice box he had taken from a glassed-in display case. Candlesticks, silver wine cups, menorahs. He was wearing a *kippah* and his back was to them.

"It's usually sit-down dinners for us," Pearl said, as she took a plate for Goldah, "and just me and Mary Royal, but there were too many people who wanted to come. This is all very cha-cha-cha for us, to have it this way, but I think it sets the mood for you, coming from Europe and all." There was now a nice mound of meatballs in sauce next to some crusted pota-toes and a healthy pile of crudités. "I'm sure someone will say it's the *goyishe* way to entertain—and maybe it is—but there really wasn't any other choice. We'll have a dinner next week sometime when it's just close friends. Hello there, Rabbi."

The man with the spice box turned. He looked at them with a well-rehearsed gaze of piety.

"Good evening, Mrs. Jesler," he said. "Always such a lovely home. And this must be Mr. Goldah." Goldah expected an extended hand, but the rabbi simply nodded deeply. Unsure, Goldah did the same.

The rabbi held up the spice box. "It's a beautiful piece. Have you seen it, Mr. Goldah? The craftsmanship is really quite remarkable."

Pearl said, "As I said earlier, Rabbi, Mr. Goldah has only just arrived this afternoon, so he hasn't had time for the full tour."

"I've just come myself," said the rabbi, "so I must have missed the introductions."

"Yes, you must have."

Again the rabbi held the box up to Goldah and pointed to the lettering. "Do you see the inscription, Mr. Goldah? You read Hebrew?"

"I do, yes."

"Of course you do. Do you see the letter, gimmel, there?"

"Yes," said Goldah. "It's in the wrong place."

"'The wrong place.'" The rabbi seemed particularly pleased at this. "That's right. Exactly right. The gimmel is in the wrong place. And do you know why the gimmel is in the wrong place?"

Pearl said, "I'm sure you're going to tell us, Rabbi."

"It's in the wrong place—and you may know this already, Mr. Goldah—because Jews weren't permitted to be gold-smiths or silversmiths. They weren't permitted to be members of the guilds, and so it was the non-Jews who did the craftsmanship. You see? The non-Jews got it wrong because they, unlike you and I, did not read Hebrew. Did you know that, Mr. Goldah?"

With no thought behind the words, Goldah answered, "No, I didn't. Fascinating."

"Your husband bought it for you in New York, Mrs. Jesler. On one of his trips?

"Yes, Rabbi," said Pearl, "that's right."

"As I said, a wonderful piece." The rabbi continued to stare at the silver. "You, of course, have firsthand experience of such injustice, Mr. Goldah. Far more terrible injustice, of course. I can't imagine what it is to carry that with you. But if you should ever want to sit and to talk—"

"Thank you," Goldah said with great restraint. "You'll excuse me. I need"—there were so many things he needed at this moment—"I'd like to get some air."

Goldah started to go and the rabbi held his arm.

"Know that you are among Jews again, Mr. Goldah. Jews who are alive and who are living."

Goldah felt the weathered hand on his sleeve and with it the taste of his own quiet rage. What was it, Goldah wondered, that was so appealing in the living? What was it he was meant to reclaim? Rage and despair, indignation and longing? There had been none of these in the camps because there had been nowhere to hold them. Such things were kept safe only in the pockets of the living.

"Yes," said Goldah. "Comforting to know." He drew his arm away. "But I really do need some air. You'll excuse me."

He chose not to see Pearl's reaction as he stepped alone into the hall. There was a narrow path to the front door and Goldah kept his eyes low as he sidestepped the swaying hands filled with glasses and cigarettes. At the screen door he heard

Jesler's voice out on the porch. Goldah placed his hand on the door to step through but stopped when he heard Jesler speak.

"I mean it's understandable," Jesler said. "We've all seen the films. The camps. But then you take that and put it in your home, that's just—"

"It's queer," another man's voice said. "I agree with you. Absolutely queer. Fannie had to get up from the theater. Up in New York. We saw it in the newsreel and she just had to get up. I can't say I wasn't happy to go with her."

"But he doesn't look it, does he?" said Jesler. "I mean, you wouldn't know it to look at him?"

Goldah brought his hand down and continued to listen.

"Of course not. The man looks fine, Abe. It'll just take some getting used to, that's all."

"That's right. Getting used to. It'll be fine," said Jesler.

"He's a grown man. He'll want his own place sooner than later. Make his own way."

"Exactly. That's exactly right. It's what I've been thinking all along. But you know Pearl. She might not want to hear it. A man like that, and her . . . well, you know. But he's a grown man, after all."

"He is. No question."

"Show him the ropes. Let him see what fits."

"Absolutely, Abe. No question. And he's a good-looking fella, too. A bachelor. Think of the time he'll have. Can't say I don't envy him."

"I'll be sure to tell Fannie that."

"You *do* tell her that. You go right ahead. Let her know I might get myself footloose and fancy-free."

They laughed and Goldah was suddenly thirsty.

"There you are!" said the mother of the teal dress. Goldah turned. She was holding a plate of food and a tall glass, with her daughter in tow. "I saw you run off before getting your plate, so here I am. And a glass of bourbon."

Goldah found himself unable to move. He let her hand him the plate and the glass, and he drank.

———

At just after midnight, Jesler left the house in stocking feet. He felt the damp in his heels as he slid into the car, fumbled with his shoes, and kept the lights off until he had taken the first turn. This time of night, the heat carried the smell of wildflowers and exhaust, which was strange as there didn't seem to be a single other car on the road.

Up on West Broad, he glanced at the few lights that dotted the floors above the darkened shops. He remembered how Ed Cranman had just bought a building a few months back and was now burning the midnight oil to get the place in shape. Sporting goods, that was the dream. But Ed was smart. He was starting with a pawnshop. Put some money aside. That's the way to do it, Jesler thought.

He avoided the train station and took the car west into Hudson Hill. The paved road gave way to dirt and rubble, the smell of sewage and drying mud heavy among the line of row houses. On occasion a streetlamp brought a few of the tumbledown shacks into view, but most of the time the roads stayed dark.

Several turns in, Jesler pulled over and a figure emerged from behind a telephone pole. The passenger door opened and the soft-capped older black man from this afternoon ducked in. Neither said a word as Jesler took the car out. Twenty minutes on he cut the beams; he had driven them well beyond the last of the houses. In the distance a series of tall lights began to appear, over a hundred feet high, which served as a beacon to guide them through the pitch-black of the untamed fields. It was track road, with sudden dips and jolts, but Jesler felt comfortable enough easing the car along: not exactly the place to find a small wooden booth with a single bulb inside, but there it was, standing in front of a wire fence that stretched into the darkness.

Jesler brought the car to a stop and reached across to the glove compartment as a man stepped out from the booth. The man held a flashlight and raised it at the car.

Jesler said, "How's it going tonight?" He took out an envelope before straightening himself up.

The man let the beam drop and leaned into the window. He was broad in his uniform, a wide face the color of hay, with a gun holstered at his belt, and a Georgia Ports Authority badge affixed to the center of his hat.

"You got a call tonight?" the man asked.

Jesler handed him the envelope. "That's for you and Dickie up the other side."

The man stuffed the envelope into his jacket pocket and peered deeper into the car. "Riding up front tonight, are you, Calvin?" The man did his best with a loose smile.

"Raymond'll be coming up," said Jesler. "You let him through."

The smile dropped and the man pulled himself back. "All right then."

Beyond the padlocked gate, the track road continued like a strip of taut yarn along the side of a long, narrow building. Jesler drove slowly. Somewhere ahead the sound of diesel and steam engines began to roar.

He took the turn at the end of the track, and the windshield was suddenly filled with a bright white light. Beyond it, an expanse of paved ground led across to the docks where eighty-foot cranes stood at intervals, some idle, others carrying roped bundles from the two large merchant ships that had been tied off. Warehouses and workshops lined the edges, all quiet save for this particular stretch, where fifteen men maneuvered push wagons and open-back trucks in and among the growing pyramid of crates.

Jesler drove slowly past the lights and into the shadows. The sound of the diesels dulled and, a hundred yards in, he cut his own engine and let the car coast to a stop. Leaning across, he pulled a second envelope from the glove compartment before turning to open the door.

"You go get the wagon," he said.

Calvin headed off and Jesler locked the car.

The buildings were identical here, tall flat warehouse fronts with a single door at the side. Jesler came to one where the front was open, still no light, but with the smell of gasoline now thicker and the tang of melted rubber in the nose. He walked in and lit a cigarette. It was the only light in the place and he stood there, watching as the ember moved back and forth before he let it drop to the ground. Calvin appeared at the front, wheeling a cart behind him. He pulled it farther into the darkness and Jesler lit a second cigarette.

It was several minutes before the bobbing of lights appeared beyond the door, followed by the sound of an engine. The white beams grew sharper then turned and pancaked across the floor. The truck stopped and a man stepped down from the cab. He spoke with a voice that filled the space.

"Evening," he said. He had a barrel chest that sat atop a thick waist, the creases in his neck glistening with sweat. Jesler had met him once before up the coast.

"Evening," said Jesler. "Jimmy's not coming tonight?"

The man shut the door to the cab. "Thought I'd come down myself, see how things are going."

35

"Not much to it."

"Never is, is there?" The man glanced around. "Jimmy told me you always have two boys with you?"

"The other's on his way."

"Well I guess this one can get started on the loose boxes while we wait, can't he?" The man poked a thumb toward the truck and pulled a handkerchief from his pocket. "It's the ones on the left, boy. Make sure your hands are dry." He ran the handkerchief across his neck.

Calvin brought the cart up to the back of the truck, wiped his hands on his shirt, and climbed up. The man pocketed the handkerchief and brought out some folded papers. He said, "Gonna need you to sign these tonight."

The man found a pen in his other pocket and Jesler said, "Excuse me?"

"Need you to sign these papers."

"Sign?" Jesler heard the rawness in his own voice; he regretted it.

"Nothing to worry about. You take a look at them if you want."

Jesler dropped his cigarette, crushed it out, and took the papers. He read. "This is in Italian," he said.

"It sure is."

"Why would I sign something in Italian?"

The man laughed to himself. "Oh, I don't know. Why would you have yourself standing in the middle of an empty warehouse at near two in the morning? I said not to worry. No one sees those papers except the Italians on the boat. They gotta have *something* to show their folks back home. Dropped off, signed, paid in full, that sort of thing."

"I see..." Jesler continued to glance through the pages. "I'm not sure I should sign anything."

"You're not?" The threat had such a carefree quality to it. "I guess Jimmy didn't explain well enough what we got going on here. This makes, what . . . your third pickup?"

"Third. Yes."

"Then you know how things work, at least on this end."

"I thought I did."

"Go on and flip to the back pages." The man waited. "You see that signed import form there, that tax registration? Either of them got your signature on it?" Jesler shook his head. "No," said the man, "they don't. But they're signed all the same. Know why we need them? 'Cause the Italians need to see them. And your name's gotta be there right along with everyone else's. That way the Italians can put it in some file back in Rome and keep on sending us the merchandise. You getting it now? No reason for them to wonder if some Abe Jesler is *actually* paying the import fees or the registration tax. No reason for them to talk to anybody at the port." The man watched Jesler but he wasn't waiting for an answer. "All the Italians need to know is that Abe Jesler is a part of it, that this Jesler is gonna keep on *being* a part of it. We *all* need to know that. And everybody gets to stay happy."

Calvin appeared at the back of the truck and hopped down with four small boxes held against his chest. He placed them in the cart. The man held out the pen. Jesler took it and signed.

"Oh," said the man, "and there's some extras this time out. The fella in the tax office needs a little more cash up front. Couldn't be helped. Thought it'd be best if I come down and tell you myself."

"Extras," said Jesler.

"Nothing you can't handle."

"How much?"

"Hundred and fifty."

"Hundred and fifty?" The rawness returned to his voice; Jesler wondered if it had ever left. "That's almost two dollars a pair."

"I guess it is. That's not a problem, is it?"

Jesler knew there was no point in pushing back, but damned if he was going to let himself give in so easily again.

"It depends," he said.

"Depends?" This time there was nothing to veil the threat. "Depends on what? You think it'd depend for Sussman or Wagger? Maybe it don't have to be Jews getting the advantage on the merchandise here."

"Except the Jews are the only ones willing to pay."

It was a dangerous few seconds before the man laughed again. "Well, ain't that just the way." He folded the papers and placed them in his pocket. "My associate Jimmy tells me you folks made Savannah. Rag sellers, meat grinders, now ladies' shops and city markets. That's quite a thing. So I guess you're just keeping up traditions, aren't you?"

Jesler pulled the envelope from his pocket and handed it to the man.

"You can get me that extra hundred and fifty by Wednesday."

The man pocketed the envelope as a second truck pulled into the warehouse. Its lights spilled along the far wall before coming to a stop. A young black man, the one from the store this afternoon, stepped down from the cab. He, too, had a chest that strained against his shirt, but here it was all muscle.

"Sorry I'm late, Mr. Jesler. There was a confusion at the booth."

"Don't worry about it, Raymond." Jesler imagined the "confusion": the man at the gate, keeping a thick hand on Raymond's chest, holding the "boy" in his place, and feeling the power beneath the black, black skin, and all Jesler felt now was his own helplessness and a pen in his hand. "Just get yourself up in the back and help Calvin with the big crates."

"Yes, suh."

Raymond hopped up, and the man said, "There's always one nigger that's late, ain't there? I'll take a cigarette."

Jesler blinked for a moment and tapped one out, and Raymond's head peered out from around the back. "Mr. Jesler. Calvin says there's a couple a boxes been crushed down. Some loose heels and such inside."

It took Jesler a moment to refocus. "How many?"

"Four or five."

The man smiled willfully. "It wasn't like that when I drove up. You tell your boy to be more careful."

Jesler stood in the silence and waited for this last wave of resentment to pass. "Tell Calvin to be more careful."

"Yes, suh, Mr. Jesler." Raymond disappeared into the truck.

Jesler lit the man's cigarette and said, "Maybe there won't be any broken boxes next time out."

The man spat a stray piece of tobacco to the ground and inhaled deeply. "Maybe."

2

THE FIRST government letter from the State Department arrived on Friday. The Atlanta office had scheduled an appointment with Goldah in three weeks' time. It was a single sentence followed by an equally short apology for any inconvenience this might cause. No mention of why, only that the material in question was too sensitive for correspondence and therefore required his presence. They had included a voucher to pay for Goldah's train ticket.

Jesler stared at the page as he gnawed at the last of his lamb chops. Pearl had kept the letter unopened in her purse all day, bringing it out only now, just before dessert.

"You'd think they'd have more sense," Jesler said. "A government letter asking you to report for no reason. No concern for how familiar that might sound to you."

The thought hadn't even occurred to Goldah. "I didn't take it that way."

"Then you're a better man than I am, Gunga Din." Jesler set the bone on his plate and ripped off a piece of the challah. "I'm sorry for this, Ike. I'll close the store for a couple of days. Maybe I can get some business done up in Atlanta."

"Oh, I can go with him, Abe. No reason for you to close up. And there's a better selection of suits in Atlanta anyway."

"Pearl, please. I'll make a few phone calls. See if we can't find out what's going on with this." Jesler picked up the letter and read it through again.

With a sudden cheeriness Pearl said, "I was thinking you could wear the new blue tie to shul tomorrow, Ike. That would look very smart."

It was Goldah's first Friday with the Jeslers. He thought all the ties she had bought him were blue.

He said, "I wanted to say again how much I appreciate all you've done."

"Now stop saying that." Pearl took great pleasure in this particular chastisement. "There's no need. It's a joy. And it's a joy for Abe as well, isn't it, Abe?"

Jesler took a last look at the letter and set it down. "A joy," he said absently. He saw Pearl staring across at him. "A real joy."

"And the service, Abe? Don't you want to tell him about the service?"

Jesler now recalled how she had instructed him on this. Somehow he had let it slip his mind.

"Oh, it's a good service," he said. "Traditional. If a Jew came to town—even a Jew from New York or Philadelphia—and wanted to know where he could find a regular Shabbas service, they'd send him to us. No question about it. There's no separating the men and the women. We're Conservative now but just about as close to Orthodox as you can get. You grew up Orthodox, didn't you?"

"I didn't. No. Not at all."

"Really? I thought most Czechs were religious. Laying tefillin. That sort of thing." Jesler eyed another bone and picked it up.

"That was more Poland and Lithuania."

Jesler nodded.

42

Pearl said, "Were there Reform?"

"You mean Methodists?" said Jesler. He shook his head with a smile. "I'm just joking with you, Ike. It's a little joke." He made a sucking sound through his teeth.

"And your family?" said Pearl.

Goldah found it odd that this was the first time they had thought to ask about the family. He said, "I think perhaps I won't go tomorrow."

Jesler and Pearl shared a glance. She did her best with a smile.

"No?" she said.

"If that's all right?"

Another glance.

"No, no," she said, nodding, "of course. We completely understand." And then, as if she truly did, "It's not the rabbi, is it? It wasn't your meeting the rabbi?" She looked again to Jesler for help but he was back working the chop. "He's a very nice man but he's, you know . . . a rabbi. And rabbis are . . . well, they're rabbis. You know what I mean. Well-meaning. A little full of himself. But very learned. He's a very learned man. Wouldn't you say so, Abe?"

Jesler nodded as he ate. "Very learned."

Goldah said, "The rabbi seemed very kind."

"He *is*," said Pearl. "He really is."

Jesler examined the chop. "If he's not inclined to go, Pearl, then he doesn't need to go. You're not inclined to go, are you, Ike?"

"I'm afraid I'm not, no."

"Well, there it is." Jesler set the food on his plate and took hold of his napkin. He chose not to feel Pearl's glare from across the table. "Mary Royal'll be here in the morning for breakfast and lunch. We like to get there just before the Torah reading so maybe we'll leave here around nine, nine fifteen, back by twelve thirty. Might go a bit longer. The sermons have a tendency to grow the closer we get to Rosh Hashanah. I think he likes working up the muscle, make sure we're primed for the big ones. Maybe a quarter to one?"

Goldah felt the genuineness in this. "If it would be better—"

"Nothing about this is better or worse," Jesler said easily. "I like to go. Pearl likes to go. Simple as that. We've never thought to ask any questions about it. I imagine you have. You're in our home, Ike. You find what you need and we're here to give it."

Goldah watched as Jesler looked at his wife. "Isn't that right, Pearl?" Goldah saw an unexpected warmth in Jesler's eyes.

As if breathing it in, Pearl said, "Yes, that's right." She looked at Goldah. "You find whatever it is you need, wherever it is you need to find it."

Goldah heard himself say, "You're very lucky, the two of you."

"Yes," said Jesler. "We are." He folded the letter and placed it inside his jacket pocket.

———

Goldah waited until after ten the next morning before heading downstairs. He had brought an orange up the night before to tide him over. It was Pearl's favorite phrase.

Mary Royal was standing at the sink washing up when Goldah stepped into the kitchen.

"Hello there," Goldah said.

She was taking great care with the glasses and plates, peering through each at the window as if to measure the sunlight in them.

He said, "I hope I didn't startle you."

44

"I'd've dropped the glass if you had, Mr. Ike. See, I'm still holding it. You want something to eat?" She set the glass down and wiped her hands on her apron. "I got some nice melon, bread for toasting I made this morning, maybe some eggs and grits? Or you just want to start with coffee like usual?"

"Coffee would be good. Thank you."

"You go on in and I'll bring it in to you. There's still the papers on the table." She stepped over to a cupboard.

"I can eat in here, if it's easier for you."

"Both is easy."

The light through the window came in like a spray of ice and played in gray spots on the wall. Just below them was a small table near the door to the back porch. For some reason Goldah was wanting the brightness. He stepped over and pulled back a chair.

"I think here this morning."

"That's fine." Mary Royal brought a cup down and poured from the percolator. "Miss Pearl said you needed to have some eggs. And she was wondering if you got yourself ready for those grits yet."

"Not ready."

She was remarkably quick at splitting and whipping eggs. Goldah hadn't realized how hungry he was until he smelled them in the pan. She slid them onto a plate and cut up a few pieces of melon and laid them alongside.

"Mr. Abe likes to fry up his pastrami. He just got it new yesterday. You ever try fried pastrami?"

"I haven't, no."

"It's pretty good. I think Mr. Abe done it the first time 'cause a how much he love the smell a bacon. He told me how he used to smell it down in Yamacraw when they was young and living there, coming up along the street and just knew it

45

was the best thing he ever smelled in his whole life." She set the plate in front of him and brought over a fork and knife. "He can't eat it, a course, on account it not being koshuh. There's lots a stuff he and Miss Pearl don't eat on account a the koshuh. But he says fried pastrami just about as close as he's going to get to that smell a bacon without it actually being the bacon. I can fry you up some, if you like?"

"Thank you, no." Goldah took a sip of the coffee and started in on the eggs.

"You know, I ain't asked you yet. You koshuh, Mr. Ike?"

"No."

"Not at all?"

"Not at all."

"So that's something some Jewish folk do and some don't?"

"I suppose. Yes."

"I didn't know that." She smiled, and Goldah noticed the fineness of her cheeks as they rose toward the deep brown of her eyes. She went to the percolator. She checked something in the oven and then went across to a large cupboard.

"That's the same with praying?" she said.

Goldah was struck by the directness in her question. He wasn't sure how to answer. She said, "You can stop and start with that, too?" She refilled his cup.

"I'm afraid I don't know the answer to that one."

"Miss Pearl none too happy you not going with them this morning."

Goldah felt this more strongly than perhaps he had expected. "Did she say something?"

"She don't need to say nothing. I know when she's feeling something, and this morning she was feeling she wanted you with her."

"Maybe I'll go next week."

46

"Oh—so you'll be getting your believing back by next week?" He smiled and she picked up a cloth, opened the oven, and brought out a long pan. The smell was of apples and raisins and she set it on the counter. She sprinkled a handful of sugar from the tin over the pan, then brushed her hands, set the pan back in the oven and closed the door. "You like fresh tomatoes with your eggs?"

She was at a bowl with a knife before he could answer. She cut the tomato into thick wedges and set the pieces on his plate.

"You leave any of that on the plate and Miss Pearl'll really find her anger, and I'll be in more trouble than you."

There was a knock at the door and Mary Royal peered over through the thin curtain. She wiped off her hands and bent down to catch her reflection in a tin tray on the counter. Goldah had never seen—or perhaps couldn't remember—such tenderly plied preparations for a man. Mary Royal pressed at her hair, rubbed her finger across her chin and cheeks, then straightened her blouse as she stepped to the door. Goldah saw only her back as she opened the door and said, "Raymond Taylor, I can run a clock on you. Mr. Ike having his breakfast inside."

Goldah saw a moment of unspoken communication between them before Mary Royal stepped back to let Raymond Taylor in.

He was the young man on top of the ladder from that first day, not much taller than Mary Royal but far darker. His hair was cut close to the scalp with a thin part on the right, and he had small ears that sprouted like two sprigs of mint. He was carrying three large brown paper bags across his chest, each filled to the top. Goldah saw the deep strength in his forearms and the size of his shoulders, but it was the care between them that struck him most.

Mary Royal quickly took the packages from Raymond Taylor and set them on the counter. He smiled and nodded to Goldah. Goldah stood and extended his hand.

"Hello, Mr. Taylor. Good to meet you."

Raymond's eyes flashed. His smile remained fixed even as he shot a glance at Mary Royal, whose back was to them. She continued to unpack the bags.

"Take his hand, Raymond. He's putting it out there for you."

Raymond bobbed another nod and then took Goldah's hand and shook it. "Yes, suh, Mr. Ike. Pleased to meet you."

Mary Royal said, "Raymond comes every Saturday with groceries when Miss Pearl and Mr. Abe praying."

"And I do deliveries sometime, too, for Mr. Jesler. I got a truck, take it down to Jacksonville or up to Charleston. Every third week or so."

"He don't need to know your schedule, Raymond. He knows it soon enough working with Mr. Abe in the store and all."

Raymond nodded, as if to remind himself. "Mr. Jesler tell me about that. That sounds fine, Mr. Ike."

"Raymond was in the war, too," she said. "In Italy. I keep all the letters he sent, and I got a scarf he get me." She opened the icebox and set a few packages in paper along the shelf. "He was in the fighting, not like most. Most Negro boys who come back did graveyards and mopping up. Raymond was a fighting man in Italy. We all real proud a Raymond." She went back to the bags.

Raymond said, "She's bragging on me too much, Mr. Ike. I just did what I was told."

Goldah said, "Doesn't make you any less brave." He saw Mary Royal smile at this as she placed the last of the boxes on a shelf.

"Why don't you take Mr. Ike down to the store," she said and closed the cupboard. "He ain't seen the store inside and

I got things to do here and you got to get yourself going. That sound good to you, Mr. Ike?" When Goldah didn't answer, she said, "Raymond'll have you back in time for lunch. Then when Mr. Abe take you down this afternoon you already feel like you know the place. You meet Calvin and Jacob. Make it easier on you."

Goldah realized the decision had been made long before he had come down this morning. "Yes," he said, "that sounds fine."

Raymond stepped over to Mary Royal and she put her hand on his chest. "He knows you get to kiss me, so you don't need to show it in front of him. Take him down Drayton by the big park so he sees everybody walking out."

She took a rag and stepped over to the drying rack and started in on the plates. Raymond leaned over and kissed her on the back of her neck before quickly heading for the door.

"That's just fresh," she said as she continued to dry.

"But mighty brave," Raymond said. He opened the door and waited for Goldah to step past.

Out in the truck, Raymond said, "I drive a bigger one for Mr. Jesler when I make the city runs." Raymond kept his elbow propped out the window as he took them by the park. In the wind his arm seemed larger still. He said, "This one just for inside Savannah."

It was a Ford from before the war but Raymond had kept it up, the engine easing into gear each time he shifted. Goldah had placed his white fedora between them on the seat and was tilting his head toward the window so as to feel the air run past him. Goldah liked the way Raymond spoke.

"Sometimes I take Mary Royal and her people out to Tybee for picnics and such. We do some fishing, dancing. Make a day of it. You been out to Tybee, Mr. Ike?"

Goldah watched as the large houses began to grow closer to each other, the porches with only narrow strips of land between them.

"No," he said. "Not yet. Pearl said the beach is better when the weather cools down."

"That's smart. Too hot right now. Better when the weather cools." Raymond looked over at Goldah. For a moment he seemed unsure of himself. He looked back at the road. "That's a fine hat, Mr. Ike."

"White for the heat," said Goldah. "Pearl made sure it was white for the heat."

"White hat's good for a man in Savannah come June and July. Maybe even as far as October sometimes."

Again Raymond looked across at him, and this time Goldah turned just as Raymond was looking back at the road.

"Is something wrong?"

"No, suh, nothing wrong." Raymond nodded to himself. Then, "Awful kind a you to give me your hand with Mary Royal, Mr. Ike, but maybe you shouldn't be doing that no more."

Goldah looked at the eyes focused on the road. If there was anger or resignation in them, Goldah couldn't see it. "Because you're black?"

"Yes, suh."

"And I shouldn't offer my hand to a black man?"

"No, suh."

Goldah took a breath and thought, Was it really that easy to land on the other side of things?

———

Five minutes later, the truck came to a stop along a dirt alley that ran behind the store. Farther down, two men were unloading what looked to be glass jars of hair tonic, electric blue glinting in the sun.

"I'll let you say your hellos," Raymond said. "I got to make a quick trip. No more than half an hour and I'll be back. You okay with that, Mr. Ike?"

At the back door, Raymond used his key, then pushed through. The door stuck on the cement floor and he put his shoulder into it.

"Me and Jacob fix this door up next week, Mr. Ike. He's good with his hands. He'll try to wriggle out a it, but I'll make sure he does it."

The smell of dank cardboard and shoe polish filtered through the ceiling-high metal shelves, each stacked with boxes. Raymond led them through. They came to an archway. Across from it hung a curtain that draped to the floor and, at the side, a narrow hall. Stools, ashtrays, and a cooler stood alongside the walls. This was where the carpeting began. Goldah heard voices from the other side of the curtain.

Raymond said, "We can wait here 'til Jacob comes back. Calvin should be here. Don't know why he ain't." He shrugged. "You want something to drink, Mr. Ike?"

Raymond reached over to the cooler and fished two Coca-Colas from the ice. An opener was hanging from a string on the wall and he popped them both open. He handed one to Goldah.

"No reason we can't cool off while we waiting."

They heard footsteps before the curtain drew back. Calvin stepped through. He was in a white shirt, dark pants, and a bow tie. If he was surprised to see them he didn't show it.

"Morning," said Calvin.

"This here's Mr. Ike," Raymond said. "Mary Royal thought'd be good for him to come down early."

"Morning, Mr. Ike. Raymond here try and kiss my grand-daughter this morning?"

Goldah found himself smiling. "I believe he did, yes."

"Well, between you and me, one day I think she might just let him."

"'One day,'" Raymond said. "That's rich."

"Good to meet you, Mr. Ike." Calvin turned to Raymond. "You drop off them groceries?"

"Yes, suh. Dropped them off. What you doing dressed up like that?"

"Mr. Jesler says I get boxes on Saturday mornings so Jacob don't have to leave the front empty when he needs them. Any more questions, Romeo?"

Raymond smiled. "No, suh, no more questions."

"Good." He took Raymond's Coca-Cola. "Then go back and get me lady sizes six and six and a half, wide, Naturalizers, black. You going to need the ladder."

"But I got them deliveries to Delaney's . . . oh, never mind." Raymond looked over at Goldah. "You take care a this old man, Mr. Ike, while I'm getting him his boxes. Make sure you help him to his seat."

Calvin said, "Just get the shoes, son."

Raymond stepped through the doorway and Calvin pointed to two stools.

"Care to sit, Mr. Ike?"

The two sipped at their Coca-Colas, Calvin staring straight ahead and taking his time with each sip. He had learned how to steal these moments for himself. There was nothing too considered, no glance at Goldah. Calvin's was an absolute stillness; its depth was one Goldah understood only too well.

Raymond returned with the boxes and Calvin set down his empty bottle and stood.

"I'll tell Jacob you here," he said. "Then you can come on out." Calvin took the boxes from Raymond. "And you gotta fix that door to the alley, son. It's still sticking."

"The door?" said Raymond. "I just said I got to get them Kaybee crates over to Delaney by noon otherwise he ain't going to take them."

"That's fine with me, but that door ain't going nowhere. It'd be here when you get back."

"Fine." Raymond looked at Goldah. "Don't you worry, Mr. Ike. I get you back in time for lunch even if I have to saw that door in half."

"Sounds about the usual kind of fixing you do," Calvin said. He pulled back the curtain and stepped through to the store.

Raymond waited until the curtain had swung back before reaching over to the cooler for another Coca-Cola. "I see you later, Mr. Ike."

Goldah sat and drank. He finished the bottle, set it down next to Calvin's, and imagined this life as his own. It was a foolish thought, imagining what was clearly here: the frayed edge of the carpet, the carbonation in his throat, and the sound of footsteps approaching.

"Ike?"

Goldah stepped to the curtain and pulled it back. The store was empty save for Calvin and a white boy of perhaps fourteen. The boy was dressed in a perfect little suit, with a blue handkerchief folded at the breast pocket and his red hair slicked down to a razor-thin part.

"Ike," the boy said again, his hand held out. "Jacob Gersons. Good to meet you."

Goldah stepped through and took the hand. It was rough for a boy so young, and strong. "Hello."

"You look well, Ike. No wear on you."

Goldah imagined the boy had been practicing what to say. "Yes. Thank you."

Jacob did a quick inventory of the store with his eyes. "Pretty good, ain't it? And you and me getting right in on it."

Goldah had trouble following the boy, not just for the words but for the accent. It was duller than the Jeslers', heavier, and without the polish. Goldah nodded.

"You were a newspaperman." said Jacob. "That's what I hear. Newspapers and writing. I been thinking about that, too."

Calvin said, "Jacob thinking about a lot a things, Mr. Ike. Why don't you show him the store, son."

"In a minute, Calvin. In a minute. I'm getting to it. Men got to be able to make introductions, ain't that right, Ike?"

"'Men,'" said Calvin dismissively. "Why don't you show him the store, son."

"Yes, men. Like me and Ike. Ain't I in a nice suit and hand-kerchief in my pocket?"

"You is, son. You is. Jacob here lives down in Yamacraw, Mr. Ike, but he's getting himself out a there real soon, ain't that right, Jacob?"

Jacob rolled his eyes. "Why you go and tell him that, Calvin? Got to go and tell him about Yamacraw and me here in my suit, and my hair pressed down. What you tell him that for?"

"Well, you *do* live down in Yamacraw, and you *is* fetching to get yourself out."

"I'm making introductions here."

"I suppose you is, son." He turned to Goldah. "Mr. Jesler have Jacob here on Saturdays when he doing his praying. He gives him the suit. Got a cot in the back so the boy can stay

54

sometimes the night before if we starting in early. Suit stays here the rest a the week hanging in the back. Don't know where the boy gets his pomade."

"'Where the boy...?'" said Jacob. "I pay for it with my own money, if that's what you care to know."

Calvin laughed. "I know you do, son." There was genuine caring in the way Calvin spoke to the boy. "It's good what you doing. Mr. Jesler pick a good boy with you, and you get yourself out a Yamacraw real soon."

"That's right, he did. Mr. Jesler come up from Yamacraw same as me. And one day I get some boy to do my working when I go to shul for my praying. And Calvin still be here when I do it."

"Well that's just a lot a nerve coming from a boy," said Calvin. He stepped over to the curtain. "You still want them boxes out here?"

Goldah turned to the front door just as the bell jangled and a young woman stepped inside. She wore her hat low on an angle, hiding much of her face from view. Calvin let the curtain fall as he took his place standing at the wall.

Goldah had turned—with the bell or before it, he didn't know—but something had made him turn, and he now continued to watch the woman as Jacob smoothed down the back of his hair.

"I'll be right back," Jacob said quietly. "Just watch. See how it's done."

Jacob moved between the chairs and, with a voice Goldah had yet to hear from the boy, said, "Good morning, madam. Is there anything I can be of assistance with?"

The woman remained by the shelf, her back to them.

"Boy's a natural," Calvin said under his breath. "Smooth and clean. He's moving her to the new ones in from Europe, even though he knows she's coming in just to look. She'll be trying on one a those before she knows it."

Sure enough, Jacob had her in a chair within a minute. He called Calvin over. Goldah watched as Jacob gave the styles and the size. Calvin moved quickly back toward the curtain.

"Okay if you come back with me, Mr. Ike?"

Goldah followed Calvin through.

"Best leave the boy to himself. Okay with me standing in the corner, but he don't feel so important with you looking over him. Good for Jacob to feel important. He's a good boy."

They came to a stack near the back and Calvin's eyes darted up and along the boxes. "Seven narrow," he repeated to himself. "So you was in newspapers, Mr. Ike?"

Goldah had been letting his mind wander to other things, pleasant things. It took him a moment to answer. "Yes. I was a journalist."

"And now you in shoes."

"Yes, now I'm in shoes."

Calvin found the box toward the bottom and crouched down for it.

"We got a newspaper here in town. Pretty good. Got some Jewish folk working on it. Not fancy like in Europe with the war, but maybe you want to do that some time, it'd be there."

"Maybe," said Goldah.

Calvin stood with the box in hand. "You go to college for that?"

"I did. Yes."

"That's how come you speak English so good?"

"I suppose so."

"That's real fine. And now you in shoes."

"Yes. Now I'm in shoes."

Calvin pointed over to another shelf. They found two more boxes and headed back to the front. At the curtain, Calvin handed Goldah the three boxes.

"If it's okay with you, Mr. Ike, you go on in and hand them to Jacob. It'll make him feel good to have you helping him. Important for a boy like that. Unless that's not a good idea according to you."

"It's a fine idea, but I think maybe the boy finds himself important enough already."

Calvin smiled. "Maybe he do."

Jacob was standing by the shelf, the woman seated with her back to Goldah. He brought the boxes over, placed them on the floor, and Jacob said, "And this is the newest member of the Jesler shoe family." Again Goldah heard the precision in the words so carefully practiced. "Mr. Jesler's cousin—from Europe—Mr. Ike Goldah."

The woman looked up from under her hat and for the first time Goldah saw the sharpness of her eyes and the paleness of her skin. He had no idea of it then, not even the smallest sense, but a feeling of wonder was once again his.

———

Goldah remained by the back wall with Calvin as the woman paid. She had said only two words to him—"Hello" and "Welcome"—but she had watched his face and Goldah had managed only a weak smile before Jacob had started in on the fitting of the shoes.

She now moved past them. The bell rang and she stepped outside. Goldah watched her past the large front windows, even after she was gone. And Calvin, watching Goldah watching her, headed for the boxes.

Jacob was finishing behind the register. "Knew she'd buy two pair," he said proudly. "Two pair of six-dollar shoes. Not bad."

"And how'd you know that, son?"

"I just know these things, Calvin. I just know."

57

"It wouldn't be that she was a De la Parra, would it?"

Goldah had been listening with more interest than he cared to admit as Jacob continued to work through the math. "And how'd you figure that, Calvin?"

"Because you and Mr. Abe always going on about them Saffees. You knew who she was the moment she come in, and you knew she was going to buy them shoes."

Jacob closed the register. "Well maybe I did and maybe I didn't but that's twelve dollars in the drawer. Tell Raymond he needs to deliver the boxes this afternoon."

Calvin said, "Raymond's got enough on his plate, son. No one's stopping you from delivering them."

Jacob stood there for a moment, and then said, "I'm using the toilet."

Jacob stepped out from behind the counter and quickly moved through to the curtain. Calvin had the boxes at the counter and set them down.

"I'll take them back when he's done. Jacob likes his privacy."

Calvin rested his back against the counter while Goldah kept his against the wall. The two men stood like this listening to the rattle of the fan as the heat seemed to gravitate to the walls. It was a strange and comforting silence until Calvin said, "You look real smart in that coat and tie, Mr. Ike. Nice fit. Hard to fit a thin man. I should know. Where'd Miss Pearl take you for it?"

"Levin's."

"Shirts as well?"

"Shirts as well."

Calvin saw a speck of something on one of the chairs. He reached over and flicked it away.

Goldah said, "I've never heard Italians called Saffees." He knew it was a poor attempt at spontaneity.

Calvin looked up, momentarily confused. Just as quickly his face cleared and he brushed something from his hands. "She was pretty, wasn't she?"

"Pardon?"

"I said you was thinking she was pretty."

Goldah had been thinking just that. No reason, then, to step around it. "Yes," he said.

"Good. It's good to notice a pretty woman."

Goldah imagined it was.

Calvin said, "Come in all by herself. That's strange. Women usually work like shoes. They come in pairs."

Goldah smiled under the heat.

"De la Parra is Jews in Savannah, Mr. Ike. Old Jews. Over two hundred years. Older than me and my own been here. They ain't no Italians."

"Really?"

"Yes, really," Calvin said with a quiet laugh. "You like hearing that, don't you?" He pulled his handkerchief from his pocket and dabbed at the back of his neck. "I'd be careful there, Mr. Ike. Like I say she's a Saffee. That's a whole different kettle a fish from Mr. Abe and Miss Pearl."

Goldah had heard any number of names thrown at Jews. Saffee was not among them.

"Saffees is temple Jews," said Calvin, as if reading Goldah's mind. He folded the handkerchief into a neat square and placed it back in his pocket. "They get their praying done by eleven. Mr. Abe and Miss Pearl, they go to the AA. That don't finish up until twelve thirty, maybe one o'clock. Less praying for a Saffee."

Goldah understood: Pearl had explained it on one of their drives, albeit not in so many words. Saffee Jews were Reform Jews. She had even shown him the temple—"A church with

59

a few Jewish stars stuck on it." It was the Sephardim who had been the first to arrive—"Two hundred years of Jews in the South"—but there weren't all that many of them left. Now it was the German Jews who had brought their easy faith and their assimilation to the temple, "And see how well that turned out for you." Pearl had grown bolder talking about his past.

Goldah imagined Calvin had never heard the word Sephardim. *Saffees is temple Jews.* It was as simple as that.

Goldah said lightly, "It's nice to see you keep such a close eye on it all. Who prays when, how long they pray."

"I been with Mr. Abe close on twenty years," Calvin said. "My son was fifteen years before he get killed in the war. And now Mary Royal. I even tell you who sits where on Saturdays. Mr. Abe and Miss Pearl close up front but not as close as them Kaminskys. Mr. Kaminsky always right up there on the left. He'll get you a good car if you need it."

"I'm sorry about your son," said Goldah. "I didn't know."

Calvin let the weight of it pass. "Yes, suh. Italy 1943. I'm sorry, too."

Jacob reappeared at the curtain. "Raymond's back. He says he'll take you home, Ike."

Goldah pushed himself away from the wall. Calvin pushed himself up as well. "You got a nice story to tell at lunch today, Mr. Ike. A Saffee coming here all by herself from the temple. Got to get her some Jesler shoes right away. You tell Mr. Abe that. He'll get a kick."

———

Outside the synagogue, Jesler milled about with the rest of the congregation and thought God might have been kinder on a Shabbas. Then again kindness wasn't really God's way, was it? You had to earn everything, even a breeze after two hours trapped inside the sweltering heat.

Jesler lit a cigarette and knew he had made a mistake. He had let Pearl wander off with the girls, leaving himself open to the likes of Mel Green. Jesler tried to look away but Green already had him fixed in his sights.

"*Buongiorno*, Abe," said Green with too much affection. "Can't say I know how to say 'good Shabbas' in Italian, but there you go. How you doing?"

Mel Green was never one to miss a service. He saw the last few rows of the sanctuary as a sort of second office, a chance to get a foot in during moments of private meditation. He had made his greatest killing during Sukkos of 1942, ten thousand yards of cotton to an army supply officer who was visiting from Charleston, and who just happened to be in need of thread. The deal had been struck somewhere in the middle of the haftarah. Green's shaking of the lulav was, some say, particularly robust that year.

"Good Shabbas, Mel."

"I tried to talk to you inside. Been hearing things."

"I got that. The '*buongiorno*.' Very clever."

"It's a bold move."

"And what's that?"

Green took a pull on his cigarette. "You got someone up in Atlanta? You're going to need someone in Atlanta, Abe. I've got a New York Jew up there. Very discreet. If you ask me that's the way you need to go."

"Sure," Jesler said noncommittally. He was trying to figure out how the news had reached Green. Green was always bringing something in through the port. It could have been anyone.

"So what are you moving, Abe? Three hundred a month, five hundred?"

"The way I hear it," said Jesler, "you need to be careful with those New York Jews. They're smarter than us, Mel, or at least that's what you've got to let them think."

"That's right, Abe, that's right. But this one knows the ropes. And he knows New York. He knows those unions. So you going to let me make the introductions?"

Jesler dropped his cigarette to the ground. "Always good to know people in Atlanta. We'll see."

"Good, good." Green spotted another opportunity. "So I'll call you."

Green was gone before Jesler could answer.

Unions? What in hell did this have to do with New York unions? Jesler lit another cigarette, exhaled, and wondered how Mel Green had gotten wind of things.

3

GOLDAH CHOSE not to mention Miss De la Parra that afternoon or any afternoon for that matter. It seemed something for private consumption, at least until he could figure out why. Not that there was a lilt to his walk or a warmth in his chest. He knew he would never recover that kind of ridiculous sentimentality, but the thought that something was now purely his own set him thinking in this new way. If he could have recognized it as anticipation he would have called it such, but he couldn't and so kept it to himself.

It wasn't all that much of a shock then when, at week's end, he saw her again at the ice-cream shop just a few blocks from the house. Goldah had developed a taste for malteds, a perfectly wonderful American treat that he gave himself each night after dinner. Ice cream was off the menu at the Jesler's most evenings — meat the main course — and, as Goldah was too tired to wait the three hours for the kosher rules to kick in, he snuck away to Leopold's for a little walk and a thick chocolate malted.

She was at a booth in the back, with two other young women, when he stepped into the shop. Goldah picked a seat at the far end of the counter that happened to be nearest her. He had gotten in the habit of bringing a newspaper with him to read as he drank, and tonight he made sure to read through every last article. He was dangerously close to the back page when he saw the three women begin to get up. Goldah turned on his stool just as Miss De la Parra was standing.

The hat was smaller this time, a dark blue, leaving her face free and open below it. He was once again caught by the paleness of her skin but now he noticed the small brown birthmark just below the left eye. On a different face the mark would have drawn attention. Here it served only to amplify the quality of the rest.

She caught him staring; she smiled and stepped over. Goldah stood.

"Hello again, Mr. Goldah."

"Hello."

"Eva De la Parra. We met at the shoe store." Her voice was warm and assured and just as he had remembered it.

"Yes, of course," he said. "It's where I seem to meet everyone."

"In stocking feet."

"Hazard of the trade."

"I hope you don't remember mine."

There was something so wonderfully bright in this familiarity, he thought. It wasn't scattered or small talk but ease, the kind that made Goldah feel no less bold.

"How could I forget them?" he said.

Her smile widened. "I see you've discovered one of our favorite pastimes."

"Yes. It's quite wonderful. Terribly sweet."

"That's the best part. I like the chocolate as well. And I see you enjoy our local newspaper."

"I do. Yes."

"Well, thank goodness for that. My father is one of the editors. It would be quite disappointing if you didn't." A thought came to her. "I believe I read you were also in newspapers at one time. I could introduce you, if you like?"

"I should like that very much. Thank you."

She seemed to want to say more but her friends appeared behind her and she quickly introduced them. "We're off to the movies," she said. "The new William Powell. Have you seen it?"

"I haven't, no," said Goldah. "It sounds quite wonderful."

He watched as her smile reappeared—a quiet, thoughtful smile—and she said, "Yes, it does." She nodded at his glass. "You should have another. Treat yourself. I would." The smile stayed in her eyes as she offered her goodbyes. Goldah watched her walk to the door like so much untried promise and ordered himself another of the same.

———

The second State Department letter arrived two days later, a confirmation of the appointment in a week. It put Pearl on edge. Even so, Goldah told the Jeslers he wouldn't be joining them for services again. And, again, Pearl managed to accept it, this time on her own.

Instead, the next morning Goldah returned to the store with Raymond. It was something of a surprise for Jacob as Goldah had spent the week learning the ropes. The boy didn't like it.

"He knows we can handle it just fine, don't he?" A hint of accusation laced the young voice as the face grew redder. "Mr. Jesler knows *I* can handle it just fine?"

"Son," Calvin said evenly, "if Mr. Ike wants to come in, he wants to come in. That's nothing to do with you."

"First it's you coming and helping on Saturdays, and now Ike. Does he think I'm not up to it? Because I am. I *am*."

Goldah said, "I didn't tell Abe I was coming, Jacob. He doesn't know I'm here."

"He didn't send you?"

"No."

Jacob tried not to show too much relief at this. "Well that's different, then"—and, with a bit more air in his lungs—"that shows initiative to me, Ike. I can appreciate that."

Calvin said, "Yes, I'm sure he's glad you appreciate him, son. Ain't that why you here, Mr. Ike?"

Goldah did his best to ignore Calvin's gaze and spent the morning shelving and spraying shoes. By eleven o'clock his jacket and tie were long off and his shirt wet through as he handed boxes up to Calvin on a ladder.

"I think maybe I should clean myself up," Goldah said. "In case Jacob needs me out front."

"In case Jacob needs you," Calvin said before snorting a harmless laugh. He stepped to the floor. "You don't think it's clear as glass why you come in this morning? I just want to know why you so certain she's coming back?"

"Are you any less certain?" said Goldah.

"No. I'm just asking why *you* is."

At ten past eleven Miss Eva De la Parra walked into the store. She was alone. Jacob started toward her but Calvin placed a light hand on the boy's arm and said, "I think Mr. Ike's going to take this one, son."

Goldah was already moving through the aisle. He imagined the penny just now dropping for the boy.

Miss De la Parra stood by one of the shelves, looking at the shoes, and seemed to know just when to turn.

"Well, hello again, Mr. Goldah."

"Hello." He knew he'd spoken with too much eagerness. "Did you enjoy your movie?"

66

"I did, thank you. Did you have your second milk shake?"

"I did indeed."

"Good for you. I'm glad to hear it. You should know I've had quite a few compliments on the shoes I bought last week. Please tell your young man he has excellent taste."

"I will, of course." Goldah almost forgot why he had stepped over. "Would you be looking for another pair?"

She held his gaze for what seemed a very pleasant passage of time and then, as if an afterthought, smiled. "No, I don't believe I would."

Goldah felt a momentary lightness in his head. He had spent so little time with women—young women—that he found her candor both remarkable and terrifying. But this was America. Women were permitted their boldness. What else was he meant to expect?

She said, "I've taken the liberty of putting some clippings together from the paper. Editorials my father has written, politics and so forth. I thought you might find them of interest."

It was only then that Goldah noticed the large envelope she was carrying. She held it out to him and he had no choice but to take it. He tried not to show his disappointment. He said, "You're very kind."

"If you should have any questions, I'd be happy to answer them."

Moments of courage require so very little—a lie of hope, a piece of sugar for the dying—and Goldah said, "Perhaps you'd care to take me through them now?" He was hoping to see more in her expression. "I have a break and there's a very nice square around the corner. Unless, of course, this isn't the time?"

She hesitated. Goldah felt the lightness return to his head when she said, "All right. That would be very nice."

Outside the sky was moving in thick, white clouds. Rain had come midweek and brought a cooling to the air. It felt almost breathable. Had he been standing still, Goldah might not have felt his perspiration, but this was early August. His chest sweltered under the jacket and tie.

They walked in silence, stilted only for him as she seemed completely untouched by the heat or the sudden realization that they were together. They moved past storefronts and people out for a morning shop. No one seemed to take notice of them, which suited Goldah just fine. They came to a crosswalk and she said, "Do you mean the square down here?"

He might have. He didn't know.

"Yes," he said with perfect certainty.

"I like that one, too. I don't think I'll talk about the weather, although it has been surprisingly cooler. I hope you're feeling the change."

"I am. Yes."

"It becomes quite lovely in the next month or so."

"I'll look forward to that."

She smiled as if she, too, knew that anything beyond this simple back-and-forth was beyond them. Even so she couldn't help but add, "Mother always appreciates when the holidays are late. Easier for everyone without the heat. Unfortunately this year they're so very early. Will you be planning on joining the Jeslers at the AA for the holidays?"

Mention of the Jeslers chafed at him for a moment. He said daringly, "I knew you would come again."

Her silence nearly stopped him.

"Did you?" she said. "I'm glad."

Real or not, he now felt her closer at his side.

They reached the square, where the trees showed a moment of wind. Stepping across the road, they found a bench and sat. They both looked out at the park and watched as a young mother placed her baby in its pram. The woman's maid stood at her side. Goldah set the envelope between them.

Eva said, "One of the articles is about you. I hope that's all right?"

"Of course."

She pulled the pages from the envelope and began to leaf through them, even as he continued to watch her.

"There wasn't much detail, but people know how to fill in the blanks these days. Easier with a plane or a boat going down—'thirty of the crew of twelve hundred'—that sort of thing. I suppose we all grew used to that, but yours was something entirely different." She stopped and looked up at him. "I hope you don't think I'm making light of it?"

"Not at all."

"You must know how terribly shocking it was. The horror of it."

"Yes."

"And then, of course, here you are."

Goldah couldn't think of anything to say to that.

Filling the silence, she said, "It wasn't a terribly good picture of you."

Goldah knew the photograph—Pearl had shown it to him—along with the article: "Welcome from the war," "The warmth of newfound family," "The courage of a single man," and so forth. The photo had been taken at one of his first DP camps, suit and tie and hair smoothed down, and eyes with a look of absolute vacancy. His face had been so gaunt then, so tired and yellowed, and all he had been were those eyes and that nose caught in the eternal grain of black and white.

The woman across the way pulled the hood up on the pram, and she and her maid began to move off.

"I thought it was an excellent picture," Goldah said with a first stab at charm.

"Did you?" Eva looked out at the square again and followed the path of the woman. "It's funny, but Savannah gets its hottest in the late afternoon, five or six o'clock. Have you noticed?"

He hadn't.

"You will. It's a surprise at first, but then you know it. It's as if the heat can't find anywhere else to hide and just lets itself go. You can't really find fault with something if it can't be helped, can you?"

He was enjoying the effortlessness of this, the kind of ease the untested and the very young confuse with love. And he liked the way she spoke of the city as if it were her intimate, a friend who needed protecting, or at least one who deserved the admiration she felt for it. Goldah remembered having greatly admired that quality in people.

She said, "Have you seen the pavilion out on Tybee Island?"

"I haven't. No."

"We'll have to remedy that, won't we?"

They glanced through several of her father's editorials, the first few written during the war, one simply titled "Did They Know?" There were more recent ones about the GI Bill and Mrs. Roosevelt—her father was a great enthusiast when it came to Mrs. Roosevelt—and a cautionary series on the future of Palestine. The man wrote in crisp, aggressive prose, and with a sophistication that seemed well beyond the scope of the provinces. Goldah liked him at once. It was only in an article, written for an Atlanta paper, that he finally saw her father's byline.

"Weiss?" Goldah said. "Arthur Weiss? I don't think I understand."

"Yes," she said. "My maiden name is Weiss. De la Parra is my married name."

And with that the air in his chest became a dry heat. He thought: I've missed it, haven't I, missed it entirely—the pity and the unwanted kindness. She had gone to such lengths, offered so much of herself, that to call this malice would have been a mark of his own callousness. It was inadvertent, nothing more. Or perhaps in her eyes he was someone not to merit such ideas, not to be capable of those things beyond the most basic needs of a life. He had seen himself as a man. She hadn't. It was as simple as that. He reminded himself that the fault had been his.

"Yes," he managed, his eyes focused on the black and white of the printed page now in his hands. "Of course."

She said, "I've kept his name, my husband. He was killed in March of 1945 in Germany."

The shock of this second blow struck Goldah with equal force. He looked up and saw the unimaginable stillness in her face. There was nothing halting in her voice, nothing to match his own self-pity, which, by comparison, seemed all the more pathetic.

"We received the telegram in May after V-E Day," she said. "That was very hard. We thought he'd been celebrating but, of course, he hadn't."

Goldah nodded as if to console and felt shamed by this intimacy. "I'm sorry," he said.

"I only mention it because you asked."

He noticed he was still clutching the clippings in his hand and all he wanted was to stand and to run.

She said, "Are you all right?"

"Yes."

"Perhaps you need to get back?"

He nodded. She started to get up and he said, "I haven't spent much time with women—young women—not for a very long time. I apologize if I seem unfeeling."

She looked genuinely touched by this. "You don't at all, but perhaps that's something else we'll work on." She stood. "Would you walk me back to Broughton? I have my car there."

He walked at her side, feeling relief and a strange sensation that he took for safety. He hadn't felt it in years and only much later would he recall it as happiness.

————————

Pearl was sitting on the porch swing when Goldah got home. Her short legs reached just to the ground and her toes were on point as she pushed herself back and forth. Goldah wondered if perhaps she was in one of her moods: She hadn't taken the slightest notice of him as he walked up the path.

"Hello," he said cheerily, surprising himself with his tone. "Did you enjoy the service this morning?" He moved up the steps and she looked over, her stare empty, peaceful, unnerving all the same.

"Yes. Yes, I did. That's very kind of you to ask. All about endings. The old year done, the new one about to begin. I think Abe liked it as well."

"I didn't see him down at the store this afternoon."

"Oh, so you've been down to the store?"

"Yes, since this morning."

"Good. Good for you. Did you get some lunch?"

"I did." He was doing what he could to maintain the artifice of this. "Jacob introduced me to Gottlieb's."

"Oh, Gottlieb's. What a treat. I love Gottlieb's. Did you try a chocolate chewie for dessert?"

"I did. Yes. Delicious."

"They call them the come-back cookies because you just keep coming back for more. Isn't that funny? Abe's been on the telephone since after lunch. He's in a bit of a mood. Not before lunch but ever since."

Goldah said, "Is he inside?"

"He is. I was wondering, Ike"—there was just the smallest hitch in her tone—"while you were down at the store, if you happened to spend some time with a Mrs. De la Parra? I've had a telephone call myself. From Irene Jelinek. She takes her newborn for a walk during the sermon at the AA and she called to say that she thought she had seen you with Mrs. De la Parra. Was Irene Jelinek correct in thinking what she saw?"

Goldah was struck more by the words "De la Parra"— strangely emanating from Pearl's mouth—than by the revelation that the two of them had been seen together. It took him a moment to answer.

"As a matter of fact, I did. Yes."

"Really?" said Pearl no less buoyantly. "And how would you have come to meet Mrs. De la Parra and spend such intimate time with her?"

Intimate time, he thought. Evidently uncomfortable phrases were going to be at a premium. He said, "It turns out Mrs. De la Parra heard I had been a journalist before the war."

"And how would she have heard that?"

"From the article you showed me," he said easily. "It mentioned I had written for a newspaper in Prague."

Pearl hesitated then nodded, perhaps too quickly. "Yes, that's right. Of course. The article. And how would that article have brought Mrs. De la Parra to a bench in Johnson Square?"

Goldah appreciated the strong detailing in Mrs. Jelinek's report.

"Is there something I should know about Mrs. De la Parra?" he said. "I hope it wasn't a mistake of mine to meet with her? She seemed quite pleasant."

"Of course she's pleasant," Pearl said without losing steam. "I'm sure she's a lovely person. And to lose her husband. I know all that. It just seems strange to me that on a Saturday morning, after she's been to the temple, she finds herself in close quarters with you on a bench in downtown Savannah with everyone in the world to see the two of you together. So I'm simply asking how it is that such a thing might have happened when I know myself you spend all your time either here or at the store or on an evening walk—all by yourself—which I must say is probably very calming for you."

Goldah listened and nodded—always at the right moments—and now stepped over and held out the envelope. Pearl stared at it and Goldah said, "Mrs. De la Parra's father is an editor at the newspaper."

"Yes, I know that, Ike."

"Yes...and these are a collection of some of his editorials. She came by the store and thought I might like to see them. It seemed very...thoughtful to me."

Pearl continued to stare at the envelope, her mouth pursed. Phrases formed, inched ever closer to the lips, and then retreated before she finally said, "Well that *is* thoughtful. Of course it is. I just don't see how that would have prompted her to take you to Johnson Square."

"She didn't take me. I was the one who suggested it." Goldah realized this might lead to another barrage. He quickly sat with a conciliatory nod; there might even have been a quiet smile behind it. "Perhaps it was my mistake."

"I'm not saying there's been a mistake."

"If only I'd known."

"A gentleman can suggest any number of things but it's a young *woman* who makes her own decisions. That's all I'm saying."

"Yes, you're right," he said, enjoying this perhaps more than he should. "A young woman does make her own decisions. This wouldn't have anything to do with her having been at the temple this morning, would it?"

"And what is that supposed to mean?"

"I just know you and Abe don't approve of the Reform Jews."

"Approve? That's not what I . . ." Pearl's voice trailed off as she shook her head. "Ike, you have to understand how things are. I'm sure the De la Parras and the Weisses have their ideas about how we go about things, and I'm not sure I'd care to hear them, but I will say there's a good deal of looking down noses—and I'm not saying that's *always* the case—but you should know better than anyone how certain Jews look at other Jews, and some don't even want anyone to know that they're Jewish. But that's neither here nor there. It's about the way a woman *behaves*."

"Yes," said Goldah, "you're absolutely right. Although she did seem perfectly respectable."

"Ike." Pearl was coming to the end of her rope. "I just don't want you getting hurt by any kind of person. That would just kill me, you know that, after everything you've been through, and what we've done to have you come here."

"I appreciate it all, you know that."

"I do. I do. And that's not for you to say. You know I don't like hearing it. We just care for you so much. You fill our house. That's what you do. You just fill it. And if I want everything to be perfect for you, well then *I'm* the one to be blamed. That's all I'm saying. You know that we're here, and if you need clippings and such, well you just ask and I'll go get them. I really

75

will." This brought a smile and a little laugh. "You see what I'm saying?"

"I do. Yes."

She patted her hand on his knee. "Well good." She stood. "So enough about that. I just wanted you to know. Between you and me. No need to bother Abe with any of this."

"Of course."

"And I made you a strudel. How about that?" She was at the door when she turned. "Oh, and I completely forgot. Abe said he's not coming tonight. He's just not in the mood after... Well—he just wouldn't be any fun."

"Of course," said Goldah, feigning understanding. He had no idea what she was talking about.

"And I'd hate to cancel, so I told Fannie and Selma you'd make a sixth and they're ecstatic. You don't have any plans, do you?"

The pleasantness of the day slipped quickly away as Goldah knew it was only a matter of hours before "And how are you enjoying Savannah?" would send him reeling into the grip of untold weariness.

———

"And how are you enjoying Savannah?"

Goldah sat at the center of the banquette, keeping his elbows in as he tried to spread some butter on his corn-bread roll. Two rounds of martinis had squeezed him ever tighter between Pearl and Fannie, a tall narrow woman with strikingly blue eyes that seemed always in need of a receptacle for their caring. Her husband, Herb, sat on the other side with the Kerns—Selma and Joe—owners of Kern's Grocery on... Goldah nodded and smiled as if he knew the place and now tried to re-angle the bread.

"Here," said Pearl, reaching over, "let me help you with that."

Goldah was quick enough to get his knife free and set the piece moving toward his mouth.

Beyond the rise of Fannie's hair lay the wide oval of the dining room, flush with tables and linen cloths, and smelling of cooking oil and men's cologne. Johnny Harris's was packed on a Saturday night, plate after plate of ribs and chicken drowning under Harris's famous brown sauce. Fannie had poured some onto her pinkie and was now insisting that Goldah take a lick.

"Careful there," Herb said with too much geniality, "that's a married woman." The laughter carried them past the second round of drinks and onto a short discourse on the art of barbecue.

"Well of course we're kosher," said Herb, "inside the house. Outside it's beef and chicken and fish. Wasn't it that way where you grew up?"

Herb was a man who saw his own experiences as everyone else's. It made him either endearing or a boor. Goldah hadn't decided which.

Selma said, "I'm sure they were eating much more exotic than that, Herb. Doesn't it have a nice tang to it, Ike?"

They were in one of the booths that ringed the dining room, quieter here, although the conversation seemed to bounce off the dark wood of the walls before disappearing into the domed white of the ceiling. At one point Joe had mentioned Prohibition and curtains, but Joe wasn't terribly good at finishing a story. Orbed lights hovered above, the most pronounced sprouting from a single column at the center of the room, where strips of mirror reflected what seemed to be every possible angle. Had there been the grinding sound of a calliope, Goldah might have mistaken the place for a carousel.

Fannie pressed the service button. "I'll get you some more bread, Ike. It's a madhouse tonight so it might be a little while for the food."

"You might have to wait a bit," said Herb, "but you never go hungry in Savannah."

Goldah all but expected the requisite look of abject apology for this slip of the tongue but, to his credit, Herb plowed on. It was a relief.

"Must be a little much for you, all this," Herb said. "Heaping plates and such. Fannie and I saw the newsreels up in New York—"

"Herb!" said Fannie.

"He doesn't have to answer—you don't have to answer, I'm not doing it to provoke—but he must know it's what we've all been wondering. I'm not going to pretend."

Goldah appreciated the honesty, and Pearl said, "I'm sorry, but I think that's highly inappropriate."

"The man's lived through one of the great evils in history," said Herb. "He must have something to say about that."

Pearl said sharply, "Well I don't think it's for you to ask."

Goldah had his finger on the last of the crumbs on his bread plate. "It's all right," he said vaguely. "You probably have a better idea of it than I do. I haven't seen the reels so I have a rather small idea of the history."

Fannie's eyes showed shock, then slipped back to their usual caring. "You haven't seen them? Any of them?" When she realized why, she said, "No, of course you wouldn't have. I'm so sorry."

Pearl said, "Fannie, why don't we talk about something else?"

"I'm fine, really," Goldah said. He spoke with enough calm for the entire table. "There are certain things I don't care to talk about, but the rest..."

The door had been opened a crack, and it was all any of them could do not to step through.

"Well that's very brave," said Selma. "You have to know Pearl's told us so much already."

He did know. How else would it be? He had been through it all endless times elsewhere; why not here? They started in on the basics—which camp, when he had gotten there, how many of his family had been lost. He answered each in turn even as the food arrived. Father, uncle, younger brother. His mother had died from a cancer of the liver in 1937 and so had been spared any of it. Selma took this as a small blessing.

Herb said, "So almost two and a half years?" Herb had gone in for the fried chicken. Goldah had been told one was meant to use one's fingers.

"Yes," said Goldah. "Fourteen months in Terezín, the rest in Birkenau."

There was no need to explain these once trivial names on obscure rail lines. They were now a part of the vernacular.

"And Terezín was the holding camp?" said Herb.

Goldah had gotten the fish. It had been a mistake.

"No, not really," he said. "It was a city, a fortress. The Germans created it for propaganda so everyone would think we were being treated well enough."

"How terrible," said Fannie.

Goldah nodded, if only to let her feel that this had been the right thing to say.

"And then they moved you," said Herb, "and you stayed with the same group from the first place?"

Goldah had trouble understanding the question. "'Stayed with...?'" he repeated.

"I think what Herb is asking is did they keep you together from the first place?" Selma seemed proud of this clarification even if it made no more sense to Goldah. He shook his head.

"And did you know where they were taking you?" said Herb.

"We did. Yes."

"You knew it would get worse?"

Goldah moved the fish with his fork. "I imagine so." He was now concentrating on the potatoes. "Or maybe not. I don't know. It's hard to remember when exactly you knew and didn't know."

The two couples shared a glance and Goldah kept his eyes on his plate.

Herb said, "And inside the camp?"

"It was cold. Very cold. And wet."

"And all of it was forced labor?"

"Yes," said Goldah. "We made rubber."

Fannie asked, "And what if you became ill?"

Goldah noticed how the cream of the potatoes seemed to keep the barbecue sauce at bay.

"Became ill?" he said. "No—you didn't become ill."

"But surely in all that time—"

"If you became ill you were chosen, so you weren't ill."

Again the four shared a glance. Goldah knew they were desperate to stop asking if only they could. It was why he kept his eyes fixed on his plate.

Joe said, "And did they tell you that from the start?"

Goldah could feel it coming now. "Tell us not to get ill?"

"No," said Joe with no small amount of confusion. "I mean—did they tell you about—"

"The selections?" said Goldah. "No. They didn't tell us about that."

"But you must have been thinking, How can they do this?"

80

And there it was: the question that always came. How this? How could they be so inhuman? But that wasn't the question they were really asking. What they really wanted to know was: How could you have let this happen to yourself? Surely you could have seen something early on, understood. *We* would have seen it, wouldn't we?

"It wasn't the guards who were inhuman," Goldah said distantly. "It was us." He watched as the sauce seeped through. "If we'd been allowed to keep anything of what made us human, it would have been far worse. And we all knew it." He finally looked up. There were never any questions after that. "I'm sorry," he said. "I'm not sure that answers your question."

Joe continued to stare across the table. He nodded pensively. "No . . . it does. Of course."

Selma said quietly, "It's all so very brave."

Goldah felt a tightening in his head. He thought he would have been able to manage more of this. He took another bite of the potatoes.

A black boy stepped over with a pitcher of water. Herb slid his glass to the table's edge for a refill. "I don't know how you make it through that," said Herb.

Goldah waited for the boy to finish and thanked him. The boy moved off and Goldah said, "I suppose you just do."

Pearl said, "Oh my God."

They all looked at her. She had her head flat against the booth and was staring out at the dining room.

"Don't look, Selma—I *said* don't look—but guess who's just walked in?"

It was an unnecessary caution as no one in the place was showing the least bit of interest in any of them. Even so, Selma brought her head back.

"Sit back, Joe," she said, "I can't see." Selma looked out and her eyes widened. "Well that's just perfect, isn't it?"

Goldah recognized no one. Herb was also staring out.

"Who are you talking about?" Herb said.

"Nothing," Pearl said. "Never mind." She raised her eyebrows to Selma.

"Well what is it?" said Joe. "I'm looking out at the Karps, the Ringelmans—I think that's the fella who just moved down from Atlanta with his wife—and there's Art Weiss and his wife—"

"Well imagine that," said Pearl, still looking at Selma.

Joe looked at her. "Why am I looking at Art Weiss?"

Goldah now understood what he was meant to be looking for, even if he had no idea which of the men was Weiss.

"The tall one," Herb said, helping him along. "With the pretty wife, in the blue."

"She's not that pretty," said Fannie.

"Yes, she is. She's always been pretty. That's why the girl is such a knockout."

"I'm glad to see you've taken such an interest."

"I can tell you a woman's good-looking, Fan, and still save all my undying love for you."

"You better."

The conversation continued—a seamless string of muted words—as Goldah watched the Weisses follow a young man with menus across the other side of the room. Weiss was slim and tall with a shock of white hair, premature on a face that was at most in its early fifties. The wife was tall as well, elegant in the way she sashayed between the chairs and the tables, her husband's hand gently nestled in the small of her back. Goldah saw the resemblance to Eva at once.

The Weisses sat and Goldah turned to Fannie. "Do you mind?" He pointed beyond the booth.

The table became quiet, and Pearl said, "Where are you going, Ike?"

"I thought I'd introduce myself."

He felt Pearl's hand on his arm under the table.

"And why would you want to do that?"

Goldah conjured the smile from this afternoon on the porch. "He wrote a very kind article about me. It seems only right to thank him for it."

Selma said to Joe, "Ike had lunch with Mrs. Eva De la Parra this afternoon."

"It wasn't lunch, Selma," Pearl said sharply. "She brought him some newspaper articles. That's all."

"I thought you said—"

"Ike was a newspaperman back in Europe." Pearl's eyes widened as if to say, Leave it alone. "It was the thoughtful thing to do." Pearl let go of his arm. "You go right ahead, Ike. You be courteous."

Fannie slid out and Goldah moved into the dining room. He imagined he had Pearl's eyes boring through him the entire way.

The Weisses were in a booth, glancing through their menus, when Goldah drew up. He stood for several seconds waiting until Weiss pulled his reading glasses from his eyes and looked across the table to his wife.

"That was easy," Weiss said. "Ribs for me tonight." He slid the glasses into his breast pocket and noticed Goldah. "Hello there." Weiss spoke in a friendly way. "Can I help you with something?" Before Goldah could answer, Weiss said, "Oh, of course. It's Mr. Goldah." Weiss slid out and stood. He extended his hand and they shook. "What a pleasure to meet you. Are you here with friends tonight?"

"Family," said Goldah. "You're very kind to recognize me."

"I like to look at a man's picture before I write about him. I have to say yours was a tough one."

"I'm afraid I'm not the most photogenic."

Weiss said, "Allow me to introduce my wife. Marion, this is Mr. Goldah. I believe I might have mentioned him to you once or twice."

Her smile was far more reserved. "Yes, of course. Hello."

Weiss said, "And are you enjoying Savannah, Mr. Goldah?"

"I am. Yes."

"Good. That's good. You know I managed to track down some of the pieces you wrote before the war. The *Herald Tribune*. Some wonderful stuff. You were their native correspondent in Prague, is that right?"

"I was. Yes."

"I did a stint with the *New York Herald* a hundred years ago. During my woolly years after college. I came back down to Savannah just as quick as I could. Not quick enough for some, but..." Another icy smile from Mrs. Weiss before Weiss said, "You know you've got a wonderful command of the language."

"Thank you," said Goldah. "As do you. I've had the pleasure of reading several of your editorials."

"Yes, but despite what people might think, English is my *first* language. I was duly impressed, I truly was, especially for a man your age."

"You're very kind."

"Kindness has nothing to do with it. Believe me. Would you care to sit for a drink or do you need to get back?"

Had it been Weiss alone Goldah wouldn't have thought twice about abandoning Pearl and the rest. But it was clear Mrs. Weiss had other plans.

"That's very thoughtful," Goldah said, "but I wouldn't want to interrupt your evening. Perhaps another time."

"I'd like that." Weiss pulled a silver case from his jacket pocket and handed Goldah his card.

Goldah said, "I'm afraid I haven't had any printed up just yet."

"Not to worry. That's the office and that's the home. Feel free to call either."

Goldah said his goodbyes and the two men shook again. There was a last bob of the head from Mrs. Weiss, and Goldah started back. He felt a wonderful surge of purpose moving past the chairs and the waiters. There was something here that resembled a life he had once known. He felt invigorated by it.

The sight of Pearl and the others brought him quickly back to earth. Before any of them could catch his eye, Goldah decided on a quick trip to the bathroom.

Five minutes later he stepped from the men's room and saw Mrs. Weiss standing in front of the ladies'. The lights were dim but he recognized her at once, an awkward moment between them as they stood in the little corridor: odder still as Goldah felt as if she had been waiting for him.

"Hello again, Mr. Goldah." Her voice was no less distant.

"Hello."

"You'll forgive me, but this seemed somewhat more private."

Evidently he had been right.

"Yes," he said, not knowing why.

"My husband doesn't know you've met with my daughter or that the two of you have spent time together. If he did I'm certain your conversation would have gone a very different way. You understand that, of course."

Goldah didn't but nodded all the same.

"I think I'll say my piece and then be done with it. Is that all right?"

The unspoken threat was voiced with such gentility that Goldah had no choice but to nod again.

"I'm sorry for all that you've gone through," she said. "I truly am. And I'm so pleased that you've been able to find a home here with your people. But my daughter is still very fragile, even now, and there are things you can't possibly know or understand about what she is going through. I believe the word they like to use these days is 'susceptible,' and you, Mr. Goldah, are the perfect vessel for a woman in that state. A man who needs help. A man broken by this war. You can understand that, too."

Goldah realized he wasn't meant to answer, just nod.

"You may have her pity, Mr. Goldah, but please know that pity is all it can ever really be, despite what even she herself might come to think. I have no doubt your own experiences tell you such. Am I right?"

This time Goldah simply stared and Mrs. Weiss said, "Yes, I imagine you do. I do hope you enjoy the holidays and I wish you and your family a very sweet and happy new year."

4

THE SEVEN A.M. Nancy Hanks got them into Atlanta just before two p.m. They had spent half the trip in the grill car, Jesler praising the Georgia Central for its steaks—the best of any of the lines, he said, even the ones up to New York. Goldah agreed and let Jesler finish the slab of meat that remained on his own plate. It was little more than a thick spine of fat and veins when the boy in the white coat came to clear the table.

Out in the cab the streets beyond the station grew wider while the buildings—littered with signs and awnings—moved past at full assault. Goldah had let himself forget the pace of a real city. He settled back and listened to Jesler drone on as the streets moved by in a blur.

Their hotel, the Georgian Terrace, was a grand affair, with white columns and a series of red-striped canopies out front. It lived up to its name, with a side terrace where early drinks or late lunches dotted the tables among the legion of tuxedoed servers.

Goldah felt the heat at once as he and Jesler stepped from the cab. It was a different heat here—different from Savannah—drier, and Goldah wondered if it was possible to miss a thing he had only just come to know.

The sixth-floor room was plush, with sitting chairs and a small ottoman. Goldah pressed his hand onto the mattress and it gave with his palm; he imagined the pillows would do the same. Jesler had tossed his jacket and tie onto his bed and was now in the bathroom running the water.

"You can see the Tech campus from the window," Jesler said between splashes.

Goldah was already staring out. In the distance he saw a few green patches—trees, red brick—congregating in a small oval. Elsewhere pockets of height broke through the endless stretches of thick, packed-down stone, all of it gray and drab. Goldah had seen the city burn at the cinema years ago, magnificent on the screen. This, he now saw, was what had come after.

Jesler was patting a towel on his neck as he stepped into the room.

"So," he said, "we'll meet back here at around seven? I'd take you with me but it's going to be one store after another. You could walk to the campus from here. Take a look around. It's very pleasant. Or you could catch a movie just across the street. I didn't see what was playing. Then we'll have some dinner and be up and ready for tomorrow. Sound like a plan?"

"It does."

"Good. And look—I don't want you to be worried about any of this government stuff. They like to keep it all very close to the chest but I'm sure it's nothing. They'll ask you a few questions. Probably just about how you're getting on. So we'll head down to the offices early, get it over with, and get back on the train."

"I'm not worried."

Jesler tossed the towel onto his bed. "No, I don't imagine you are. Wish I could say the same."

"It'll be fine, I'm sure."

Jesler pulled his collar up and reached for the tie. "You never seem to flap, do you? Always calm with things. Have you always been that way?"

Goldah knew he hadn't. "I don't know. Maybe."

"I guess you just have to be." Jesler brought the tie to a knot, and Goldah watched as the skin around Jesler's neck strained against the collar. Funny how some people took silence for calm. Jesler said, "Just take things as they come, I guess." He nodded then put on the jacket and checked himself in the mirror. "You have money?"

"I do."

Jesler pulled out his wallet and placed a five-dollar bill on the bureau. He turned back to himself in the mirror.

"Just in case," he said. He straightened his hair. "And if you bring a girl back, leave a signal for me on the door. You know, shoes outside or a tie." Goldah started to answer and Jesler smiled. "I know, Ike. Just don't spend it all in one place."

The door clicked shut and Goldah turned again to the window. He waited a few minutes until he saw Jesler step out onto the street. Jesler got into a cab, and Goldah watched as it pulled away.

The room was remarkably still. Goldah thought perhaps he had never known such quiet. Within minutes he was asleep.

———

"Hats, girdles, handbags...it's all the same in the end, Abe, lucky for us. You see what I'm saying?"

Meyer Hirsch was small and very thin, and when he spoke, his words tumbled into each other, tied together by a nasal bridge, as if he was constantly humming. It made it difficult to get a word in. His desk was at the back of a vacuum repair shop, although Jesler guessed that Hirsch wouldn't have known the difference between an Electrolux and a Hoover: The machines all stood on the shelves like undusted trophies.

Hirsch said, "So Mel Green tells me you've never done this sort of thing."

Jesler was eager to move past Green. He said, "I can't say I know exactly what you mean by 'this sort of thing.'"

"Sure you do, Abe. Otherwise why would you be sitting in my shop talking about New York unions? You're moving up, making an advantage for yourself. Nothing wrong with that. Just that maybe certain things are best done not out in the open. Fewer hands reaching out. You see what I'm saying?"

Jesler was wondering how many hands they would be talking about.

"There's nothing illegal," Hirsch went on. "At least not on my end. You say the Irish are handling the tax and import men, yes? Always important to have someone good handling the import people. Making sure they're comfortable. *Very* comfortable. That way no tax notation. No tax notation, no import log. No import log—you see what I'm saying. Then it stays very private, very local, which is what you want. And why you've come to me. You haven't signed anything, have you?"

"No," said Jesler.

"Good. That's good. You let them take care of all that. Still, there's a danger. Naturally there's a danger. The unknowns, who gets wind of what's doing, so forth and so on."

"And how often have you done this sort of thing?"

The nasal hum became a momentary laugh. "He wants to know how often. That's good. *Very* good. It's a good question. You're sure you want the answer? No, I'm just joking. Enough. I do it enough to know how to make sure that what happens here doesn't catch anyone's eye up in New York...or Newark, maybe even as far north as New Haven. Some union boy all the way up there hears what's doing down here…" He bobbled his head, smiled. "We don't want this to happen. Simple as that."

"Forgive my ignorance, Meyer, but I'm not exactly clear why any of them should care about what happens in Savannah."

"Abe. Please. Longshoremen, Teamsters…these are serious people. They need to know that they're…how should I put it…that they're *involved*. That nothing comes or goes without they get something for themselves. You see what I'm saying. They'll want their piece. But, really, do they need to involve themselves with something like this? Of course not. So we make sure they…"—the words trailed off into a long breath out—"that we don't bother them with this. That they don't feel bothered. Simple as that."

"And when I begin to ship the shoes—"

"Merchandise, Abe, merchandise. Much better that way."

"So when I begin to ship the *merchandise*…here to Atlanta or to Charleston or Miami, maybe even to Chicago—"

"I'm going to stop you there, Abe. Not to be rude of course. Only for clarification. You have to understand, this isn't for Chicago." Hirsch shook his head vigorously, his hands up for emphasis. "No Chicago…Chicago, Cleveland, anything north of Richmond. We have to understand this from the start. You draw your lines, you stick to them, and you put enough money in your pocket to make yourself more than happy. Now, if this was booze or textiles or fruit—"

"Fruit?"

"Sure. Fruit is big, very big, trust me. You don't want to go near peaches, God forbid plums. Then every union boss up to Boston would be down here quicker than you'd care to know. But you're smart, you picked something small, specialized, coming in from Europe—even better. It's not worth it to them, as long as they don't find out. This part of the world, it's pishers, Abe…believe me…small potatoes. You're a pisher, which is nothing to be ashamed of. Plenty of money as long as you play it smart. My job—I help you play it smart. Then we all make a lot of money."

Jesler was beginning to feel uneasy, but with a man like Hirsch in his back pocket—or he in Hirsch's, he didn't fully know—maybe the boys up the coast would see things differently, especially when it came to all those "extras."

Hirsch said, "And you're sure these Irish know how to handle the import people? Maybe I help them there a little, too. What do you think?"

Jesler said, "So how many other folks in Atlanta do what you do?"

Hirsch looked mildly disappointed. "Abe, you want I should get you a list of references? I'm the only game in town."

"You misunderstand me, Meyer. I want to make sure that no one else down here feels deprived, someone who might be inclined to send information up north to those unions boys out of spite."

Jesler saw a moment of caution in Hirsch's eyes, then something he wasn't expecting: respect. Hirsch said, "That's smart. *Very* smart. And careful." Hirsch nodded as if he'd just convinced himself of something. "Good. I'll need six hundred up front to get things going."

The sudden shift caught Jesler off guard. "Six hundred?" he repeated.

"What—we're not wasting each other's time, are we, Abe?"

"I don't think so."

"You sure?"

For the first time, Jesler felt the threat from across the desk. Where the hell was he going to get another six hundred dollars?

"Because I'd hate for you to see the whole thing go up in smoke. I'm the only game in town, Abe, and I happen to know everything about what you want to be doing. Believe me. You've worked it beautifully on your end. I'm very impressed. Putting merchandise like that on your shelves, distributing the rest throughout the region. Very nice. Clean. But keeping things quiet on something like that, especially when it's coming in from the coast, that takes organization, planning. Someone goes talking... You see what I'm saying?"

Jesler wasn't sure whether to appreciate or blanch at Hirsch's directness.

"Six hundred," said Jesler. "So when do you need it?"

———————

Goldah followed a man named Hilliard into a narrow office on the third floor of the new post office building, the State Department's home in Atlanta. Jesler had agreed to wait outside.

The place held no surprises, all of it stark and in keeping with Hilliard's creased lines and gray suit. Hilliard asked if Goldah wanted water, Goldah declined, and Hilliard sat. He opened a drawer and removed a single file. He seemed to hesitate before looking across at Goldah.

"I'm afraid we've had no choice in this, Mr. Goldah, so I apologize if any of it becomes uncomfortable for you. As I said, we simply need your help, nothing more."

"I understand."

"Good." Hilliard opened the file. "You're here because of a Miss Malke Posner. Am I pronouncing the name correctly?"

Goldah was staring down at the file, the letters upside down. He had the sudden thought that he might never catch his breath again. But he did and looked across at Hilliard.

Hilliard said, "Why don't I get you that water."

Goldah drank deeply. Hilliard refilled the glass and Goldah drank again.

Hilliard said, "I'm guessing from your reaction I'm pronouncing it correctly."

Goldah set the glass on the desk and found his voice. "Yes."

"You were close to Miss Posner before the war?"

Goldah stared at Hilliard's face and his neatly parted hair, the lines around the eyes and the small discoloration near the ear. Hilliard's lips were thin and pale, and Goldah thought he smelled a woman's soap beneath the tang of the cigarettes. But there was nothing feminine to Hilliard, nothing smooth to the face or narrow in the fingers. The knuckles were red and meaty, and the hands looked as if they had held things that men were meant to hold. For Goldah, though—in this place, now—he saw another face, one he had told himself, time and time again, he must learn to forget . . .

———

She is small, smaller than he, her skin fine, not like a doll's but soft in a way that the other girls envy. They say she can pass for a non-Jew, her hair light, her nose close above the lips, and her eyes a light blue that makes them seem distant. She stares up at him as the train slows. He sees the cold on her skin and the redness in her cheeks. He has cried as well, and he stands with his brother who is staring out through a small crack in the wood. The train slows and his only hope is that it will find speed again, better that than the stopping. The light is now so

94

white and so bare through the cracks, and she steps into him as the train lurches to a stop.

The swill of the shit pail splashes to the boards and there is a need to speak, to say farewell, to look at the others packed so tightly in and say what no one has said for all these days locked inside. Farewell. No fear, only farewell.

The door opens with a crash and the light is somehow less bright. There is barked German in the ear, beyond it a vast platform with reflectors, and still she is with him. Luggage here, luggage afterward. They, the two, stand outside, every-thing now silent as men of the SS march about as if waiting for the next train, easy questions in barked German—How old? Healthy or ill?—and everyone is healthy but still there are two ways to go, and she is told to the left toward the sound of the water, pulled from him to go to the left, while he must stand in a line and look down. Together again after-ward, they are told, together with the calm assurance of simple duty and everyday life. Afterward, they say. And he marches, she now behind him and gone, and he tells him-self to feel more but he is already one of the lucky few who knows he does not.

————

"You were close?"

Hilliard repeated the question. He was a decent man, not a Jew, but he had learned to show the necessary sensitivity during the last few years.

"Yes," Goldah said, "we were close."

"So you recognize the name?"

"I do."

"She was deported with you?"

"Yes."

Hilliard marked something down. He now expected the usual line of questions: Had they found something of hers? Did she have relatives here? Had a family member survived?

"Is she alive?" said Goldah.

The question caught Hilliard by surprise. He hesitated. "Why do you ask that?"

"Because it's the only question that matters."

Hilliard had never heard things presented so plainly. He was accustomed to passing on information, to console or to advise cautious optimism. Yitzhak Goldah was asking for none of these. "I suppose that's true," Hilliard said. Goldah remained silent and Hilliard added, "It's not exactly clear."

"Not clear that she's alive?"

"Not clear that the woman in question is Miss Posner."

There was a moment before Goldah said, "I see. And why is that?"

"There's been some memory loss, physical scarring. It's not clear the woman is who she says she is."

"Is this common?"

"It does happen from time to time."

"Is she in the United States?"

"She's in a sanatorium in Virginia. Miss Posner has relatives there."

"The Lubecks," said Goldah, surprising them both with the speed of his answer. "I met them. Once. They visited Prague before the war. Do they think this woman is Malke?"

"They saw her only the one time. They believe she is."

"You mean they hope she is."

Hilliard tried to read Goldah but there was nothing in the eyes. "I don't mean to sound presumptuous, Mr. Goldah, but I was expecting something of a stronger reaction."

Goldah continued to stare across at him. "I'll take another glass of the water, if I may."

Hilliard poured it out and watched as Goldah drank. "We have a photograph," Hilliard said, "if you'd care to see it."

Hilliard leafed through several pages before arriving at a large black-and-white photo. He slid it across the desk and let Goldah take it.

———

"He seemed like a good man."

Jesler was the first to break the silence. They were in the elevator where an older black man stood at the lever and watched as the numbers on the brass plate lit their descent.

"If it's something we need to talk about," Jesler said, "you let me know."

Goldah nodded. They reached the first floor and the man placed his large hand across the metalwork gate and pulled it open.

Goldah knew he would have to tell Jesler something: a name, someone from the camp, anything. It was so much easier to find a fiction than to think of that photograph, the paleness even in black and white, and the emptiness. Was it her? He had known her face so well, and now he couldn't say. He truly couldn't. The hair was so thin, the color gone, the nose not hers, and the dip along the cheeks...Why ask this of him? Wasn't it enough to carry his own helplessness, to see it in his own eyes? Now to have hers. It was too much. Didn't the future have to be more than a shared hollowness?

97

5

"IT'S THESE goddamned Micks at the docks."

Jesler sat at his desk, tucked in behind the shelves and the shoes. He was on the phone when Goldah stepped through with a cup of coffee. It was Thursday and all hell had broken loose.

"No, I don't want you to worry about that," Jesler continued into the phone. Goldah hesitated and Jesler waved him over. "He'll be there Monday with the small truck and I'll let you have twenty-five... Yes, twenty-five boxes." Goldah set the coffee on the desk and Jesler nodded his thanks. "It's what came in, it's what we've got... No, just ignore all that... No, I don't know who would have been calling... Okay... Okay... Yes we'll square all that... No, not to worry... Okay... And mine to Louise."

Jesler hung up and took a quick sip of the coffee. His shirt collar was open and damp through, the tie loose, and there was an empty glass on the ledge behind him that looked as if it had held whiskey. Jesler pulled a bottle from the bottom drawer and poured some into his coffee.

"You want a drink?" he said and took another sip.

"It's a bit early."

"You know I had four calls at home on Saturday. *Four*. They call on a Saturday because they know it's going to put me in a position, and they can say, 'Well, you picked up the phone, it can't be a problem if you're doing business on a Saturday.' And of course I'm doing business on a Saturday when they're talking about some fella in Jacksonville and maybe moving the whole distribution down there." He tipped another splash of the whiskey into his cup and put the bottle away. "Jesus." He took another drink. "What am I supposed to do—not pick up? Let them tell me today, 'Well, we didn't hear from you so we didn't think you were taking it that seriously,' so of course I have to pick up. And then Pearl gives me that look."

Jesler was still thinking things through when Goldah said, "I'm sorry."

Jesler looked over and shook it off. "No, nothing to be sorry about. These things happen. Anyway—you doing okay? I hear you're taking out a young lady."

It took Goldah a moment to respond. He hadn't seen or talked to Eva since Saturday. And there was still the matter of the chat with her mother.

"Am I?" he said.

"Be careful," said Jesler. "Pearl overreacts but she's not far wrong. It's a different kind of thing."

"I'll keep that in mind."

"Good." Jesler pushed himself up. "No one's been by the store, have they? I mean asking questions, that sort of thing, when I haven't been here?"

Goldah shook his head.

"Good." Jesler tightened his tie and smoothed back his hair. "We're getting some more inventory in today. Make sure Calvin tells Raymond he'll need to be here by five thirty. You can cut out early. Get yourself a new tie for your young lady friend." Jesler pulled the jacket from the back of his chair and put it on. "All seriousness, Ike, be careful there. That isn't going to work the way you think it is."

Calvin was standing by the far doorway. It was clear he had been there for some time.

Jesler looked over. "What is it?"

"You got someone here, Mr. Jesler."

"The sign says lunch, Calvin. Tell them we'll be back in half an hour."

"They got badges, Mr. Jesler. They ain't here for no shoes."

"What kind of badges?"

"Just badges."

"Well are they police or government?" Jesler said sharply. "What kind?"

Calvin shrugged. "Maybe government, suh. They was real quick with them."

Jesler stood staring across at nothing in particular. Finally he said, "You tell them I'll be right out." Jesler tried a careless smile for Goldah but there was too much care in it. "Well, I guess we'll just have to see what they want. Why don't you stay back here."

"I'll come with you."

"No need. You wait here."

"How about I come with you?"

"There's nothing to this, Ike. Trust me."

"I'm not sure you believe that."

"Whether I believe it or not, no point in having you talked to by some men with badges. I think you've had enough of that for one lifetime."

Goldah had thought this pride or fear, but all Jesler was trying to do was protect him.

Goldah said, "I think I'll take my chances."

Two men were waiting in the store, brown suits and shoes, hats in hand, and the same kind of cheap government tie knotted too tightly at the neck. They were carbon copies of each other, tall and gaunt, except the one at the counter wore a pair of wire-rim glasses that pinched at his ears behind his thinning black hair. The other stood hovering over the men's Italian shoes, his narrow nose dangerously close to the leather. Calvin was keeping an eye on him.

"Good morning, gentlemen," Jesler said. "This is my associate, Mr. Goldah." Jesler moved to the counter. "You can head back and finish those boxes now, Calvin."

"Yes, suh."

All four watched as Calvin moved slowly through the curtain and into the back.

The man with the glasses was the first to speak. "Mr. Jesler?"

"Yes."

"Mr. Abraham Jesler?"

"Yes. Abraham Jesler. What is it I can do for you gentlemen?"

"We're here—"

"I believe I heard there were badges," Jesler said easily. "If I could?"

The men pulled them out. They were from the Ports Authority. Jesler glanced at them. "Excellent. Thank you. Now what is it I can help you with?"

The man with the glasses brought out a small pad. "Just a few routine questions," he said. He scanned the pages as he began to leaf through. "You have occasion to use the Ocean Terminal on West River Street for the receipt of shipments, is that right?"

"I do."

"And you also have a depository in one of the warehouses?"

"Yes, as does every other businessman in Savannah. What is this about?"

"And you've had occasion to use them"—the man stopped on a page and read—"since June of 1942?"

"That sounds about right."

The man looked up from his pad. "Are you aware there was a recent theft of goods from a warehouse within the same block and sector as the one you're currently using?"

"I wasn't. No."

"We just want to make sure there hasn't been anything suspicious that you might have seen during one of your trips to the port. Anything that might have seemed out of place."

Jesler studied the man's face for a moment. "And what kind of goods were taken?"

"I'm afraid that's not information we can provide at this time."

Jesler continued to hold the man's gaze. "I don't recall anything out of place. It's just me and two of my employees who go out with a truck during the day."

"The boy we just saw—he's one of those employees?"

Both knew it was an unnecessary question. "He is. Yes."

"I'll need his full name and address."

"And why would you need that?"

"Is that a problem?"

Jesler waited a moment too long before giving him Calvin's information.

"And the other?"

He gave him Raymond's as well.

The man flipped his pad shut and put it back in his pocket. "Well, you've been very helpful, Mr. Jesler. And I hope we didn't alarm you in any way. As I said, just routine. Of course, if you do hear of anything, don't hesitate to get in touch." The man pulled a card from his jacket pocket. "That's my office."

Jesler took it.

When the two reached the door, Jesler said, "If you see Harry Cohan down at the port office, you give him my best. He's an old friend."

The man with the glasses waited, then said, "I'm afraid I don't know Mr. Cohan personally, but I certainly will if I see him."

The bell jangled and Jesler watched as the two men passed by the window outside. Jesler's breathing became more pronounced and he slammed his hand onto the glass. "Goddamned Micks."

The sound of the slap hung in the air before Goldah asked, "Who's Harry Cohen?"

Jesler was checking the hand, flexing it. "Co-*han*," he corrected. "Irish. Like George M. Mr. Yankee Doodle Dandy. You can come on out now, Calvin. They're gone."

Calvin stepped through the curtain and said, "I'm at *three* forty-six, Mr. Jesler, not two forty-six. You got that wrong."

"Did I?" Jesler shook out his hand one last time and moved to a chair. "I guess they're going to have to knock on some doors if they need to find you at home, aren't they?" He sat heavily, letting his head fall back. He stared at the ceiling and let out a long breath. "Harry Cohan is the man who makes sure everything runs smoothly, Mr. Doodle Dandy down at the Ports Authority. And if Harry Cohan isn't getting what he needs, then Harry Cohan sends a message." Jesler brought his head forward. "These two fellas were delivering that message to me. And I made sure they knew *I* knew exactly where it was coming from."

"Harry Cohan," said Goldah.

"Harry Cohan," Jesler repeated; even the sound of the name exhausted him. "That's right." He moved himself forward on the chair as if he was about to stand. "Nothing's been stolen,

Ike. No warehouse goods. These two fellas were here to tell me that things *might* go missing if I don't play ball. Pay up. And the cost keeps going up. More and more and more. What they call 'extras.'" He stood and rubbed a thick hand through his hair. "That's what Harry Cohan wanted me to know."

"I'm afraid I don't understand."

Jesler let out another long breath. "Why should you? I barely understand it myself. Immigrant capitalism, Ike. That's what I call it. And everyone's got their own set of rules." His eyes wandered; it was as if he was talking to himself. "You sign something, can't get out of it, and then you get yourself squeezed beyond a point where you can pay."

"I still don't—"

Jesler snapped himself back and looked over at Goldah. "I know." He looked as if he might say more. Instead, he took his hat, and said, "The sign says lunch. Maybe we should go get some."

———

That night, Eva mentioned Tybee Island and a picnic lunch. If the weather held—if he could take the time—she would show him the beach. They would go on Monday. It was now Monday.

She drove with the top down while Goldah's eyes squinted through the shaded glasses she had bought for him. A few miles back they had passed the last of the drawbridges. The marsh water was now close on either side, edging against the road with cordgrass that was bleached a yellowed green. Eva had tied a scarf around her hair and the wind was catching it each time they took a curve.

Hers was a familiar enough look from countless magazines—dark glasses, red lipstick, the cream-colored blouse that pressed hard against her chest—but Goldah couldn't recall a single photo showing a man so utterly foreign to this: He had seen lakes before; he had seen rivers and the Atlantic in white-capped waves; this, however, was not any water as he had known it.

A series of hand-scrawled signs, each hawking fresh shrimp and crab, began to dot the siding. Shacks appeared, then houses, and farther on the red roofs of a cluster of buildings. Goldah assumed they were a hotel's and Eva said as much as they drove past: the De Soto Beach—Saturday-night dancing and drinks for members of the Cabana Club. Eva preferred the pavilion, which was open to the public and where she had seen Red Nichols and His Five Pennies perform before the war. She became quiet after that and turned off the main road. A pier came into view and she pulled over. There were one or two other cars parked along the narrow lane, but it was a weekday. No one was out for the morning sun.

Goldah took the basket from the back and followed her along the sand and dirt. The path rose and they came to a thicker sand, where she stopped and placed her hand on his shoulder. She pulled off her shoes, he did the same and, rolling up the cuffs of his pants, he felt at once the heat and the grit on his soles. He walked unsteadily behind her until, stepping atop a raised mound, he saw for the first time in his life a stretch of ocean beach.

It wasn't the breadth that struck him—the drifts of pale sand and rock amid the dull coloring of clustered shells—but the enormity of the water against it: steady and vast. For a moment, a thought of both wonder and fear took shape in his mind, but he couldn't find the words for it, his lips dry, the memory mercifully clouded by the heat. He felt a momentary pain in his lungs as he walked behind her and wondered if the sensation would pass.

The sand grew harder underfoot and she stopped to spread out the towels she had brought. Standing over them, she took off her scarf and glasses and began to unbutton her blouse.

"My suit's underneath," she said, seeing his expression. "I've brought one for you, if you like. They have a changing room up on the pier."

She pulled off her blouse and then unzipped her skirt and let it fall down her legs. The swimsuit skirt clung tightly to her slender thighs and Goldah's instinct turned him away.

"It's just a swimsuit," she said, with a care he hadn't yet heard. "If it makes you uncomfortable, I'll put my skirt and blouse back on."

He turned back. She looked more puzzled than modest. It was a relief.

"I've seen a bathing suit before," he said.

"I'm sure you have."

"Yours is quite lovely."

She held out the men's black to him. "This should fit, I think."

"No, it's all right. I'm better this way."

"You're sure?"

He nodded and she dropped the suit onto the towels.

"I'm going to have a swim," she said. "It seems a waste not to. Do you mind?"

"Of course not."

Only now, as she smiled, did he see a moment of modesty.

"All right, then," she said. "I'll be back."

A few yards down the beach she turned her head. For some reason she waved. He waved as well and she began to run to the water. She splashed in and dove under, and he watched as her arms rose and fell, the strength in her body a marvel all its own as she moved along the surface.

He sat like this with his hands behind him, deep in the sand, before he closed his eyes. He felt the heat bring the first beads of sweat to his back, down along the muscles of his covered arms, into the creases of his knees. He let it drench him, the welcome feel of liquid skin, until he heard her steps in the sand. He opened his eyes into the glare and saw her, wet with water, standing above him. She peered down and he knew he would always keep this with him.

"If you slide over I can sit."

He made room and said, "Do you want a towel to dry off?"

"No, I like it when it dries on me. Lets me remember I've been here."

She sat and he felt the heat from her arms and legs next to him. She smelled of oranges, and they both stared out at the water.

"You've never been to a beach, have you?" she said.

"I haven't, no."

"It was in your face. I'm so pleased to be the first to introduce you to it. It's marvelous, isn't it?"

"It is."

"I thought at first you spoke so very little because of the language, but that's not the case, is it?"

"No."

She laughed lightly. "You see, there it is again."

It took everything he had not to turn to her. "I don't need to say much with you."

He heard the depth of her breath, and she said, "I think that's a very kind thing to say."

They found themselves looking at each other. The water was still in her hair and small beads of it had gathered on her shoulders and cheek. When their mouths met he tasted the lipstick and the salt on her lips. He waited for her to pull away and, when she did, he saw the perfect flush of sun in her cheeks. She looked out again and smiled gently.

"Will you start speaking more, now?"

He put his arm around the base of her back and let his hand rest at the side of her thigh. She drew closer into him and he felt the wet through his shirt and his pants. It had been so long since he'd felt this kind of woman's softness, the curve and the frailty in it.

"So this is America," he said.

She laughed quietly to herself. "Is that what you think of us?"

"Think what?"

"That we're all so ready and carefree."

"Is that what you are?"

She brought her knees up and wrapped her arms around them. "Wouldn't it be nice to feel that again?" He said nothing and she asked, "You have felt it before, haven't you?"

The sound of steps behind them drew close before a man and a boy with fishing rods moved past. The man turned and nodded. "Morning."

The two moved on and Goldah watched as they found a spot by the water.

"I don't know," he said. "Maybe. Yes."

"'Maybe. Yes.' Either you felt it or you didn't. Either you needed to love someone or you didn't."

"So it comes down to need?"

"With love, yes—it does."

He said, "Then I don't know."

"That seems strange to me."

"Does it? I'm sorry."

She stared out for a few moments and then said bravely, "I have a son. His name is Julian. Have the talkers thought to tell you that?"

Goldah had grown accustomed to the recklessness in her moments of revelation—perhaps only for him. He couldn't imagine ever growing tired of them. "The talkers?" he said.

"The voices of reason. Your Pearl, Irene Jelinek, my mother. I'm sure the list goes on."

He heard the weariness in her voice.

"No," he said. "They haven't."

"So she managed to keep that to herself when she saw you out at Johnny Harris's? Yes, I know she spoke with you. She likes to make sure I know all about her grand gestures, even the ones she means to keep secret from me." She looked at him. "I have a son. He's five years old. Do you regret coming here?"

He was so taken by her honesty that he barely noticed her caution should he turn tail and shut her out. He reminded himself that she had kissed him and spoken of love.

"America is such a strange place," he said.

"Is it?"

"I think your mother—"

"My mother is my mother. She has compassion from a distance and she's very protective of her place in the world. I think Judaism for her is a necessary inconvenience, which makes her protective of me for all the wrong reasons."

He recognized the finality in that. "No," he said, "I don't regret it. Is that why you brought me here?"

"To tell you about my son? No."

"You brought me here so I would kiss you."

"Yes."

"And the rest just followed?"

He watched as her gaze wandered across his face. "You don't regret it, then?"

"I'd like to kiss you again."

Her smile returned, hesitant then strong. "You would?"

"Yes. I'll even talk more if that would help."

Her eyes flashed. "All right, then. Go ahead."

He looked out at the water and saw the man kneel down and help the boy with his rod. The boy kept his small hand on his father's back as he watched the line slowly come uncoiled.

When Goldah spoke, his words came just as easily.

"I've been asking myself—I can't help it and I know maybe it's unfair—but I want to know, was it like this during the war, sitting here, in places like this? Was it possible to come and find this and forget all the rest...? I know. No one can ever put something like that aside, but to have this, to know it was always here within reach...it's impossible for me to understand. At dinner, in the store, the simplest words, and I can't help but think, was it like this even then? It makes it all almost unknowable." He turned to her. "I'm sorry. I know what you must have suffered through, but—" He shook his head. She kissed him. His hand pressed against her back—her suit wet against his skin through his shirt—and he knew, whatever else might come, that this was how a future was made.

———

On the ride back they caught the worst of the sun, the glare off the water on the windscreen almost impenetrable. He managed it, even with his free hand in hers. She had insisted he drive.

When they turned onto Thirty-Sixth Street she slid back to the passenger side of the seat, just in time to see Pearl on the porch. She wasn't sitting. She was holding the telephone on an extension line and, when she saw them drive up, she quickly hung up. She set the telephone on the rail and started down the path. Goldah saw the panic in her step.

"Ike," Pearl said, not bothering to acknowledge Eva, "you need to come inside. I need to stay by the telephone."

Goldah was stepping around the hood of the car. "What's the matter? Where's Abe?"

"Abe?" Pearl said. "Abe is fine. Why would you ask about Abe?"

"This is Eva—"

"I know who she is," Pearl said tightly. She finally looked at Eva. "Good afternoon, Mrs. De la Parra. I would invite you in but I'm afraid this isn't a convenient time."

Eva said, "Is everything all right, Mrs. Jesler?"

"Everything is fine, Mrs. De la Parra. You're very kind to ask."

"What's happened?" said Goldah.

Pearl said, "We need to go inside."

Eva slid over behind the wheel. "I should probably get home."

"No," Goldah said more firmly. "Pearl, what's happened?"

Pearl's face grew hard. She glanced at Eva, then at Goldah. "I'd like to go inside, Ike."

Goldah said calmly, "I understand that, but I'd like to know—"

"Raymond's been beaten and his hand has been shattered." Pearl's expression showed a bitterness Goldah had never seen in her. "I would have preferred to tell you inside, but now, there you have it." She looked at Eva. "Raymond is a boy who works at our store, Mrs. De la Parra. It's quite a terrible thing."

Goldah moved toward Pearl but she said, "I wasn't aware you were going off today, Ike. To the beach, evidently. How very pleasant for you. We've had people trying to reach you, but obviously that wasn't possible, was it?" She looked at Eva.

"You'll forgive me, Mrs. De la Parra, but I took the liberty of telephoning your parents in the hopes of finding Ike. They were not aware that the two of you were off together today."

Goldah matched the sharpness in her voice. "Where is Raymond now?"

"At his home."

"With Abe?"

"Yes. And a Negro doctor. I'm trying to find a surgeon who will take a look at the hand."

"How is Abe?"

"How do you think, Ike? How do you think Abe is? I need to get back inside to the telephone."

She started to go and Goldah said, "I'd like Raymond's address."

Pearl turned back. She stared coldly, then gave it to him.

Goldah said, "I'm going to go."

"You do what you like," Pearl said and turned again for the path.

———

The row houses each had a box porch above the stoop, with three plank steps leading up to a front door, wood beams browned and rotted. Goldah saw Jesler's Ambassador parked on the dirt road in front of one and he told Eva to pull over.

Mary Royal answered the door. Her eyes were red. She was done with her crying and showed only a moment's surprise at seeing Eva.

"How is he?" said Goldah.

"Bad, Mr. Ike. Real bad. He won't get no more use out a that hand."

"They're sure?"

"The doctor's come and gone. Raymond's sleeping."

"And Abe?"

Calvin's voice came from the distance behind her. "Who's at the door?"

"Mr. Ike, Pawpaw."

"He alone?"

"No."

"Invite them in," Calvin said.

Goldah followed Mary Royal and Eva down a corridor. He felt the need to duck his head even though he had a few inches to spare. They passed the door to a kitchen, where three women and a young boy stood and sat around a table. They barely looked over as the three moved past.

Mary Royal stepped through a narrow doorframe and into the back room. It was small, the floorboards painted white, with a throw rug by the metal bed. The mattress was wide enough for two but Raymond lay by himself, propped up at its center, deep in sleep. His hand was in white bandages and rested on a straw pillow, traces of blood where the knuckles would have been. His face was bloated from the beating, and his breathing was hard. Jesler sat in a chair leaning forward. His elbows were on his knees, his head on his clenched hands, as he stared at Raymond. At the other side of the bed, an older woman pressed a wet cloth to Raymond's brow. She, too, had been crying. Calvin stood in the corner.

Goldah said, "Pearl's been trying to find a surgeon."

"It won't do no good," Calvin said. "Evening, Miss Eva. Can we get you something to drink?"

"No. No, thank you," she said solemnly, her eyes on Raymond. "They gave him something?"

"Doctor give him a shot. Morphine, I think. Said it'd let him sleep."

Goldah said, "Hello, Abe."

Only then did Jesler look over. His eyes were blank. He nodded quietly and turned back to Raymond.

Calvin said to Mary Royal, "Why don't you go get something to drink for Miss Eva and Mr. Ike. We have tea and lemonade, Miss Eva." He brought a chair over to her. "I can have another brung in if you want."

Eva sat.

"When did it happen?" said Goldah.

"Early. Out at the warehouse. He was loading up for the Jacksonville run. We got a call down to the store just before lunch. Someone find Raymond against the truck."

"And no one saw anything?"

"'Saw anything'?" said Calvin. "I'm sure there was a mess a boys who saw it. Ain't no one going to do nothing about it."

Mary Royal returned with a tray and a pitcher. She set them down on the dresser and poured out a few glasses. She handed one to Eva.

Calvin said, "I got something to show you outside, Mr. Ike, that is if that's all right with you, Miss Eva?"

"Of course. Is there anything I can do?"

"No, ma'am. Just sit with Mary Royal if you would."

"Of course."

Goldah followed Calvin down the corridor and outside to the porch. The dirt street was empty under dusk, save for some boys a few houses down, tossing a rock or a ball. Calvin stepped to the edge of the porch and placed his hands on the railing. He stared out at the street and waited until Goldah was with him.

"You go off with Miss Eva today?"

"I did. Yes."

"Out to Tybee?"

"Yes."

"And you stop by Miss Pearl on the way back?"

"She was the one to tell us."

Calvin spat something to the dirt. "There ain't nothing I got to show you out here, Mr. Ike."

"I didn't think there was."

"Just didn't want Miss Eva or Mr. Abe hearing, that's all."

"Hearing what?"

Calvin continued to stare out. "You seen him. He ain't right about this. He said maybe three words when he come in, and then he just set there. He knows it's on him what happened to Raymond and I ain't going to tell him otherwise, but he's got to snap himself out. Whatever he done, he done, but it only gets worse if he don't find his way. You understand what I'm saying?"

"I think I do, Calvin."

"Them Irish sending their message all right this time, sending it through his nigger."

Goldah had never heard an edge in Calvin's voice; he was glad for it but said nothing.

"That boy ain't never going to use that hand again. And no telling for sure about that eye neither. They used a bat, Mr. Ike. A bat. That's a war hero laying in there, and they used a bat. Think Mr. Abe understanding things now?"

"I know."

"Yes, I know you know. And I know you know better than most. I understand, but this ain't like what you had in the war in those camps. I'm sorry to say it, but it ain't the same. They tried to kill you, all a you, all at once. I seen that. But here they kill us one at a time and that's a difference."

They had never spoken about the war, about anything before Savannah. Goldah had told himself there had been no need. They knew each other, knew the shared silences to their cores. Now Goldah saw how naïve that had been. There was a ranking, even to victims, and severity had no cause against time.

"Yes," said Goldah. "It's a difference. You're right."

Calvin continued to stare out. Goldah left him there and moved back inside. From the dark of the corridor he saw Eva sitting with her hand in Mary Royal's, Jesler behind them, his shoulders rocking in his chair. He was a Jew in prayer. For what, Goldah could only imagine.

PART TWO

6

MARY ROYAL SAT with Raymond on the small porch of the house. His good eye was still having trouble adjusting to the sunlight and she brought the brim of his hat lower on his face so as to lend him some ease. His bandaged hand sat on his lap like so much rotted fruit: hints of a shape that was familiar, with an odor that required constant tending. His other held a bottle of Coca-Cola, its straw absently resting on his lip.

They heard the car before they saw it, its carriage bouncing along the tiny hillocks of churned dirt.

When it came to a stop, Mary Royal said, "Hey there, Miss Eva." Mary Royal always did her best to hide the exhaustion in her voice. "We sitting outside today. First time."

Eva had made a habit of dropping by every few days. She stepped around the front of her car, and said, "I can see that, yes. It's a good day for it. Good for you. I've brought some apple butter. Mr. Ginsburg sent it along, no charge." Eva placed the jar on the rail as she moved up to the porch.

"The Ginsbergs is good people," said Mary Royal. "Raymond helped them move themselves upstairs in the store a few years back, you remember that, Raymond?"

Eva said, "Mr. Ginsburg mentioned that, yes. Hello there, Raymond."

Raymond licked at one corner of his mouth, the other still swollen, and slowly pulled the straw from his lip.

"Afternoon, Miss Eva." His words were slurred. The doctor had said it was still a few days before the jaw and throat would find their full mobility.

"You're sounding so much better," said Eva. "Maybe you could get in some walking today?"

Raymond continued to stare out at the street. "Yes, ma'am."

"Walking can really do the trick."

"Yes, ma'am."

Eva heard the hollowness in his voice. Worse, she heard the need in her own and thought how petty and foolish these words must sound—the consolation and the caring—and recalled their hollowness when her Charles had died.

Mary Royal said, "No Mr. Ike today?"

"No," said Eva. "He's down at the store...or with the truck. I forget."

"He's always down at the store these days."

"Yes." Eva forced a smile. "Shall we have some of this apple butter?"

Raymond said, "We been eating just fine, Miss Eva. Mr. Abe sent all sorts a food. Feed an army on it."

"Good—that's good. I'm glad."

Mary Royal said, "Not that we don't appreciate what you brung. It's very kind."

Eva saw the strain in the girl's eyes. She tried to share a moment with her, but Mary Royal kept her sadness to herself.

Eva said, "And when was Mr. Jesler here?"

"He ain't," Raymond said plainly. "Just sent it. We be fine on food for a while. No need to trouble yourself no more. Or Mr. Ike. We be fine. That'd do the trick."

Eva heard the quiet scorn—the brazenness in the word "trick" thrown back at her—and she let it pass. "Yes," she said. "Well, I just wanted to check in. I'll leave the apple butter here, shall I?"

Mary Royal said, "That'd be fine. And you tell Mr. Ike we appreciate all he done, taking over the deliveries and such."

Eva nodded. "Yes. I surely will." She thought to place a hand on Mary Royal's shoulder but knew it would do neither of them any good.

———

The smell of sweat and varnish filled Goldah's nose as he sat on the bleachers and watched the boys in their short pants and sleeveless shirts move across the wooden floor. There was a squeal of rubber each time one stopped. Jacob, the smallest and fastest, showed no fear of darting in between the rest.

He had been asking Goldah for nearly a week to come and "catch a game," a phrase that had caused several moments of confusion until Jacob explained that Goldah would not, in fact, be "suiting up." This next phrase had brought its own set of problems, though it proved less confounding than the rules to the game itself. Suffice it to say, tonight was Goldah's first visit to the Alliance and a basketball match. Thirty years ago someone had decided that the poorer Jews in town needed a place to socialize, a place to blend in and forget their shtetl pasts. Now there was glee club and summer camps and stage revues... and a great deal of basketball. It brought a certain pride: nothing too Jewish, and nothing like the workmen's circle or the communists. Better to throw a ball around for a few hours than to get involved with any of that.

A whistle blew and the boys gathered. The small crowd began to stand and Goldah realized that the game had come to an end. He headed over.

Jacob's red hair was matted against his brow, the ball tucked under his arm. "Pretty good, huh? You could follow?"

"Enough," said Goldah. "I take it you won."

"Killed 'em. Wouldn't want to be on that bus ride back to Jacksonville tonight, I can tell you that."

Goldah had to remind himself he was talking to a boy: Jacob spoke with the tired swagger of a man who had won these kinds of victories beyond the playing fields and gymnasiums. Goldah said, "They were much bigger than all of you."

"Jacksonville Jews is big Jews, but they're slow, so we just run 'em until they get winded and then we take care a business. We'll see them again in October, but they'll be just as slow. It's the Charleston Alliance boys you got to worry about."

"Well... it was a good match."

Jacob looked around as if expecting to see someone.

Goldah said, "Lots doing these days at the store. I'm sure Abe tried to make it."

"Yeah. Sure. I know."

As if on cue, Jesler appeared at the doorway. He was winded from the three-story climb, his face red and glistening under the bare bulb of the stairwell light. Goldah smelled the booze as Jesler drew up to them.

"Dammit," Jesler said, with a weak smile, "I missed it, didn't I? We had a shipment come in late." Even he didn't seem to believe it. "Anyway. You run them?"

"Yup," said Jacob.

"How many'd you get?"

"Twelve."

Jesler pulled out his cigarettes and lit one. "You liked it, Ike? Think we can suit you up for the next game?"

"Jacob was excellent."

"Good, good. You still want that ice cream, son? A win's a win."

"I'm good," said the boy. "I think maybe I'll just take a shower and head home."

Jesler smoked through whatever he was feeling. "Sure. Okay." He took another suck. "How about you, Ike? You want some Leopold's?"

Goldah hadn't seen much of Jesler in the past ten days. The store had been quiet with Jesler at the warehouse or in meetings or anywhere but the store. His absence was the surest sign that what had happened to Raymond was no longer up for discussion, for good or ill. Goldah had begun to wonder if, in fact, they were all thinking that the beating had never happened: no police inquiry, no outrage, not even a word from Calvin. And yet none of them had moved beyond it.

"I'm heading out as well," Goldah said. "Maybe tomorrow night."

Jesler looked as if he might say something funny or clever but knew it would be neither. Jacob jabbed a thumb in the direction of the locker room. "Well," he said, "I guess I'll see you Saturday unless you need me to sleep in on Friday if we got something coming early."

"No, nothing early," said Jesler. "Not these days."

"Okay, then. Thanks for coming."

Out on the street the humidity trumped the heat and Jesler offered Goldah a ride.

"I'm getting picked up," Goldah said. He had been playing his part as well by finding any excuse he could to eat away from Pearl's table.

"Mrs. De la Parra going to drop you off at home?"

"That's the plan."

"The plan. Good to have a plan. Always got a plan." Jesler tossed the butt of his cigarette to the pavement. "You're sounding like a regular American, Ike. So is it dinner, dancing? Pearl always wants to go dancing."

"I don't know. I'm not much of a dancer."

"That's not the point, is it?" The smile was no better than the one up in the gymnasium: It was hard, thought Goldah, to help a man so intent on going nowhere. "Okay, then," Jesler said. "I should probably—"

A pair of headlights turned onto the street and slowed.

"Well, look who's here," Jesler said with sudden enthusiasm. He waved a hand as Goldah looked to see Eva's Cadillac pulling to a stop.

Jesler leaned his head into the passenger window. "Evening, Mrs. De la Parra."

"Hello there, Mr. Jesler. What a pleasant surprise."

Jesler settled his forearms on the window frame. "You missed quite a game. Sent those boys packing back to Jacksonville with their tails between their legs. You should come out to the Alliance for the next one. Jacob's a real fine player and I'm trying to convince Ike here to take it up. He's got the size."

"He surely does."

"You have a beautiful car, Mrs. De la Parra."

"Why thank you."

Goldah had stepped around and was opening the driver's door. Eva slid across to the passenger seat and Goldah got in.

Jesler said, "Taking him for some dancing tonight, Mrs. De la Parra?"

"I'm not sure we've decided just yet, Mr. Jesler."

"It's Abe. Please."

"Of course. Abe. And I've been meaning to ask about your young Raymond. Has the doctor said anything more?"

Jesler seemed to lose his focus. "That's very kind of you to ask," he said. "Doing the best he can, that's where it is. Looking good on the eye, but the hand—that's a different story. We'll just have to see. But he's strong and young. He'll never have a worry as long as I'm around." He was searching for something else to say and settled on, "Well...you have a pleasant night, the two of you." Even Jesler's well-wishes held a kind of hopelessness. "You come when you want, Ike, make your own time."

Jesler stepped back and Goldah pulled out, watching in the mirror as Jesler stared after them. Jesler turned, uncertain for a few seconds as to where he had left his own car, and walked off.

"Poor man," said Eva.

Goldah took the next turn. "He's all right."

"Don't be unkind."

Is that what it was, thought Goldah—unkind? Unkind to expect something more of Jesler, of himself. The world was once again moving forward, getting on with things, taking care of itself. But he had seen it in Mary Royal's eyes, in Raymond's. They would never look at him the same way. The familiarity in their silence reminded him of his own resentment, one that Goldah had learned to choke down long ago. But to find it here...Unkind. It was a word without meaning.

He reached his hand over and held it open. Eva took it, and he said, "There was a time when I wouldn't have seen a difference between Raymond and me. I shouldn't forget that."

This time he had caught her off guard. She said, "Only you could see it that way." She ran her thumb over his palm and, staring down at it, said almost to herself, "Foolish to think a little apple butter would make a difference."

"What?"

She looked up. "Nothing," she said. "Mr. Jesler must be feeling the weight of the world on him. He'd been drinking."

"I imagine he'll figure it out."

"You really should think about finding your own place. It would make it easier on him."

"Would it? And what do we think Pearl might do with that? She's already so pleased with how far we've let things progress between us."

"Is she?" said Eva. "I'd be happy to set up a luncheon between Mrs. Jesler and my mother at the golf club so they could share in their untold happiness."

"Are the tables at the club fire-resistant?"

"I'd have to call ahead and ask." She shifted almost imperceptibly and said, "So how far have we progressed in all this?" Eva never failed to find a singular moment to catch him off guard. He took another turn, and she said, "You're taking us back where we came from."

"Am I?"

"You have no idea where we're going, do you?"

"In this car? No. I don't suppose I do."

She was looking at him, his face in and out of the lamplight. "So how far?"

Far enough, he thought, if questions like this could come so blithely.

"I saw your father yesterday," he said. "Downtown. He was having lunch at that pharmacy on Bull."

"Pinkussohn's," she said and let him move them along. "Every Tuesday. With Jack Stern and Sid Friedman. They've been doing it for twenty years."

"He's always so generous with his time."

"It's because he likes you."

"He hardly knows me."

"He knows enough to know. If the store is so terrible, why not leave and write for my father? You know he'd love that."

Goldah saw they were about to pass the Alliance for a second time. He accelerated and said, "So you've had a chat with your father."

"I have lots of chats with my father. Yesterday we talked about a patch in the garden that doesn't seem to know how to grow. He was rather concerned. You've just driven past the Alliance again."

"I'm making sure everyone got out safely."

"He knows how good you are. He wanted to know if I could bring it up subtly so as not to seem pushy."

"Oh dear, there's that chance gone."

"Hush. But he understands how important family must be to you and how you might not be inclined to step away from that. But what a shame, he said, with a young man who has such talent. Take the next left."

"Why—is he waiting for us somewhere on Gaston?"

"Yes, he wants to take you dancing."

Goldah pulled the car over. Nothing too dramatic but he felt the need to look at her, tell himself that this was real, regardless of everything else.

"What's the matter?" she said, but even her concern couldn't touch this moment.

He turned to her and reached his hand across to her waist. It was always the waist and the smallness of her hips, the feel of them beneath the crisp, taut layer of cotton, and he pulled her closer into him.

"Oh, I see," she managed before he gently kissed her, then with greater need. She was still holding him when she said, "You surprise me when you do that."

"Do I do it too often?" He felt the heat from his collar between them.

"No . . . Maybe."

"And it worries you?"

"It's not a worry, no. It just feels—"

"As if I don't trust you're here."

"Yes." There was more strength in her voice. "Why doesn't it surprise me that you'd know exactly what I mean."

"I'm sorry."

"It's as if somehow you need to convince yourself of what you're feeling. You *are* feeling it, aren't you?"

"Of course."

"It's unfair, I know—what with everything you've been through. I can only imagine."

"You can't," he said perhaps too bluntly, then more gently, "and that's the way it should be. I'm sorry if I'm not terribly good at this."

"You're wonderful at this and you know it. You're not asking for anything beyond what this is right now."

"But I am."

She sat quietly, searching his face, and Goldah wondered how it was that he could question what was so clearly in front of him. How easy life would be, he thought, to blame it on his past, that crucial everything-he'd-been-through that she and everyone else gravitated to as a way to make sense of him. How much more of a shock to admit that this reticence, his numbness, had been his long before the camps and that, perhaps, his survival was simply proof that such detachment had its own worth.

"A few rooms," he said. "So how does one go about finding those?"

———

Jesler placed his keys on the hall table and felt the ache of the failing booze in his neck. He'd been drinking too much lately, he knew it. Hirsch didn't care about Raymond. He said the boy was a Savannah issue, nothing to do with the unions. Pay the Irish what you owe them. That's how it works. Any trouble with the Micks was Jesler's problem. In fact, if Hirsch had known Jesler was playing it this way from the start—"I told you not to sign anything"—it was too late now.

Jesler saw the lights on in the parlor. Pearl was usually upstairs this time of the evening. She was spending a great deal of time upstairs these days.

"Abe? Is that you?"

Her voice had more life to it than he expected. He stepped in and saw her with a glass of tea, sitting across from a young man he had never seen before.

"This is Mr. Thomas from the *Morning News*," she said with an equally unexpected pride. "He says he's been trying to get in touch with you for several days."

Thomas was on his feet. He seemed an amiable enough fellow: tall, reedy, blond.

"You'll forgive me, Mr. Jesler," Thomas said. "I telephoned your office downtown and left several messages. I thought I'd try and leave a note for you here."

"And I just happened to be out on the porch and here we are," said Pearl.

Jesler noticed the half-eaten piece of pie and several small cookies on a plate.

"Mrs. Jesler was very kind to offer me a glass of tea," said Thomas. "I would never have thought to intrude at this hour."

"Nonsense," Pearl said, standing. "No intrusion at all. The newspaper wants to talk to my Abe, that deserves a glass of tea. I'll leave you gentlemen to it."

She moved across to Jesler with what could only be described as a bounce in her step. Jesler wondered which of the two—the pie or this final flourish—was more disconcerting. Closing in on him, Pearl raised her eyebrows and leaned in: "Now everyone's going to know about the expansion. Put everything back in line."

Unable to look away, Jesler watched her to the stairs before turning back to Thomas. Jesler knew his head wasn't clear enough for this.

"Have a seat, Mr. Thomas, please. I'll take a glass myself?"

Thomas poured one out and handed it across. Jesler said, "You did an article on me when I opened the store. The paper did. Mrs. Jesler was very pleased with that."

"Yes," Thomas said, clearly uninterested. "I cover the docks." He pulled out his pad and pencil and Jesler took a hasty sip of his tea.

Jesler said, "The docks. I didn't know the paper had a man just for that."

"Docks, treasury, city hall, that sort of thing."

"Very interesting. And you've been at it long?"

"About eight months. I came down from Roanoke."

"Into the swampland of the South."

"Yes, it does get steamy here."

Another sip—Jesler felt the awkwardness even as he drank—and he said, "So what is it you think I can help you with?"

Thomas scribbled something. "One of your employees was beaten recently. A Raymond Taylor."

Like a constellation, the conversation now opened up in front of Jesler—point to point to point—and with no way to navigate around it. "That's right."

"He was making a delivery down to Jacksonville. Nothing was stolen."

"Yes."

"Would you care to comment?"

"Comment? Comment on what?"

"You don't find it strange that an employee of yours was beaten for no apparent reason?"

There were any number of things Jesler was finding strange these days—his own sour reflection not the least of them—but he said, "I find it terrible, Mr. Thomas. Strange? Well...you've been in Roanoke. I'm sure you understand."

"I'm looking into corruption at the docks, Mr. Jesler. So coming down from Roanoke—no, I'm afraid I don't understand."

"Corruption." Jesler repeated. "That's a thick word, isn't it?" He knew another sip would only come across as weakness but he took it all the same. "No—our Raymond was a war hero. Decorated. That's unusual for a Negro. Some folks haven't been all that kind about it."

Thomas saw where this was going. He nodded indifferently. "I see." He placed his glass on the table. "Your wife mentioned an expansion. That must be exciting."

Jesler didn't know if this was a coup from having just overheard or if Pearl had jumped the gun over pie. Either way, everything was coming to a head.

"Did she?" Jesler said casually. "Yes, very exciting, but as she knows we're only *thinking* about an expansion. Not really on the front burner what with Raymond still recovering." He set his glass down and stood. "But when we do, I hope it merits another article in your paper. Always good to have a little free advertising. Was there anything else?"

Thomas had been through the drill. He was cordial in his goodbyes as Jesler walked him to the door. The world was caving in around him and all Jesler could think of was the woman upstairs, patiently sitting and waiting for a celebration.

7

AS IT TURNED OUT Goldah enjoyed driving a truck. He liked the weight of it on the highway and the height of the cab, and felt, even if it was only boxes of shoes, he was doing something of importance. His father had always disparaged truck drivers and menials—not in any direct or conscious way—but a lifetime of comments had been enough to let him distinguish between himself and those who got their hands dirty in order to survive.

"You wouldn't want me digging a ditch, Yitzhak," his father once said. "It would be a terrible ditch. An editor of a journal needs to know only how to *write* about the man who does the digging. You see?"

By then, Goldah had given up trying to lay bare the veiled condescension. It would only provoke a slightly less uncomfortable response: "But Yitzhak—I said I'd make a *terrible* ditch. Why have me do it?"

It was the more direct volleys, always posed innocently enough to Goldah but in clear earshot of his father's victims, that Goldah learned to filter out entirely: For the mechanic, "Does the man think it takes a genius to change a tire?" For the washerwoman, "Wouldn't she have been smarter to post a little sign 'Wet Floor' before starting to mop?" And his coup de grâce, for the cabbie, "Can you explain to me, Yitzhak, how an idiot of a driver can't find the clutch...?"

It is Pasco, the little Italian, who asks the question.

He sits with Goldah in the back of a transport truck, both of them smelling of wet wool from the blankets the Russian soldiers have given them. Goldah knows that the man across from them is already dead even as the driver grinds away, and Pasco, indifferent, steals Goldah's father's favorite grumble: "Doesn't he know I have no kidneys left?"

Pasco refuses to be silent with the rest. He refuses to see redemption as a solemn thing. He says as much: "He's dead, you know. They'll discover it the next stop and look at us with even greater incomprehension. 'They ride with the dead and say nothing? Who are these ghouls of men?' But who else would we ride with? You know I'm right."

Goldah sits and feels the unimaginable cold—imaginable as he has known far worse—but finds the sight of his own breath mesmerizing because it is there in front of him and he can touch it if he chooses. Even now he has trouble remembering the *Lager* as it was, the same trouble with the liberation camp, where they were free to dig out the snow for their Russian saviors. They dug, of course, not because they were still prisoners—although what else could they have been?—but because none of them, when placed face-to-face with it, felt worthy of real freedom.

Goldah admits to Pasco that he has already begun to forget the look and the smell of certain places in the *Lager*, places he saw every day. Goldah says it is like the face of a family member or a friend who has died—blurred and distant—and Pasco tells him this is a lie. Heat and anger fill Pasco's voice, not because he doesn't believe Goldah but because he knows it is an impossibility.

"The laws of nature," Pasco says. "Gravity and the planets. Memory plays no role with these things. There is the shape of the world and the draw of the moon and the tides. It is the same with the *Lager*. You think somehow memory will let us see ourselves otherwise? You think we will find a way to enter the world beyond the *Lager*? I understand that, but you must know that *this* is the lie because the real world for us lives only in the past. This is why we ride..."

———

A Packard raced by—a quick press of its horn—and Goldah sat alone with the memory.

The guards had made his father dig his own grave. They had told him to fill it with water, to stand in the freezing pit, drenched and shaking, before shooting him. This, they said, was for Goldah to stand and watch. It was nothing his father had done or said. It was simply to show it could be done.

A second car passed and Goldah thought, Yes, this is why we ride with the dead.

———

Calvin crouched next to the bottom shelf and counted out the boxes of size sevens. No matter the style, the sevens were always the first to go. It would have made more sense, he thought, to set them up on a middle shelf, but his knees always took him down on instinct, so maybe it was better to leave them where they were. He heard a glass fall to the cement floor the other side of the stockroom and moved out from the shelves thinking, What in the world is that boy doing back here now?

It was Jesler standing by the desk. He was leafing through a stack of papers and hadn't noticed Calvin or the shattered glass. It looked as if he hadn't been sleeping. His face was pale and he had a shine on him from too much liquor.

Calvin said, "You want me to sweep that up, Mr. Jesler?"

Jesler turned, his eyes wide as if he had been caught at something: What it was didn't matter.

"Calvin," Jesler said. "I didn't see the truck in the back. I thought you were doing the Jacksonville run."

"No, suh. Too much for me these days. Mr. Ike's been doing it since Raymond. He'll be back soon enough if you need him."

"No...no. That's all right. Jacob's out front?"

"Yes, suh."

"Good...good. You doing okay?"

"We haven't been seeing you."

"What? Oh—yes—things have been picking up. Lots on the plate. Store looks good."

"Yes, suh." Calvin took the broom and dustpan and stepped over. He said, "We getting through it, me and Jacob."

Jesler looked as if he might answer but they both knew there was nothing for him to say.

Calvin began to sweep up the glass. "I ain't blaming you, Mr. Jesler." It was the starkness of the statement that let it pass untouched. "Not my place, whatever it is that got that boy all tore up. And I'm reaching the end a my anger, which you can understand is natural enough. But that's not for me to have you thinking about anyway. I know that." Calvin knelt down and swept what he had collected into the pan, every grain, back and forth. He didn't care to see Jesler's face. "Maybe it ain't my place neither to be talking about it now but I know you long enough and thought you should know." He brought the pan over to the trash can and dumped it out.

Jesler nodded again; his face had grown paler. "Yes...Of course...That's right."

"Always talk right about you and your people, Mr. Jesler. Always have. How you do things, take care a things. Ain't something I ever want to regret. You understand, don't you?" Calvin stood for a moment before he placed the broom and pan against the wall. "I'll get back to the shelving now. Mr. Ike be back soon enough."

Calvin moved off and Jesler felt an overwhelming need to sit. His hands began to shake, not from the booze but from this strange and weighted absolution that made even shame feel like a kind of relief.

8

THE FIRST PINK of evening settled on the puddles along the street and Jacob, standing at the curb, gazed after a car that was splashing up a thick stream of water.

"It'll be a ghost town down here come *yontif*," he said.

Goldah stood with him: He hadn't given a thought to the holidays. "Not every store, surely."

"You come down a couple of weeks from now and see for yourself. Goyim gone, too. Not enough to make it worth their while."

Goldah hadn't thought of that, either.

Calvin poked his head out the front door and said, "We got boxes to be shelved. I'm done waiting on you two. Ain't no time to be taking the air." He was gone before either of them could answer.

Jacob stared out at the street; his face had aged in the last week. "Calvin's got to get past it. Ain't doing no one no good."

Goldah said nothing. Another car drove past and Jacob sidestepped the spray before heading for the store. Goldah took a last pull on his cigarette and flicked it to the curb, intending to follow, when a car pulled up. The passenger window rolled down but there was no one there.

"Mr. Goldah?"

Goldah bent low and saw Art Weiss leaning across the seat.

Weiss said, "I thought it was you. Do have a few minutes to take a drive?"

Goldah looked back to the store and saw Jacob watching him from the door. The boy really had become something so much more than a boy in the last weeks. He nodded to Goldah and mouthed the word *Go*.

Goldah turned back to Weiss. "I think I can manage a few minutes."

"Good. Hop in." Weiss pulled the car out. He offered Goldah a cigarette and they both lit up. "You like Americans? The cigarettes, I mean."

"I do," said Goldah. "They're very nice."

"Good." Weiss took a pull and said easily, "A little strange pulling up like that, I know. I hope I didn't alarm you."

"Not at all."

"Good. Then I think I'm going to get this out of the way right at the start. I don't think I'm going to care how close you get to my daughter, Mr. Goldah. It's not that whatever makes her happy makes me happy—that's just never the case and, if you ever have children, you'll understand—but I don't think I'm going to care."

Goldah felt an odd sense of déjà vu. From his first go-round with Mrs. Weiss, he knew to say nothing.

"What?" said Weiss. "You've got nothing to say at all?"

Goldah tried to mask his surprise. "I...didn't think you were expecting me to answer."

"I'm not my wife, Mr. Goldah."

There was something refreshing in the way Weiss laid things out.

"No, of course. So...I make Eva happy?"

"Why don't we just play this straight. We both know the girl's in love with you. Has she introduced you to Julian?"

Goldah regretted having made light of things. "I haven't met him, no."

"Good. At least she's being cautious there." Weiss took a turn.

"Can I ask," said Goldah, "why is it you're not going to care?"

"Oh, I'm going to care, Mr. Goldah. I care right now. The grand history of Jews in Savannah has been all about that caring. And I know it probably doesn't make much sense to you, given what you've been through. I can't imagine the SS officer who put you on that train asked which synagogue you were affiliated with. I know that. And I know it must make us seem rather small in your eyes, and maybe I'm not so sure I wouldn't agree with you."

Goldah had never expected this kind of candor. "I've tried to understand."

"I know you have. That's what makes you a remarkably decent fellow. But I still have Mrs. Weiss at home and I won't say there isn't a part of me—a very *big* part of me—that doesn't agree with her one hundred percent. So here's what we're going to do. You're going to write a column for me. I haven't figured out what that might be, but you're going to do it. You see, I've tried to be affable with my daughter about getting you to agree, but that doesn't seem to have made an impact. And maybe I appreciate your reticence because of that decency, but it's not going to work for any of us. So you'll write for me, then something a bit more after that, and then—because you *do* make my daughter happy, and if you ever have children, you'll realize that's the *only* thing that truly matters—we'll find a way to keep everyone in line. Maybe not happy the way the two of you are, but well enough. So you see, Mr. Goldah, I can go on just like my wife. Must be why we've been so happy together for all these years."

Somehow they were back at the store. Weiss put the car in park.

"It's a damn good thing you're such a fine writer, Mr. Goldah. Everyone would think me a fool not to use you. Otherwise I'm not sure how we would have squared this. You have yourself a pleasant day."

———

At dinner Goldah mentioned he might be interested in doing some writing for the newspaper. Pearl was in a surprisingly festive mood, and not just for his appearance at the table. He hadn't realized it was more than a week since his last dinner with them—a fact Pearl blithely let slip once or twice—but there wasn't the usual silence after each dollop of guilt. These were simply the facts, and she seemed to be holding on to one of her own as if it might change the world entire with its arrival.

Jesler paused at the mention of the newspaper. "The sort of stuff you wrote in Prague?" He reached for the bread.

"I'm not sure," said Goldah. "It's all very tentative."

"Well, that's good, isn't it? Get to meet some new folks. People who share your interests."

Pearl said, "He said it was tentative, Abe. And speaking of the newspaper"—the moment had come, the heavens and the earth conceived—"what a coincidence, but you'll never guess. They're planning on doing an article on the store, Ike. Abe and you and the expansion. Isn't that exciting?"

"The what?" Goldah said.

Pearl pressed on: "Now there'll be no time for distractions for the two of you, will there? Maybe I'll even come down and lend a hand. Get my picture in the paper. Isn't that exciting?"

Goldah tried to gauge his own reaction by Jesler's but it was impossible to discern a singular emotion in the man's face. The best he could decipher was confusion and that seemed the wrong approach entirely.

"Congratulations," he managed.

"To you, too, Ike. To you, too," Pearl said. "You're a part of this now. A big part. I know you've been finding your legs, but now there's something bigger on the horizon. And we couldn't be happier that you're such an essential part of it, could we, Abe?"

Jesler continued to gaze blank-faced across at his wife. He then turned to Goldah. "So what kind of writing are you thinking about?"

"Abe," Pearl said. "I just mentioned the big news. We can talk about that later."

"What kind of writing?"

"Abe," she said, like a slap on the wrist. "Some little thing Ike might be writing—he might not even have time for it now, will you, Ike?"

Jesler continued, "Is it something you might want to think about as a regular thing?"

"Abe Jesler! I'm talking to you!"

Jesler looked across at his wife. He said calmly, "We're done talking about that, Pearl. I think you know that. And I'm very interested in what Ike might be finding for himself."

"'What Ike—'" The words caught on her tongue. Her disbelief quickly gave way to something darker. Goldah had never seen a smile with such tightness and immediacy, as if her every muscle from cheek to jowl had been pressed in starch. Sitting above it was something more familiar, rage, constrained in the narrow slits of her eyes and indiscriminate in its focus.

"I see," she said with hollow pleasantness. "You're interested in what he might be finding for himself. Tell me, Ike, are they wanting you to write about your experience in the camps? I'm sure Savannah readers would be most interested in that."

"Watch yourself, Pearl," Jesler said easily. "You don't want to do this now."

"Do what, Abe? Tell me, what is it that I'm doing? Or should I call Mrs. Eva De la Parra and ask her why her father is throwing a bone to Ike? How embarrassed that man must be, a little Czech Jew and his daughter, and here he is trying to wash it away. Would that be better, Abe? Would it?"

Goldah said, "Perhaps I should—"

"No, Ike," said Pearl. "You and Abe obviously have a great deal to talk about that doesn't concern me."

Jesler said, "Pearl, you need to calm yourself down."

"It must feel quite grand to have come into our home and feel so much more welcome elsewhere. It's only a livelihood and an understanding that we wanted to give you. But I'm sure the chance to write again—that must fill *all* the holes that have been left. And so very fortunate to have it be the father of the girl you've taken up with."

"I said careful, Pearl."

"The girl and her little boy." There was a meanness now in her voice. "What a *wonderful* little family they have there. Just perfect. She gets to have a little boy and Ike—" Pearl stopped herself. Tears now commingled with the rage. The whole face was shattering as she stood. "I'm afraid I don't have much of an appetite for dessert. Mary Royal stopped by today. A Key lime. She said she'd heard you enjoy that, Ike. I'm sure you do. I'll leave you to it."

Her eyes moved haphazardly along the table—to Jesler, to Ike, to Jesler again—until, with a sudden purpose, she stepped around the table. It looked as if she might move past Goldah but, in an act of desperate compassion, she leaned over, placed her arms around his shoulders, and kissed him on the top of his head.

"You're a good man, Ike Goldah. A good man. I need you to know that. That's all. I just love you so much." She straightened herself up and spoke through the tears. "I'm feeling a bit tired, Abe, so I'll say my good nights. You boys enjoy your talk."

She moved through to the hall. Goldah waited until he heard her on the steps before saying, "Do you need to go after her?"

Jesler listened, waiting for the sound of their bedroom door to close. His eyes were distant when he turned back to the table. "She'll be all right." He looked at Goldah. "She's not far wrong on Weiss, though. He's not doing this for you. You do know that, don't you?"

"I do. Yes."

"Rare that a man does something for someone else just to do it."

Goldah knew Jesler was wrong; he just happened to be right this time out. Goldah said, "I've been thinking—"

Jesler stopped him with a long breath in and turned to Goldah. "You've been thinking about getting a place on your own. I know. I'm afraid I haven't done you much help with that tonight."

For the second time in the last few hours, Goldah tried not to show his surprise. "Yes."

"It's not as if I haven't been encouraging it. I think that might be the right choice."

147

"I'm sorry for this."

"For what? For getting on with things? I wish I had some of that myself."

"You've been—"

"I know. We've been kind. Terribly, terribly kind. It starts to sound a little empty after a time, don't you think?" Jesler smoothed out the tablecloth in front of him and said, "So here's what we'll do. I'll help you with Pearl and you help me with a little something down at the newspaper. You think we can work that out?"

———

At just after eleven p.m. Goldah lifted the latch on the Weisses' side-yard gate—as he had been instructed—and pushed through. The whole thing seemed slightly foolish, juvenile even, but Eva had sounded so wonderfully mysterious on the phone, what choice did he have? Even so, he kept close to the fence and checked to see whether the bedroom lights were on upstairs. The house was dark, the crucial parties asleep, he imagined. He had never been to the Weiss home, so coming at it for the first time in this flanking maneuver seemed to him somehow more audacious.

He inched along the grass—unable to see more than a few feet in either direction—when his shoe hit cement. It was a puzzling sensation. He tried to find his bearings but the tree cover was too dense: not even a bit of moonlight to help him along. He took another step, and he heard Eva say, "Careful."

Goldah strained to see her through the darkness but it was no good. "You have me at a disadvantage."

"I know."

"So we just stand here?"

"I'm not standing."

There were any number of things that passed through his mind—first and foremost the best route back to the gate—but Eva turned on a bright light, and the Weisses' swimming pool suddenly appeared some twenty feet from him. She was sitting on a lounge chair in her swimsuit. She held up a pair of black trunks for him, and said, "You wanted American. It doesn't get more American than this."

Goldah's instinct told him to look back at the house. He expected a light to turn on at any moment.

"They're out at the cottage on Tybee," Eva said. "With Julian. They give me a night to myself every so often."

"And this is how you choose to spend it?"

"I do."

"There's a cottage?"

"There is."

"How very nice."

"Yes. Are you going to come over and take the suit or are you expecting me to hand-deliver it?"

Goldah glanced around at the remaining chairs and small tables, one of which was sprouting an unopened umbrella. The pool itself was simple but elegant, blue and white tile, with an ever-widening set of steps leading down from the far corner. As with everything to do with the Weisses, Goldah had seen it all before in a magazine. Eva had placed two folded towels on the chair next to her. A bottle of wine and two glasses sat nearby, poolside.

He said, "As I won't be putting the suit on, I don't think it makes much of a difference."

"Ooooh. How *very* bold of you. Skinny-dipping the first time you try out our pool."

"Skinny what?"

"Dipping. Naked. No clothes. You shock me, Mr. Goldah. But how American. Look at how quickly you're picking up on things." She stood and Goldah found himself leaning back against the fence. She said, "You must really hate the water."

Goldah wanted so much not to lose touch with her playfulness, but memories, he knew, were rarely that accommodating. It was all he could do to keep the more ruthless of them at bay. "Not at all."

She moved toward him. "You can't swim, can you? I saw it that first day when we went out to the beach."

He said, "Not a lot of places to learn how to swim in Prague."

"I don't imagine that's true. In fact I know it's not true."

"No . . . you're quite right."

"My God, are you going to come over or not?"

His attempt at charm was quickly becoming farce—and not the good kind—and Goldah forced his right foot forward, then his left. He hoped it looked like walking.

"You can change in the cabana. There's a light inside."

It was a small space, with varnished floors, a cushioned banquette, and a cabinet. There was a separate nook for a shower, along with a few hooks for towels, goggles, and robes. Goldah undressed. He turned on the shower, stepped in, and doused himself in cold water. He had gotten used to a shower every night. It was the one way he could find to rid his skin of the heat, if only for a few minutes. He toweled off and put on the suit. He couldn't recall the last time he had left himself this exposed. Or maybe he could. Outside, she was sitting by the pool, her legs in the water up to her knees.

"We've had rain," she said, "so the water's not too warm. Your shower was probably more refreshing."

"Bracing. Sadly it's beginning to wear off."

"Oh well. Then the pool's your only hope."

"My only hope?"

He had been waiting for her smile and now had it. She said, "My father tells me you've decided to write for him."

"Did he? And that's why we're here tonight. A victory swim."

"Oh, it's not my victory. And wouldn't that depend on how well you write?"

"He tells me I write very well. You should ask him."

"I suppose I should. You know you look rather handsome in your suit."

He had almost forgotten he was wearing it. "As do you."

"Are you suggesting I try it on?"

This was an Eva he had yet to see, no less sure of herself but somehow more daring, though daring wasn't the right word. Bold. No, that was wrong, too. Bewitching. My God, that was worse. Goldah thought he might be going a bit flush. "I meant in yours," he said.

Her smile returned. "Why don't you come over."

His bare feet felt the cement more acutely than he expected, little ridges and fine grains scraping against his soles as he walked. He was nearly to her when she slid into the water. She waded out, her shoulders just above the surface. She stopped midpool and turned back to him.

"That's a dirty trick," he said.

"You're coming in. No two ways about it." She dove under, swam back to the side, and surfaced. She rested her arms on the ledge and let her legs float behind. "My father taught me to swim in this pool. He was a bit of taskmaster. Don't say I didn't warn you. Part of his job description." She saw his confusion. "It's what he always says when he has to do terribly mean fatherly things. Part of his job." She laughed quietly to herself. "He sent a boy home once, five minutes after he'd arrived to pick me up. I was upstairs and the boy was gone by the time I came down. Can you imagine? I was mortified the next day at school. Alan Rabin. My father said he was rude, a thick skull—that was the term my father always liked to use. Turns out Alan had had a little something to drink before coming by. I learned that later. 'Not on my watch.' Another of my father's favorite phrases." She laughed again and propelled herself back to the middle of the pool. "So no one taught you to swim?"

Goldah continued to stand. "Not in the job description."

"You haven't told me about your father."

"I thought I was here to learn to swim?"

"Are you in the pool?"

Goldah weighed the alternatives. He sat and eased his feet into the water. "He was a writer."

"A journalist?"

"No, a writer. An editor. Stories, essays, that sort of thing."

"Isn't a journalist a writer?"

This time Goldah laughed. At least these memories were more manageable. "I'm sure somewhere that's true. No, not for us. He thought ideas deserved more than the facts behind them. That was one of his, if we're trading favorites. Words have a deeper purpose. 'Facts are the enemy of truth.' Cervantes, but he made it his own."

"It's a lovely idea."

"I'm sure it is, although not such a good idea if you're living in Prague in 1938."

She drew closer to him and again rested her arms on the ledge. Her face was no more than two or three inches from his knees. "But he must have loved the way you wrote."

He leaned forward and placed his hands in the water. He brought them out and rubbed them on his cheeks. "He liked to find the things he had taught me in the pieces I wrote. Not so much the pieces themselves." Goldah became quiet but then his eyes widened and he gave her his best smile. "He should have taught me how to swim instead."

She mirrored the smile and took hold of his hands. She then stepped back. "I won't let you go. Just hop down."

"This is fine."

"Hop down."

He felt the weight of her pulling him in. He might have resisted but he knew there was nothing for it now. When he was standing next to her, she said, "Lie back. I'll have you, I promise. Lie back and float."

He felt his breath shorten. His heart began to race. He had yet to move.

"Please," he heard her say.

"I know how to swim," he said quietly. His throat was tightening. "I just don't care to."

"It's only swimming."

He had told himself he could find a way here, with her. He had put on the suit. He had waded out. But no. Even now, there was no way he could find the words.

"I know," he said. "I know." He took her hand. "Can we drink that nice bottle of wine?"

She waited. She knew he would tell her nothing. Instead, she let him lead her back to the side. He pulled himself out and, sitting, drew his legs out of the water as well. When she was next to him, he brought the glasses over and poured.

————

Eight days later, a young woman, fully believing herself to be Malke Posner, stepped down onto the Savannah platform from the Richmond train. She carried a single bag and had instructed the Lubecks—her distant cousins—to send on the rest of her belongings once she had settled herself in. The Lubecks, generous to a fault, had been hesitant to let her go but, as they had no legal recourse to keep her in Virginia—other than the laws of compassion and nature—they agreed, so long as Malke stayed in close contact during her travels. Even so, they remained concerned: A woman with so little English might get lost or worse. Mrs. Lubeck had even offered to make the trip with her, but Malke insisted that this was out of the question.

Malke had telephoned from Petersburg, Rocky Mount, Fayetteville, Dillon, Florence—she had missed her opportunity in Kingstree due to a somewhat stumbling conversation with a young woman from Yemassee—and then Charleston.

The woman from Yemassee, it turned out, was an Avon Lady, who showed Malke how she might best work with some of the more demanding areas of her lips and cheeks. It was all in the application and the shading, the young woman said. Malke had tried to follow as best she could and wondered if perhaps the mirror the young lady provided might not have been specially designed to help enhance these gentle deceptions, but the young lady insisted nonetheless.

Malke had purchased seven dollars worth of lip, cheek, and eye makeup, which she now carried in a small case in her purse.

When she arrived at the Jesler home in the taxicab she thought, This is what I have been hoping for all along. When Pearl answered the door and Malke recognized the deep sensitivity in the woman's eyes, Malke felt that perhaps, at long last, her suffering had come to an end.

9

"POSNER?" Pearl said.

She stared at the strange, frail young woman, with her ungainly bag and eye shadow that was several shades too dark. Pearl was having trouble understanding the accent; it was so thick and halting. She took a moment to piece things together. "You're looking for Mr. Goldah?"

"Yes," said Malke. "Forgive my English. Do you speak perhaps Yiddish or German?"

Pearl felt her own apprehension more acutely and knew it would be best to manage all this inside. She led the girl through, expecting at least one kind word about the house, but Miss Posner walked in silence—with a slight limp, Pearl thought, though she tried not to take any unwarranted notice of it.

Pearl brought in two glasses and the pitcher of tea that Mary Royal had made yesterday afternoon. Mary Royal was still slipping away for a few hours here and there—Pearl had told her it was fine—and this afternoon just happened to be one of those occasions. Sitting stiffly on the lip of the settee, Pearl felt this would have gone a great deal better with Mary Royal at her side.

"I'm not quite sure I understand," Pearl said. "You say you were a part of Mr. Goldah's family from before the war. In

Prague. Well that would mean you're a part of *our* family, too? Mr. Goldah is our cousin. Do you understand what I'm saying? That would make us cousins as well."

Pearl couldn't be sure if the look in the girl's eyes was confusion or something else—the face was irregular and so difficult to read—and, thinking back to long-forgotten grandparents, Pearl said, "*Kuzeen.* That's it, I think. Mr. Goldah is our *kuzeen.* Our cousin. *Versteht?*"

Malke stared intently and then seemed to have a breakthrough before she shook her head. "Ah, no. I am not a cousin of Yitzhak. I was to be his wife."

The miracle of finding Abe at the store, coupled with the frantic quality of Pearl's reenactment over the telephone, had him home in twenty minutes. He was now sitting with Pearl on the settee drinking something stronger than tea.

"You say you've been in Richmond?" he asked.

"Yes. Richmond. For four months. I have had some medical troubles."

"And you're feeling better now?"

"Abe," Pearl cut in gently. She shook her head, then tried a smile for Miss Posner. "And you say you found Ike—I mean Yitzhak—through the government office."

"Yes," said Malke.

Jesler said, "And they didn't recommend that you call or write before coming?"

Malke had prepared for this question: "I have your address since two days. I prefer to come myself. It is a long time. I do not wish to wait for the post."

"Sure..." said Jesler. "No, of course. Better to get yourself here."

"And I am not good so far on English in the telephone."

"Yes, I imagine that's true." Jesler took a drink. "Well...We'll need to track down Ike—Yitzhak—as fast as we can."

"He will be home soon?"

Jesler felt Pearl looking through him.

"No," he said. "He doesn't stay with us anymore. He's taken a few rooms of his own. Not far from here, of course, but once he got himself settled—you know—a young man needs a place on his own."

"On his own?"

"Yes," said Pearl. "It's a very recent development."

"And, it would seem, all for the best now," Jesler said.

Pearl ignored this latest justification. She said, "I do apologize, Miss Posner, but it's quite startling for us—not just having you here but...you should know, Yitzhak never mentioned a fiancée. This is the first we've heard of it."

It was clear things were moving too quickly for Malke. "Pardon?"

"A fiancée. A—" Pearl looked to Abe. "What's the word, Abe?"

"The word? Oh...that would be...*kaleh*," he said triumphantly.

"Yes," Malke said, not understanding why they were having such trouble. "I am *kaleh* of Yitzhak. *Verlobte.*"

"Yes," said Jesler, "but he never mentioned it. He didn't say he was waiting for someone. That seems a little odd to us, don't you see? Unless he thought—" He caught himself.

"Unless he thought...?" Malke said. "Ah, unless he thought I am dead."

She said it so plainly that it took Jesler a moment to answer. "Yes—I didn't mean it that way. I'm sorry."

With a strange sort of cheeriness, Malke added, "Well, I am not dead. I am sitting here with you."

Jesler felt Pearl's hand on his lower back, a tightening of her fingers. It was clear this woman had been through the worst of it. Even with the rouge and the lipstick—and whatever else she had done—the face was gray and drawn, contorted. The eyes, worse still, looked as if they were on alert, for what Jesler didn't care to imagine. It was as if someone had taken the trappings of good health and style and draped them over a translucence that didn't have the strength to hold them up.

Pearl said, "You'll stay with us, Miss Posner." Jesler tried to hide his shock and again Pearl ignored him. "We have a room. It was Yitzhak's so maybe you'll feel more at home there. My husband will go out and track him down—just as soon as he can—so we can clear all this up. Would that be to your liking?"

Malke sat with this barrage of words for several moments before saying, "Thank you. Yes. I am quite tired. Perhaps I could rest."

"Of course," Pearl stood. "I'll take you up right now. Abe, her bag."

Malke stood, and said, "Pardon, but what is 'Ike'?"

"Oh—" Pearl said. "Well . . . that's just what we call Yitzhak. It's easier for us here in the United States."

Malke seemed no less at a loss but tried a smile. "I see. Ike."

And, finding her own reserves of optimism, Pearl said, "But what a joy for us to have you come all this way and with such wonderful news. Isn't it wonderful news, Abe?"

———

Weiss read through the pages for a second time while Goldah sat across from him at the desk. Goldah had offered to wait outside but Weiss said he liked having the writer watch as he read through a piece like this. It helped with the editing. So be it.

Weiss kept the blinds of his office drawn—against the heat, he said—and relied on two dim lamps for light. A single fan droned from the corner.

Weiss finished and said, "It's a striking piece. Odd but striking." He leafed through the pages, stopping on a phrase here and there as he spoke. "It's not fully clear to me which way you're leaning. I might need you to be a little clearer on where you stand."

"I was hoping the power might be simply in presenting it."

"I can see that, yes. Still...you're saying something with this. You need to say it with a bit more clarity."

"So they'll know which side I'm on?"

"Something like that." Weiss set the pages down and flipped open his cigarette box. He offered one to Goldah. "First time out, you're presenting yourself as much as the piece. Readers like to know who you are." They lit up. "It's going to happen, you know. The mandate expires in, what, nine months, then the fighting will get a whole lot worse. The Arabs won't go willingly."

"I'm not sure that's the point, is it?"

"The point?" said Weiss. "You think the Arabs shouldn't have a say in this? I believe they've been in Palestine for quite some time."

Goldah was impressed. He had never imagined that a Jew, in the safety of America, would have a care for the Arabs one way or the other. "So you're concerned for the Arabs?"

"I'm not concerned, Mr. Goldah. I'm a realist. There are a million Arabs living there. A few pieces of paper aren't going to convince them that the land isn't theirs. I don't have to care about them to see that. It might be better not to have a state at all. But who am I to say that?"

Goldah said, "It's still not the point."

"Really? Then what is?"

"Guilt."

"Guilt? That's a bit wide, isn't it?"

"Perhaps." It was a long time since Goldah had spoken like this—ideas with scope and import and anything beyond his own small self. He found it invigorating. "It's the first time in history the Jews can ask for something and the rest of the world will give it. It's a moment of universal shame. I'm not convinced shame and pity should pave the way for a nation-state."

Weiss was equally struck by the candor. "Surely it's more than that. You really think Weizmann and the Zionists will care either way?"

"They can't deny it. Guilt lasts only so long. Are we really so weak? Who's to say we should want this handed to us because of a momentary crisis of conscience."

"Given the last ten years, I'd say yes, I think we are. Question is, why draw all this attention to ourselves?"

"Spoken from the very comfortable chair of the American South."

Weiss needed another moment to sort through Goldah's unabashed bluntness. "Fair enough," he said. "Still, nothing is getting handed to us—believe me, just ask the Arabs—except maybe a spotlight."

"And yet isn't it that spotlight that makes sure the world doesn't allow this to happen again? Keep the light on and they have no choice but to let the Jews survive."

"You see—that's what I mean. You're playing both sides."

"And if I say print it the way it is?"

Weiss tapped out some ash. "Not a little shoe salesman anymore, are you?"

Goldah took a draw on his cigarette and crushed it out. "I apologize. It's a muscle. It atrophies but comes back strong. If it's too much—"

"No," said Weiss, enjoying this. "It's exactly what I wanted. I won't change a word. It's always fun to see readers play with a paradox. Wait until the letters start coming in."

Goldah remembered moments like this, and the pride. He also remembered Jesler. "You're giving me too much credit," he said. "Maybe we should have another set of eyes take a look at it?"

"What—you don't trust mine?" Weiss smiled.

"Not at all—of course—but I think we both know there's more at stake here than the column." Goldah heard himself pause for just a moment. "You have a political man, don't you?"

"For the local stuff. Why?"

"I've read some of his pieces. Thomas. They're good."

"They're *very* good, that's why I pay him, but this isn't really his sort of thing."

Abe had given him Thomas's name. "No, I realize that," Goldah said, "it's just that I like his approach, that's all. I thought it might be good to have someone without the personal connection. But you're right. We can just leave it the way it is."

Weiss finished what was in his glass. "He's not a Jew but he did go to Yale. Neutral and smart. All right. I can ask Thomas to take a look. I still won't change a word."

Goldah nodded, then tossed back the last of his glass and told himself the lightness in his head was from the booze alone.

———

"And this one," Pearl said, "this was when he bought his first suit."

She sat with Malke on the edge of the guest-room bed and ran her thumb along the crease of a photo album.

"Doesn't he look smart in that," Pearl said admiringly. "He's filled out some now. Mary Royal and I saw to that but even there he looks so handsome in it." She stared a few moments longer, then flipped the page. "Oh, and this is at Johnny Harris. That's a wonderful restaurant. Ribs and chicken. Do you eat beef and chicken outside the house? Anyway, those are our friends, the Fleischmanns—Herb and Fannie—and that's the Kerns, Joe and Selma. They're very good people. We'll introduce you, take you and Ike. And there he is in front of our store. He ruined those pants doing some work on the door at the back, but that's another story."

Pearl smiled and, taking a deep breath, placed the album on Malke's lap.

"Well, you'll probably want to leaf through yourself, catch up on all he's been doing."

Pearl watched as the girl's eyes moved vacantly from image to image. Malke fixed on one and brought her hand up to it—Ike on the porch, looking out at the garden. He had been with them less than a week at the time, pensive and serious, and Abe had caught him unawares. Pearl had never liked the photo, but Malke drew her thumb to it and began to rub it across his face.

"Careful, dear," Pearl said, gently placing her own hand on the girl's. "You'll tear it if you do that."

Pearl felt the small hand tighten beneath her own. The next moment Malke was screaming out, pain and fear like the last gasp of a drowning child. She darted to the wall, her back to Pearl, face hidden beneath her arm, as she stood there shaking in silence.

Pearl sat frozen. She had no idea what had happened or what she was meant to do. She saw the album on the floor, its pages bent. She thought to pick it up but she was terrified. She felt her own breath growing short just as she heard Abe racing up the steps.

"What's going on, what happened?" he said, reaching the door out of breath. Pearl was shaking her head, her hand at her mouth. He thought she might cry. Jesler said with great care, "Hey, there, Miss Posner. Is there something I can do?"

Malke didn't move and Abe slowly sat on the bed next to Pearl. He took her hand, brought the album back up and set it on the desk.

Pearl said, "We were just looking." She was holding back the tears. "That's all. I told her not to press so hard. And I touched her hand."

"It's okay, it's okay." He put his arm around her. "Miss Posner—Malke, dear—please, we didn't know. We're sorry. I'm sure everything's okay. You understand? *Alles gut. Alles ist…sicher.* You're safe here. Okay? Why don't you come over here and sit down. Or have a lie-down. We can leave you to it. Have yourself a good *Schlaf* all by yourself. I promise…you're safe here."

Malke turned to them with a sudden hatred in her eyes. "I don't know him!" she screamed. She jabbed her finger toward the album and screamed again, "I don't know him!"

She started to move toward them and Jesler was on his feet, the girl's hands raised as if to strike him. He reached out and held them there, hardly any strength in them, as he pulled her in, her screams and thrashing cradled in the thickness of his arms.

"It's okay, you're okay," he said. "Get to the door, Pearl, get to the door."

Pearl stood just as Malke's body went limp. Jesler lifted her up and placed her on the bed, even as he heard Pearl weeping behind him.

An hour later Dr. Friedman told him she would sleep. He had found the medications in her bag, along with a letter from the Lubecks explaining the occasional bouts she might experience. Dr. Friedman had given her an additional sedative so as to help her get through the night.

On the telephone the Lubecks were beyond mortified, apologizing and explaining that they had insisted Malke give the letter to the Jeslers immediately upon her arrival. They now realized how foolish that had been.

"She's been so much better, you see, and we wanted to believe..."

Jesler was nothing but kind. He told them it had been only half a minute before she had fainted. She was resting. Everything would fine.

Now Pearl sat in her own bed, propped on a pillow and holding a whiskey, with Abe at her side. The doctor had given her a little something as well, and Abe told her the whiskey would help move things along.

"I've made a terrible mistake," she said, her voice frail and distant. "I don't know if I can handle a girl like that. What was I thinking? How could I know who she is?"

"It's okay. Don't worry."

"You're not going out now, are you?" said Pearl. "You can find Ike tomorrow. That'd be time enough, don't you think? Dr. Friedman said she'll sleep so no reason for Ike to see her."

"It's okay, honey. It's okay. I'm not going anywhere. I'll be sitting right here until you fall asleep and then I'll be right over there in that chair making some telephone calls. Okay? And Dr. Freidman said he's coming back in the morning to check on everyone."

"I've done some foolish things, Abe—I know I have—but this might just take the cake. I saw her there—and with the holidays coming up—and then knowing where things are with Ike, I just...I don't know—I sometimes care too much, I do—and then that poor girl."

Jesler nodded and gave the right responses. After a time, he stopped listening except to hear the waves of sound rising from the bed. Had there been a break he would have refocused his attention, but instead—and perhaps for the first time—he considered Ike and wondered how the boy could possibly manage this. All the time he should have been helping the boy and now Ike was helping him.

Jesler sensed Pearl was coming to the end of things and he turned to her.

"...and maybe get her some new dresses, I don't know," she said.

"Yes," Jesler said easily. "That's a good idea."

He heard the yawn and the slurred words. He took the glass from her hand, helped her under the covers, and turned out the lamp. Standing there—watching his wife slip quickly into sleep—Jesler thought how much easier life would be not having to work too hard for someone else's happiness.

————

Bill Thomas was sitting at his desk, his feet up, tossing balled-up candy wrappers at the trash can, when Goldah poked his head around the swinging door. It was late; the other desks were empty.

Thomas stepped over, retrieved three of the wrappers that littered the floor, and settled himself back in for another go-round.

"Can I help you?" he asked.

"I don't mean to interrupt."

"Well, as you can see, the office is extremely busy. I myself am waiting for a telephone call I can guarantee will never come. If you're looking for Simmons he's down at copyediting."

"I believe I'm looking for you, Mr. Thomas."

Thomas sunk his first wrapper. "Hah. There you go." He stepped over and threw out the rest. "Best to quit while you're ahead—Mr. . . . ?"

"Goldah. Ike Goldah. I think Mr. Weiss might have sent down a short piece of mine. He thought you could take a look at it."

Thomas was momentarily more serious. "Art Weiss?"

"Yes."

"Art Weiss wants my opinion on a piece you've written."

"Yes."

"Art Weiss knows my name."

"I believe he does, yes."

Thomas mulled this over, stepped back to his desk, and sat. "Then have a seat, Mr. Goldah."

The desk was piled high with stacks of papers. To the uninitiated, it would have seemed haphazard but Goldah recognized the pattern in the notes, the photos, the quotes, the contacts—all laid out to follow Thomas's particular style of writing. The better newsmen always had their own patterns, indecipherable to the rest yet perfectly logical. Goldah imagined Thomas could have found anything he wanted on that desk in less than five seconds.

Thomas began sifting through the papers. Goldah sat.

"Are you on staff, Mr. Goldah?"

"Not yet, no."

"'Not yet,'" Thomas echoed. "That's the attitude. So what am I going to be reading about?"

"I think it might be better if you go in cold."

Thomas stopped and looked across the desk. For the first time he sized up Goldah. "You're not giving me the hard sell. Which means you've done this before. Where?"

Goldah's instincts had been right: Thomas was an excellent newsman. "It was a long time ago."

"Can't be that long."

"Maybe it just feels that way."

Thomas leaned back, reached into his jacket pocket, and pulled out his cigarettes. "It's Europe, isn't it? The accent. Before the war." He took one then tossed the pack onto the desk.

"Yes. Prague. The *Herald Tribune*."

Thomas's eyes widened as he lit up. "The *Herald Tribune*. My, oh, my. Maybe I should be showing you some of *my* pieces?"

"I've seen them. They're good, clean."

"Well isn't that swell—the *Herald Tribune* thinks my writing is clean." Thomas exhaled a narrow stream of smoke. "So...you're now here in charming old Savannah, writing for Art Weiss. What's this really about?"

Goldah knew a truth, such as it was, stood the best chance of getting by.

"I'm seeing Weiss's daughter," he said. "He might not be as objective as he should."

Thomas laughed to himself. "Playing the noble card in the newspaper business. What exactly were they teaching you over in Prague? Hell, I'd ask for a daily column if I was dating the girl."

"I'll see what I can do—about the column, not the girl."

Thomas kept his smile. "You look familiar to me, Mr. Goldah. Why is that?"

Goldah recalled having seen Thomas at the store. He had come by some weeks back to speak with Calvin. Goldah had been with another customer and Calvin had told Thomas to leave. The entire episode had lasted all of two minutes.

"There was an article in the paper a few months ago," Goldah said. "It had my picture."

"No, I don't read this paper."

"And which papers do you read?"

Another quiet laugh. "You're very good. Question, feint, question, parry. I take it back. They knew *exactly* what they were doing in Prague." He tapped out his ash. "I read the papers I want to write for. Right now it's the Atlanta *Constitution*. After that I suspect it'll be the *Times-Picayune*, then the *Chicago Trib*, and, one day, when the fates smile brightest on me, the *San Francisco Chronicle*."

"Not the *New York Times*?"

"I'm a sentimental fellow, Mr. Goldah. My one character flaw. Hometown boy. Hometown paper."

"And is Mr. Weiss aware of the larger plan?"

"He'd be a fool not to be, wouldn't he?"

Goldah was liking Thomas more and more. "Good to have high ambition."

"Only thing *to* have." Thomas went back to the piles, and Goldah said, "I work at Jesler Shoes. You might have come in. I've been there since I arrived in July. Perhaps that's where you recognize me from?"

Goldah knew Thomas was too good at his job not to piece things together soon enough. Goldah would have done the same. Throwing it out there now made it seem almost innocuous.

Just in case Goldah added, "I lost most of my family in the war. The only ones left—the Jeslers—were here in Savannah."

Thomas did everything he could not to show a reaction. In fact, if Goldah hadn't been looking for it, he might have missed the slight narrowing of the eyes.

Thomas said, "I'm sorry."

"Thank you."

Thomas was juggling all his newfound information when the telephone rang. "Maybe that was it," he said, "the store. You'll excuse me. I need to take this."

Goldah stood. "Of course. You haven't read the piece yet. We can talk about it another time. Very nice meeting you."

Thomas picked up the phone, nodded, and raised a hand goodbye. "Bill Thomas here."

Goldah bobbed his head and headed for the door. He was pushing through when Thomas called after him: "Mr. Goldah—the call's for you. It's Mr. Weiss."

Goldah stood for a moment; Weiss hadn't known he was coming down. Goldah stepped over and took the receiver.

"Hello?"

The words that followed were quick, unemotional: a simple relaying of information. For years to come, Goldah would recall them with a slight buzzing in his ears. Now, standing there, all he felt was his hand squeezing tightly onto the chair, and the sound of Thomas's voice humming something about a glass of water.

———

Goldah sat quietly on the settee. The last half hour sat with him—the cab ride, Jesler's solemn handshake, the offer of a drink—all of it like shards of a reality he couldn't quite place. He had refused the whiskey and now watched as Jesler finished his own. The Lubecks' letter lay open at Goldah's side.

Goldah asked, "She'll sleep through the night?"

Jesler was lapping at the last few drops in his glass and set it on the table. "That's what the doctor said. I don't want to pry, Ike, but Miss Posner—this is why we were in Atlanta, isn't it?"

Goldah thought a moment, then nodded.

"Does Mrs. De la Parra know?"

Again Goldah waited. He shook his head.

For some reason, Jesler turned and listened at the door. They both sat in silence until Jesler said, "I thought maybe I heard Pearl. She's had a sedative as well but she's been a little restless." He leaned forward, his hands on his thighs. "Look, Ike, I called...I called because I thought you'd want to know as soon as possible. That's all. I didn't mean to get involved with whatever you're doing now."

Goldah was having trouble understanding: The words came at him the way they had all those years ago when he'd first tried his hand at English—foreign and unwieldy. He remembered sitting with his father, a book placed open on a table, a single lamp to focus the eyes. His father's finger had moved so easily along the letters—"the cat is on the hat, the rat is with the cat, the rat sits on the hat"—or was it something else? Goldah thought he might be translating in his head but knew it was only memory.

"It's fine," he said. "No, of course, it was smart to get in touch with Weiss."

Jesler tried to be consoling. "I told him there was no reason for you to come by tonight. I specifically told him that. I didn't tell him...I didn't mention the circumstances, if that's what you're concerned about. Just that the girl was here. You're sure you don't want to go up and see her? The doctor said she'll sleep soundly. You could just go and take a look."

Why, Goldah wondered? Why take a look? He knew what he would find. He had spent so many years admiring her, challenged by her, but never thrilled, never that ache to touch her. Wasn't he meant to panic out of need—for just a moment—each time before he saw her, as he did now with Eva? How had he convinced himself otherwise? Yes, Malke had been beautiful—they all told him how beautiful she was, how clever, how perfect, just for him. Even Malke told him over and over when he couldn't see it for himself. And maybe he let himself believe that was love.

Goldah said, "I think I'll have that whiskey."

"What? Oh, fine—sure." Jesler was quick to his feet.

Goldah said, "He thought it might not be her, the man in Atlanta. Hilliard. He said she'd suffered from memory loss, derangement. The Lubecks seem to have the same concerns."

Jesler poured one out and handed it to Goldah. "She seemed pretty certain to me."

"You say she screamed she didn't know me?"

"I'm not sure her English is all that good."

"But she said she didn't know me?"

Jesler took a fresh glass and poured himself another. "I guess that's what it sounded like. Anyway, Pearl's offered to have her stay with us."

Goldah had the sudden and overwhelming image of Malke here—in this place, always—the little room with the grinding fan and the too-thick drapes, the heat and the exhaustion, and he pitied her as he had pitied himself but only for a moment. Unlike him, she had come with purpose, to regain something she believed she was owed, and he knew these people would give it to her. All they would ask was for her forgiveness. No, it's unnecessary, she would say. There are no victims, only resolution and joy and gratitude for the dead come back to life.

"That's very decent of you," Goldah said.

"You know, Ike, you've made no commitments elsewhere. No one would fault you. You don't owe anyone anything."

Goldah had yet to take a drink. Ancient conversations churned through his head, and he said vaguely, "I met Mr. Thomas tonight. Excellent newsman."

Jesler was bringing his glass to his lips. He stopped. "Did he say anything? Anything about me, the store?"

It was everything Goldah could do to focus on what Jesler was saying. "Yes...? He said he'd been to the store. Why?"

"Nothing," Jesler said. "Never mind. Good, you met him. Good."

Goldah set his glass on the table and stood. "I should go. I'll come back in the morning."

"How about I set up a cot in the study? That way you could be here when she gets up."

"I think I'll walk."

"It's still raining. I can give you a lift."

"I'm fine."

Goldah recalled his first moments with Jesler: The train station and the wariness at the chance of an embrace; even a handshake had seemed too much. Now they were connected by things no less uncertain, debilitating things that made them both incapable of anything more than silence. Each carried his own weight, each stood alone, and neither pretended he might know how to find comfort in the other.

———

Goldah kept his hands in his pockets as he moved through the rain. The rest of him was soaked through, but the hands, miraculously, remained dry. It occurred to him that he had always given special care to his hands. Writing, his father said, required it. They had kept lotions and creams in the house for the winter, others for the summer. A cracked finger or a knuckle too dry and it was a day lost, even a week if the skin became too brittle. Of course Pasco had been right, too. Feet were life, shoes were life, but only in a place that took life to mean something other than what it was.

Goldah walked and thought how right little Pasco had been. One could pretend—that was the lie—or forget, but even forgetting was no hope against the past. It always found its way in. And he thought of Malke—unknown and unknowing Malke. Shredded memory only made it worse.

Goldah turned onto his street and saw Eva sitting on the stoop under his small awning. The building had been her choice, the rooms on the second floor pleasant and with a western view: less heat in the morning, she said, and a chance for a sunset in the late afternoon. She had found him a few things to furnish it with, simple but inviting. The dresser had been her husband's as a boy. She had been keeping it in her attic—who knows why, she said—and asked if he felt strange about that. Strange? She had brought him to a quiet place where he could lock a door and know that no one else could come through it. All of it was strange, and that night he had told her he loved her.

Her arms were now resting on her knees, her hands clenched beyond them and, for a moment, Goldah thought she might be in prayer. It was an absurd thought, just as ridiculous as his soaked-through appearance on this somber little street. When she looked up he was standing by her, the light from the lamp caught somewhere between them.

"You should have called a cab," she said, as if they might be meeting for drinks or a quick bite before a movie.

"You could have gone in. You have the key."

"It's cooler out here."

He recalled countless conversations like this, though nothing like this at all. "You took Julian to your parents?"

She nodded. Then, as effortlessly as before, "Is she someone you loved?"

He reached his hand down. "Let's go in."

"If you're going to tell me things are going to get complicated, I think I can do that out here."

"Come inside. Please."

"A policeman asked if I needed help. I must have looked quite a sight." She took his hand and stood.

"You look fine."

Upstairs he changed while she put a kettle on for tea. He lay his suit on a chair and hoped the humidity might let it dry by next week. He stepped into the small sitting room where she was pouring out two cups.

"You have nothing to eat," she said. "I'll make a few things and put them in the icebox. That way you'll have them."

He sat with her at the little table by the window and placed a hand around his cup. "Your father called you?"

"A young woman with a foreign name?" she said. "Of course. He said Mr. Jesler sounded quite insistent. Concerned. The next thing I knew I was sitting on your stoop. I wasn't thinking you'd come by tonight but I just couldn't get myself to leave. Isn't that silly?"

Goldah placed his open hand on the table. He expected her to place hers inside but she brought her cup to her lips with both her hands and took a sip. It was all slipping away, wasn't it?

"She was a woman from Prague," he said. "I'd known her since I was a boy."

"Was? She's just up the road, isn't she?"

"I thought she had died."

"In the camp?"

Like a bright, white light the memory crept in and blinded him for a moment. "I thought she'd been—that she hadn't survived. The first night. I thought they had taken her."

"You thought she was gone all this time?"

"Yes."

174

"I'm so sorry."

Eva set her cup on the table. She sat calmly, staring at it, the intensity in her gaze an unsettling prelude to the sudden and aimless movement she made, standing and going to the kitchen doorway. He watched as she leaned her back against the jamb—the tears he had expected downstairs forming—and she shook her head as she brought her arms tight around her chest.

"All this time," she said. "She's been waiting all this time and you'll have no choice. You'll tell yourself you have no choice."

"That's not true."

"Yes it is. And if you loved her—"

"I never did."

Goldah heard the words. He had never said them before but here they were, presented to Eva like a sacrifice.

She looked at him, not with relief but with a deep, deep pain. "Why tell me that?"

"Because it's true."

"Oh, because it's true. You think the truth takes care of it. But here she is. She's found you after everything else because she loves you—truly loves you—and you know it."

"You can't possibly know what I know."

"Don't say that."

He went to her. She made a weak effort to push him away but she let him take her in his arms all the same.

"That doesn't matter," he said.

"Of course it does. Don't be a coward. Don't hide behind that."

The word *coward* caught inside him, stark and unforgiving and all the sharper because he knew she had never intended it that way. He felt an unexpected strength in his hand and he slammed it against the wall even as he saw himself moving anywhere but near to her.

"Don't say that," he said with unaccustomed bitterness. "Don't say it. Do you have any idea—do you? My God. You think crawling back to all of that makes me brave? Love out of pity, love because fate said these are the only choices to be had?" The truth flooded in and doused whatever anger remained, leaving only a frail disbelief in its wake. "I'll never leave there, will I? It's the criminal set free but with the mark on his forehead, his arm. And they all stare and know, and who cares if it's remorse or shame or kindness—it's still the prisoner they see. And if he says 'No—'" His throat tightened. "'I won't go back, I won't be there every morning, every night,' then it's 'Shame on you for never having loved her.'" He felt his own tears. "There's your redemption," he said. "That's what we'll give you. Take it and be glad and be done with it." He crouched down, his arms to his face, and he wept.

Eva let him cry. She let the weight of everything pass, only now, knowing once they were apart it would all come rushing back and trample them both underneath.

She was next to him and he brought his head up to rest it against the wall. He saw her stained cheeks and thought he might never leave this room again, if only that were possible. Words formed in his mind but he couldn't find a way to say them.

They had never spent the night together. He had never spent the night with anyone. But he knew to wait until the morning to tell her.

10

"AND SHE ASKS, 'How you always make it taste so good, Ethel?'" Mary Royal spoke with an unencumbered glee. She sat by herself at Raymond's kitchen table, while his mother, Lilian, at the sink, pressed fruit through a strainer into a jar. "You know how proud Miss Sophie is about her sisterhood dinners, and here's Ethel in the dining room in front a all Miss Sophie's Jewish folk being asked how come her food always taste so good, and Ethel says, 'Why it's the lard, Miss Sophie. It's the lard.'"

Lilian laughed quietly, almost reluctantly, as she shook down the jar. "'The lard,'" she repeated. "Would've been better if that child had said, 'It's the Lord, Miss Sophie. Praise Jesus, it's the *Lord!*' You telling me Ethel's been cooking in that house with lard all this time, even when she's putting one set a forks in one drawer and one set a forks in the other, and she don't understand the koshuh?"

"No, ma'am, she don't. And she's still there cause Miss Sophie likes her food so much. I hear Miss Sophie's planning on going with Ethel to the market every now and then."

"I bet she is."

Raymond stepped in through the back door. He looked almost himself, save for the discoloration around his eye. His chest and shoulders were once again tight under his shirt. He kept his hand deep inside his pocket.

"What we all laughing about?" he said.

"We all?" said Mary Royal. "I didn't know you was laughing again."

"I laugh just fine depending on what it is I'm supposed to be laughing at."

The two women shared a look before Lilian went back to her work at the sink. "Well," said Mary Royal, "it seems your cousin Ethel's been serving up pig fat to Miss Sophie's house ever since she got there, proud as punch to be doing it."

Raymond thought a moment, then gave in to a smile. "Now that's funny. See? I'm laughing."

"Oh, is that what that is?" Mary Royal tried to peer around his back. "What you got there, Raymond?" His mother turned her head from the sink as Raymond brought out a piece of metal attached to a thick strip of wood—the metal curling at the end, the wood with straps and buckles up the side.

"I had Silas work it up," he said. "It don't dig into my wrist so much now. Looks good, don't it?"

"It does," said Mary Royal, "if I knew what it was."

"You know what it is. Help me get it on."

He handed her the harness, such as it was, and laid his dead hand and forearm on the table.

"Make sure it's tight, up to the elbow," he said. "You see what I mean?"

She wedged his hand up into the curl of the metal, set his forearm on the wood, and then notched each of the straps until she saw the skin spread out and whiten underneath the leather.

"Tighter," he said, wincing for a moment as she drew each strap a single hole deeper.

"It's going to leave a mark."

"Good." He pulled his arm away, twisted it at the elbow, and stared at the harness with pride. "That ain't moving at all.

You see that." He shook it out; the metal and wood remained fixed on his arm. "Now I'll show you something. Move yourself back." Mary Royal glanced over at Lilian again, and Raymond said, "Just move yourself back."

Mary Royal slid her chair toward the wall and Raymond, leaning over, placed his arms wide across the tabletop. He hooked the curled metal under the edge and lifted the table two feet off the ground, then set it back down.

"You see that? All the weight's in my shoulder and my muscle. You just hook it under, settle it in, and bring it up. And there ain't nothing my hand can't do it ain't done before. Pull on it. Try and move it. See? See how firm that is on me? And I can lift a table or boxes or crates. I even tried a barrel down with Silas and it come up easy, no pain in my arm or back. And now no one can look at me and say I can't do what I always done."

Lilian had a cloth and was wiping her hands. "Well, that looks fine, Raymond," she said with as much encouragement as she could muster. "And the doctor says you'd be okay with it?"

Raymond's breath showed his irritation. "Mama, the doctor ain't no engineer and all he cares about is the pain. If I say I ain't got no pain, then I got no pain. And when I take it off I ain't feeling strain in any part a me."

"You mean when you take it off after picking up one barrel and one crate," said Mary Royal. "Oh, and one table here. You ain't feeling pain."

She saw the beginnings of his anger and thought he might bust out through the door—he had done it enough in the last week—but he just kept looking at her.

"I ain't going to bite this time, Mary," he said. "I ain't going to show you my anger 'cause I ain't got any. I got *this*."

"And that's enough?"

"Why you doing this?" he asked more gently than any of them expected. "Why the two a you sitting here not seeing what I'm doing? Or what I'm trying to do. It ain't perfect. I know it."

"Do you?"

"Here we go . . ."

"I'm just saying—"

"I know what you saying. You think I don't know? I got a piece a bent metal bolted to a hunk a wood that's digging into my arm. I know that don't bring my hand back. I know it don't make my headaches any less. And it sure as hell don't stop me from wanting to find those boys and beat them 'til they bleed. But ain't nothing's going to do that so I got this harness instead. And if it don't work out, well . . . then it don't work out. And I'll know it then, long before either a you two."

"Mary Royal ain't saying you don't know that, Raymond."

"Mama, I can't be done. I can't sit here with a lame hand and feel sorry for myself."

"No one's saying that."

"Not yet they ain't. But I'm saying it. I ain't got no time to be no angry or thankful nigger when Mr. Jesler decides to throw me some work so he can feel better about himself. I got to show it don't make no difference."

Mary Royal said, "Even if it does make a difference?"

"Mary"—he choked back his frustration—"I don't know what you want me to say. You been telling me I can't sit back, I can't give in."

"But you giving in just the same if you say it ain't no different. It is."

Lilian said, "What about Silas's brother? He did all that training. Negro police no different than the others. He's got a badge now."

"Mama, please. I ain't talking to Silas's brother. We been through this. There ain't nothing he can do when it comes to white boys. That badge he got is for Negroes, plain and simple. He try to arrest a white boy, policeman or not, they'll do him worse than me."

Mary Royal said, "I ain't talking about that."

"No, Mary, I know what you talking about. That newspaperman. Well I ain't talking to him again. That's the *last* person I'm talking to."

"I never said that, Raymond. That's in your head, not mine."

"Then what is it you want, Mary?"

"It ain't what I want that's important," she said.

"Oh, really? Mary . . . if you saying I got to make some kind a point, show everyone—"

"I'm talking about getting *yourself* up, Raymond, getting in on what Mr. Abe and the store is doing. Nothing else." She was glad he was finding his way back, glad to hear his frustration, but his eyes had dimmed again, and she thought maybe some of that was on her. "This family's been with Mr. Abe and Miss Pearl close on twenty years. Twenty years, Raymond. He's feeling bad right now? Good. Let him. Then he needs to make it right by giving you a part in it. I ain't saying you got to make some kind a stand. No one's saying you got to take that on. This is our family and theirs. Nothing bigger than that. And he don't have to tell no one else—make some kind a point—just us, but you got to get your share, your percent. You got to make him see that. This ain't about being no angry or thankful nigger. This is about being the nigger that earned it."

Raymond continued to look at her, his eyes empty. His head ticked once, then twice as if he might answer. Instead he pursed his lips and turned to his mother. "I don't know what she wants me to say to that."

Raymond's mother wiped the cloth against the counter. "Not for me to say." He watched as she set the cloth on the edge of the sink and brushed out her hands.

Raymond said, "And what you think Calvin'd say about it, Mary? You think he'd say, 'Time to get your own, boy.' Or maybe he'd just tell me to strap on that harness and get back to what I do. You think Calvin'd say that? You thinking *maybe* he'd say that?"

"I'm thinking maybe you was done with your anger," she said. "Setting it on me don't help no one."

"I ain't angry with you, Mary. I ain't."

"Fine, but you think Pawpaw'd understand any of it? Understand what position Mr. Abe's in right now? There's an advantage here and you got to take that. It don't make me happy to say it, Raymond, but Pawpaw'd never see it that way and you know it."

The cloth fell to the floor from the edge of the sink. Raymond reached down and picked it up with his good hand and laid it on the table.

Mary Royal said, "Mr. Abe knows how he found his way up, how he stepped out a Yamacraw and took what he thought was his. You got to help him remember that and let him see this ain't no different. And when he does, all this gets put behind us. Your hand ain't the reason, Raymond. Your hand just what happened. And you got to help Mr. Abe understand that."

———

Mary Royal was a few minutes later than she said she would be. No, Raymond was having no trouble driving the truck. Mary Royal mentioned the harness and the way Raymond was managing the gears. It was just that she had lost track of time, but they would get it all back to normal just as soon as she was coming in on her regular schedule.

Pearl brought her upstairs—she might have slipped her arm through Mary Royal's just to show her how much she had been missed—and asked her if she could set Malke's hair the way she herself liked it, with maybe a wave or something in the front. Pearl said the girl was still a bit shy about going out and maybe if she had a more presentable look she might not feel so self-conscious. Mary Royal agreed and Pearl was glad for that. There were several new dresses to choose from and, once they finished with the nails, Pearl knew Malke would see the improvement at once.

When Jesler pulled up twenty minutes later—with the hair dryer he had borrowed from downtown and the boxes of shoes for Malke to try on—Raymond stepped down from the porch and said he'd be happy to move it all inside. Jesler had seen the truck. He had prepared himself as best he could but the first moments were awkward nonetheless. He stood there by his open door and asked Raymond if the arm was better—saying it with more hope for himself than for Raymond. When Raymond told him, no, the arm was done—he'd put this harness together—Jesler asked to take a closer look and Raymond deferred. He said he could take everything in through the back door, if that was what Mr. Jesler wanted, and Jesler told him not to be ridiculous and to come in the front.

Inside, they heard the women upstairs—Malke was sounding less enthusiastic than perhaps Pearl had been hoping—and Jesler laughed it off unconvincingly as he led them through to the kitchen and the plug for the hair dryer. He couldn't help but keep looking at the harness and asked Raymond if he was planning on wearing a sleeve or something over it, not for the appearance, of course, but for the comfort, maybe some padding. Jesler thought it might be digging into the flesh and Raymond said calmly that it was nothing to worry about, no different from the braces some of the other boys back from Europe were wearing, even if he had worked it up himself. But a sleeve was a good idea. Keep it out of people's faces. Jesler poured himself a coffee—more than a few drops spilling over the side, who knows why—and said he thought that sounded like a plan. Good to have a plan. And Raymond, knowing that Mary Royal might just tell him that this was his best and only chance, said that plans were a good idea, plans all around, and asked if the store was still having trouble with the folks from down at the port because, if it was, he wanted to know what they were planning on doing about it.

Jesler leaned himself back against the counter. The heat had jumped again today and he was suddenly feeling it at his neck. "The boys down at the port?" he said. "That's not for you to worry about, Raymond. I think you've had enough to do with them, don't you think?"

"I ain't talking about my arm, Mr. Jesler." Raymond continued to speak with remarkable restraint. "I'm talking about the store. And the future."

"The future? Well…I think that'll be fine. Don't you worry. We've just got to make sure you're feeling one hundred percent."

"I told you I was fine, Mr. Jesler. It ain't my health that's a concern. They trying to squeeze more money out a us? More a them extras?"

Jesler heard the *us* like a taunt chiming in his ears even as he saw the stillness in Raymond's eyes, the gaze of a man in the right. Jesler thought to himself that he had never seen that look in a Negro before. He said plainly, "They know what they have, Raymond. There's not much you can do about that."

"And what is it they have?"

"A Jew," Jesler said sourly.

"Ain't never stopped you before."

"And it's not going to stop me now. It just makes things a little more difficult."

"I suppose that's true."

Still the echo of that us, us, us as Jesler thought to take another sip of the coffee but the cup was already tepid in his hand. He set it down. "But that's not what this is about, is it? It sounds like you don't want to be stopped, either."

"No, suh, I don't."

Jesler couldn't pinpoint the exact moment he had let his guilt harden into self-damning, but it made this exchange far more palatable than he could have imagined.

"No one's ever owed anything, Raymond, you have to know that. I'm sorry for your arm, I truly am, and that's on me, but that doesn't mean you have to concern yourself with other things. That's just the way it is."

Raymond remained perfectly still. "That's twenty years we ain't shown no concern for other things, Mr. Jesler. It ain't my arm we owed for."

Jesler wondered what it was to have this kind of courage. Or was it simply an unimpeachable certainty? Either way he felt the edge of the counter digging into his back. "And what is it you think we're talking about here?"

"All them new boxes coming in, and me picking them up, driving them all around to places just as new. Some a the Negro fellas down at the docks, them union boys, telling me how no one up north's getting to know anything about that. And I tell them that ain't none a their concern, that they come and talk to me before they talk to anyone else. And they all know that's the truth."

Jesler said coolly, "Well that's the job, Raymond."

"Paying the right man at the right time also part a the job, ain't it, Mr. Jesler?"

"As I said, I'm sorry for that—"

"A Mr. Thomas at the *Morning News* also sorry about it."

Jesler nearly flinched. He hadn't seen this—not by a long stretch—and yet here it was, laid out in front of him, though just out of reach. He felt the blood leave his cheeks. "And you're inclined to talk with Mr. Thomas?"

Again Jesler saw the look—clear and firm and with no hint of a threat. He had no answer for it.

Raymond said, "You know how you come up from Yama-craw, Mr. Jesler, what you done and who done things for you. I'm just wanting to be there when you talk with them Irish at the port so they know we can straighten this out. And they know that I'm a part a it. That's all."

Jesler said nothing. He found himself looking at the harness and knew it would be there—always—to make this point for them both.

———

The small anteroom off Harry Cohan's office broiled without windows, less humid than the hallway but musty nonetheless, with the scent of stale tobacco and a woman's perspiration in the air. The taste settled at the back of Jesler's throat along with a quick draw on his cigarette. Cohan's girl sat at her desk, smoking as she typed, her fingers like darting eels along the keyboard. Every few minutes she tapped out her ash to read through what she had written—then, just as quickly, clack, clack, clack.

Jesler stared across at the line of filing cabinets. He guessed the important papers were in Cohan's office but there was probably enough inside these to shake down half of Savannah's businessmen. Raymond stood by the door, his sleeves rolled down, his frame like a fixture against the wall.

Cohan greeted Jesler with too much friendliness. The large, thick body nearly filled the doorframe as Cohan's hand squeezed tightly around Jesler's, his other rising to clasp the shoulder in a gesture of false camaraderie. Cohan told his girl to hold his calls. Jesler said Raymond would be coming in with them. Cohan's smile—a practiced flash of yellow and gums—remained fixed.

"Well, I didn't see you there, boy. Sure. Come on in. See what we can talk about."

Cohan settled himself behind his desk. A glass of iced water sweated on top of a small safe and he took a sip.

Jesler said, sitting, "No more trouble with the depositories? Break-ins have all been resolved?"

"Break-ins...? Oh, yeah. Sure. Everything's okay. What is it I can do for you, Abe?"

Cohan kept a second-rate portrait of an old-time soldier hanging behind his desk, sash and ribboned medals, with his hand resting easily on a sheathed sword. It might have been Savannah in the background but it was all open land and streamlets—someone's idea of low country and marsh. Jesler thought a bit of sweat on the brow would have made sense—all that wool and leather—but the man had a rosy hue in his cheeks and a crop of perfectly combed curly black hair at the top. A colonel, maybe...O'Shea or O'Donnell...and Jesler recalled Major Raphael Moses, a son of the Confederacy, a Jew with all the trappings, and wondered where he might be hanging these days.

Jesler said, "You can understand how I'm taking a considerable interest now that I've got more at stake out here."

"I can. That makes sense."

"Raymond here has been doing my driving. Down to Jacksonville, maybe as far as Miami by next month."

"Well…" Cohan shot a quick glance over at Raymond. "That's some serious responsibility for him, isn't it?"

"It is. We've had some growing pains, naturally, some miscommunication."

"I imagine that can't be helped."

"Water under the bridge, Harry…Anyway, Raymond's as reliable as they come and I don't expect I'll ever have cause to worry about him now that everything's fixed in place. He'd certainly never give me any reason. Would you Raymond?"

It had been strange enough bringing the boy inside his office; Cohan had let his own measured affability play in neat counterpoint to the comedy of this Negro standing here: He imagined Jesler was owed that much. But having the boy speak…that would have been taking things too far.

Raymond knew to keep his mouth shut.

Jesler said, "I'm sure you're feeling just as comfortable with your boys up the coast. It's always good for men in our position to know we've got everything under control."

Cohan shifted in his chair. Jesler thought he might have seen the colonel tighten the grip on his saber, and Cohan said, "What is it you want, Abe?"

"The money, Harry. The money's good where it is. All those extras. They've topped out, I think. We've hit a good limit. So I've got no trouble with that. You just need to make sure your boys understand. That they won't be asking for any more."

"My boys know what a schedule is, Abe. Paying on time no matter what you think you owe. We're clear on that? When the money's due? How much it is? Because as long as that's been cleaned up, I think we're fine. And sure—we can leave the money where it is. For now."

"Good."

"Just so you know—for the future—my boys work well enough without any advice from Atlanta. Hirsch doesn't need to make any more telephone calls."

"That was a mistake."

"Yes, Abe, it was. He wants to keep you off the radar up north, that's fine. Smart. But what goes on in this port, that's none of his concern. And any of his *friends* who'd want to poke their noses in here, check up to make sure that good old Abe Jesler is being treated kindly, well... that's not something he should worry himself with. We understand? There've been mistakes on both sides. I'll give you that. We can all learn to keep our enthusiasms in check from now on. As you say, growing pains, water under the bridge."

"Good. I just wanted you to know that that holds true on our side as well."

Cohan stared for a moment before snorting a quiet laugh. "Your side?" he said derisively. "What in the hell are you talking about, Abe?" Even the practiced friendliness now misted into the heat. "Your side is you and this crippled boy and Hirsch in Atlanta, doing his jobs with the unions, and everything's fine. Don't talk to me about sides. You got something smart going now. Good for you. But don't drag a nigger into my office and tell me how we've got *an understanding* when the only thing you need to understand is how to pay what you owe on time otherwise certain paperwork won't be going just to the Italians. We clear? If it makes you feel better to bring your boy, you keep doing it, but that doesn't put you in any other place than where you are. The reason we're square is because that's the best way to play this. How you play it on your end... that's up to you." He extended his hand. "Take it, Abe. Take it so we can end today on a cordial note."

189

Jesler hesitated before shaking Cohan's hand. Then he stood, and had his ears not been ringing, he might have heard the distant sound of the clack, clack, clack like nails being hammered into a coffin.

———

Hours later Jesler found himself alone by the river, across from the vacant tract where he and Pearl had had their first home. He couldn't remember the last time he had driven this far down. The place was quiet except for the sound of moving water somewhere off in the distance.

He thought how it was almost ten years since they had torn it all down, far longer since he had seen it. Not that there was a purpose in coming tonight. Why would there be? He had driven; that was all. It was a place not worth his nostalgia—memories marked by the promise of things to come, naïve things that said, once he was far from here, the world would show itself in a fuller, warmer light and reward him for having made the climb out. Yet here it was, always this close no matter how far behind him he thought it might be. But the climb, the climb... wasn't that worth something, and he chided himself for the self-pity that had tramped after him tonight like a stray dog.

He kept his lights on as he stepped from the car. Higher up the rise, the first of the new shacks showed flickers of kerosene lamps—doors and windows left open, where families sat waiting until it was cool enough to sleep. His lights led him down toward the river and he followed the tapering beams, then beyond their reach into true darkness. The grass grew higher here and his shoes began to sink deeper into the mud. The feeling was cool on his feet, and he thought he might take off his shoes, but he was so enjoying the ease of it that he kept moving, the grass now at his palms as he edged slowly forward.

He might have walked farther still, down the bank itself— for he could hear the water now—if not for a quiet "Mr. Jesler" that stopped him. The voice was less startling than the sound of his own name and he turned to see the broad outline of Raymond's shoulders and narrow frame standing in front of the car lights. Raymond's truck was parked behind, its beams trailing up the incline.

Jesler brought his hand up to shield his eyes from the sudden brightness and he waited for Raymond to speak, but the boy just stood there.

"Raymond," Jesler said. "What on earth are you doing here?"

Raymond said nothing.

"Son, what are you doing here?"

"You okay, Mr. Jesler?"

Jesler heard the genuine concern.

"Raymond—"

"You been driving a lot tonight, Mr. Jesler."

Only then did Jesler realize how long it had been. Hours, he thought. It had been hours.

Raymond said, "Things didn't seem right after Mr. Cohan so I thought maybe I'd drive with you. Make sure."

"You've been—"

"Yes, suh."

Jesler brought his hand down. How much smaller self-pity felt when set against this. He said, "I'm fine, Raymond."

"I can see that."

Jesler glanced over at the water, then back at Raymond. "I grew up in here. That's all. Just back there."

"Yes, suh, I know."

"I just thought . . . I don't know. Sometimes it's just good to see it."

"Remind yourself."

"Yes . . . I suppose that's right." He started to move but felt his sodden shoes deep in the mud, firm and rooted. It took some effort to slowly bring them out.

"You stayed behind me in your truck that whole time?" Jesler said. "That's . . . that's something." Jesler joined him at the car. He pulled off his shoes and tossed them into the back. "I'll be good from here."

Raymond stood with him for a few moments longer, deciding whether that was true. He nodded. "Okay," he said and turned to head for the truck.

Jesler watched him go—the thick hand on the wheel, the grinding of the gears, the tires hitching on the rocks and mud—and, for the first time, felt that here was a memory worth taking.

11

GOLDAH TOOK a shirt and tie from the closet and laid them on the bed atop his open suit. His shoes waited on the floor, just below the pant legs, and it struck him how the whole thing looked like a body on the verge of standing, except somehow all the life had been pressed out of it. His other suit remained where he had taken it off, still damp from the rain and curling at the collar. He doubted the jacket was even salvageable.

Two days ago he'd been handed a reprieve of sorts. Pearl had telephoned to say that Miss Posner was still not suitably acclimated to receive guests of any kind, and Goldah was happy enough to be lumped in with the rest. Who they might be—Fannie and Selma, the ever-inquisitive Mrs. Jelinek—was pure speculation, but that was less a concern than what Malke might actually be acclimating herself to: the heat, her medication, Pearl's feelings of duplicity and vindication at every turn. Goldah wondered if he might just send the suit along by itself and let it suffer through the joys of a first meeting.

He reminded himself that this kind of self-mocking wasn't cruel or frivolous: The weight of Malke's arrival lay upon him with just as much desperation and ambiguity as everyone would have imagined. How else could it be? And who better than he to work through the eternal calculations of what it was to be a person then and a person now—what was lost, what was gained, so much more believing then, so much more resilient now.

He tucked the shirt into his pants and tied his tie. He was missing Eva.

She had been beside him in bed when the call from Pearl had come through, too familiar with his single-word responses to read anything into them. When he told her they had been given a few extra days, she—saying how glad she was for their night together, truly glad—told him it would be better if she were to go. There would be too much time now to think about it, too great a chance to feel as if they were betraying something else, at least that was how she was going to feel, and so even though she would have given anything to stay here with him... no, she just couldn't. He told her then that he had never been with a woman before and she smiled gently and placed a hand on his cheek. Then, as if afraid to look at him again, she had taken hold of her rain jacket and hat and, at the door, said, "Tell her she looks well. Do that, no matter what."

"She won't believe me."

"It doesn't matter. And tell her how lucky you are to be seeing her."

"Why are you saying these things?"

"Because you are lucky. After everything, to have someone who understands it. None of us will ever be that for you." He said nothing. "She'll want to know you share that."

Now, sitting in the Jeslers' front parlor, Goldah thought the flowers in his hands a foolish gesture. How was it that a man could set himself on display in order to court his own past? Yet here he was, if in fact the past beyond that door was his: All the doubts and uncertainties—Hilliard, the Lubecks, his own terrible wishing it not so—would come to a head. He would sit with her and they would talk and he would know. It was as simple as that.

He heard them on the steps and he stood. Jesler was the first through, then Pearl, solemn and joyful as only she could manage in this contrived rite of presentation. Jesler had been directed where to stand, his nod of deep appreciation for the moment hesitant but well performed. He had done all he could at the front door to prepare Goldah for the gravitas to come. He had even admitted he was feeling this might be a bit too much for the girl—his own idea had been to send Ike up to her room by himself—but Pearl had said that wouldn't be fitting. Fair enough. Jesler mentioned he liked the flowers.

Pearl now took her place by her husband, and Goldah half expected to hear a few strains of Mendelssohn trumpeting through the doorway, but that would have required walking in time and he wasn't sure any of them could have worked that up with sufficient aplomb. For some reason he held the flowers a bit higher on his chest and watched as the woman calling herself Malke Posner stepped into the room.

"Well," Pearl said with surprising finality, just as if they had spent a long afternoon together, "Abe and I will let you have all the time you need. You must have so much to talk about." And with that she quickly motioned Jesler out—this, too, had been rehearsed—and Goldah found himself utterly alone with her.

Standing in the silence, he noticed how familiar her face was, not for anything specific but for the sallow skin and the tight gaze, those shared features from the DP camps and beyond. He recalled how women had always been so much quicker to reclaim themselves—a bit of lipstick or a pin in the hair—whatever might delineate one sex from the other. Goldah had always thought that, for them, to be human again wasn't enough: It was the feminine that brought them back. Whoever this might be—and it could very well have been her—Goldah noticed only the gentle shading on the cheeks and the smell of lilac perfume on her hair. The nose, the eyes, the chin—these were shadowy aspects of a woman he had known long ago and who perhaps was once again standing in front of him.

She said in German, "These people are absurd," and with that Goldah knew instantly this was his Malke. "Do you see how ridiculously they have me dressed? And the hair? I look like some sort of doll."

Goldah was still holding the flowers, absurd all on his own. He said, "You look well."

"Don't tell me you've become ridiculous as well?" Her lips and eyes curled unevenly into a smile. Remarkably he saw a playfulness behind them. "I think they need me to be pathetic, Yitzi, someone to be pitied. I haven't helped things much, I know, but let's sit down. I still get tired so easily." They sat, and she said, "I suppose we could embrace but that was never the way with us."

No, he thought. It wasn't. He laid the bouquet on the table and saw how easily they were setting everything aside.

"It's a palsy—my face. The doctors say it will pass but it's still here. I'm sorry."

"Well." He managed to sound hopeful. "Then I'm sure it will pass."

"Yes. No doubt you're right. And you're looking—" Her smile returned. "I was going to say 'well' but then I've just told you how silly that sounds. Although you do look it."

"Perhaps."

"More than perhaps, Yitzi."

"And you're feeling all right now?"

It was a cruel thing to mention so quickly; she was at her best when not lingering on things, and yet she was playing this out with such courage. Her stamina was something he had always admired.

"Ah, you mean my episode," she said. "Yes, how wonderful to arrive with that and then have all the hysteria afterward. No—I'm being unfair. They were very caring. Probably for the best to take a few days. They've told you about my memory, of course, but it wasn't that. You just looked...in all those photographs...you looked so comfortable, happy...in this place. It was a long time since I'd seen that. I wasn't sure if I'd *ever* known that person. I have trouble now, keeping things...well, you know it was never perfect beforehand...Can we talk about something else?"

"Of course."

"It turns out you were right. I should have taken more interest in English. I'm just terrible and it only makes things worse."

It struck Goldah how effortlessly the great question had been resolved: Here was Malke. All that was left to them was the filling of a future. He said, "Well, you'll have plenty of time now to get better at it."

"They think a great deal of you," she said. "And I saw your piece in the newspaper. I couldn't follow most of it but they say it was just wonderful. A lot of people are talking about it. How nice for you to have that again."

"Yes," he said absently. "You should know...that first night in the *Lager*. I didn't know. I thought you had been—"

"Yes," she said with a sudden hollowness. "They told me. I'm sorry. That must have been very hard for you to live with." Her eyes wandered; then, with greater strength, "Let's not talk about that now. Would that be all right?"

"Of course."

"After all, it would be so hard for you to understand."

And there it was, he thought. This morning he had imagined he would know everything she had lived through. How foolish of him. He had forgotten the one truth of the *Lager*: that nothing is ever shared. Hunger and cold, yes, but the rest...those horrors lived inside the mind in pure isolation.

"No, you're quite right," he said. "I wouldn't."

————

If he had anticipated this first encounter as their chance to ease into a distant familiarity—an hour or so sitting in quiet conversation, perhaps a walk before both agreed they needed to rest—then Goldah had forgotten how Pearl oriented herself to the unknown. The afternoon progressed much like the opening ceremony: Half an hour in, Malke was presented to the Fleischmanns and the Kerns with all the requisite pomp and circumstance—words of appreciation for her hair and dress, small gifts to make her feel more welcome, and a single, too-eager comment on how handsome the young couple looked together. Whatever jocularity Pearl had been hoping for quickly ground down to an awkward pleasantness as Goldah was forced to play the role of translator so as to make sure everything Herb was saying hit its mark: "She understands what a hamburger is, doesn't she? That's the joke. A hamburger on a roll? No—never mind. If it's not making sense, I just thought it was amusing. Does she like the pictures, music?"

Pearl's choice for dinner was Chinese, the Canton, where they spent a great deal of time making sure something called an egg roll was prepared without shrimp. Mr. Wu, the owner, played a lively Chinese fiddle while Joe took the lead and cracked one of the egg rolls open, moving his finger gingerly through its innards and pronouncing it "ninety-five percent kosher" before taking a healthy bite. "*Batel b'shishim*," he said. It was the first untranslated phrase that Malke fully understood.

"They know the Hebrew," she said quietly to Goldah, "but they use it so loosely—like a convenience. It all seems just for show."

Joe asked what she had said and Goldah explained how she was finding everything so exotic and wonderful. Nothing like this in Prague, he said, and Joe told him how he had once tried his hand at a bamboo flute that Wu kept somewhere around the place but that the whole thing had ended in disaster. Joe laughed and finished off the last of the egg rolls while Goldah sipped cautiously at his own wonton soup.

The crowning event came with dancing at the Sapphire Room downtown, where an eight-piece orchestra led by a guitarist named Gordon Gould—Gould had recently played with Frankie Carle and Shep Fields, Herb explained, up in New York and Atlanta—swung and waltzed and two-stepped beneath a canopy of plaster palm fronds and dim light. Malke smiled and, through Goldah, said she was too tired to take to the floor but was so happy to be watching everyone else enjoying themselves. Goldah remained by her side.

"So this is how it will be from now on," she said. "The war was nothing but this for them, night after night, and now they'll be the ones to show the world what a Jew is. I wonder what Lotte and Franz would have said about that."

Having died of malnutrition, thought Goldah, Lotte and Franz would have said they preferred this, but Malke was still so new to things: Why not let her keep the dead as her benchmark for a little while longer.

And yet he was already feeling his own strength slipping away. Time was moving him backward, his old self taking root. Alone he had been able to hear just the one voice: conversations with himself that sprang from memories constrained by a single string of details—out of sequence, out of time, like a dream; repeated, they had grown obscure and almost harmless. Now there was this second voice, and with it came the burden of shared memory—memory that could reshape and sharpen those details and make them unbearable again. Up against that, what hope did he have?

The music stopped. Goldah watched the Kerns and the Fleischmanns beginning to make their way back to the table.

Pearl was laughing as she sat, something she had overheard, and Jesler told her not to be so flippant even as Selma said she might as well get all her sinning in now before *yontif*. Pearl laughed again, her behavior no less manic as she took hold of Malke's hand and squeezed it tightly in her own.

"You're just the best thing ever," Pearl said. "You're hope, that's what you are. Hope for everyone around this table and I don't care if you can understand me or not, you just are. Look at her, Fannie. Look at her the way I see her."

Fannie had been trying to keep the drinking to a minimum tonight, holding Pearl in check just in case she might forget herself given all the pressures of the last few days and weeks. Fannie said, "We all see her the same way, dear."

"Not the way I do," Pearl insisted. "She has a brightness in her, and the way she calms Ike, even with her face—"

"Yes," said Fannie, "I see it. I see how lucky everyone is. Have some water, Pearl."

"We should throw a party," Pearl said, finding her own, stale brightness beneath the sheen of gin and Vol de Nuit.

"It's getting late," said Jesler.

But Joe was already ordering another round and it looked as if there was no chance of moving any of them from the table, all their idle phrases and reckless laughter springing this way and that; only Jesler showed an inclination to step things along.

He said to Goldah, "Champ Kaminsky called today. I forgot to tell you. The car came in. He's going to give it to you for a dollar."

Goldah said, "I've told him I couldn't possibly accept that."

"But you will. This time you will. You've got your own place. He said it's come up from Florida. So you'll thank him for it and take it. That's Champ." Jesler pulled his own keys from his pocket and placed them in front of Goldah. "You take mine tonight. Get Miss Posner home. Herb'll give us a ride. I'll come by your place tomorrow, pick it up."

"You're sure?"

"It's been a long day. No doubt Miss Posner is feeling it."

Goldah took the keys and explained to Malke that they were leaving. Whatever else Jesler might be going through, Goldah appreciated the concern he always showed. Malke muttered a quiet "Thank God" in Czech, while Goldah stood and helped her up.

"Oh, no," Selma said with a child's disappointment. "You're not leaving, are you? Pearl, you can't go yet. You just can't."

"We're not," said Jesler, standing with the other men. "The kids are taking my car."

"No, Abe," Pearl said no less petulantly. "I like having them here. I do. We'll take them in a little while. Drop Ike off. Don't you want to stay, Malke dear? Don't you want to...*stehen eine*..." The words trailed off as Goldah handed Malke her purse.

"It's late," he said.

Herb took the lead. "Well...this was fun tonight. I'm sure we'll be seeing a lot of you in the next few weeks. The holidays and such."

"Yes, I'm sure," said Goldah.

Selma perked up. "Oh, so you're coming to the AA? Wonderful. That's so nice to hear. I thought you'd be at the temple with Mrs. De la Parra." It was only on the last syllable that Selma realized where she had taken everyone. She quickly looked to Fannie for support but there was little chance of finding any of that.

Goldah knew Malke hadn't understood; still, silence has a way of drawing even the uninvited in.

"What are they saying, Yitzi?"

Pearl suddenly took her hand again. "You just forget that, Malke dear. That's all done with. You're here now and you have all the hope in the world."

Goldah's only hope was that Jesler might know a way to distract Pearl from her own sodden enthusiasm, but even Jesler's caring had its limits.

"I'll tell you at home," Goldah said before they made their quick good nights.

Ten minutes later he was pulling the car out when Malke rolled down her window and said, "It was a woman they were referring to, wasn't it? The high drama at the table."

Goldah might have shown surprise, but why pretend when he felt none. He remembered how, if nothing else, Malke was never one to indulge in sentimentality. He nodded and told her everything she might need to know about Eva. He made no apologies.

When he was done, she said, "It's not like you." There was no accusation in her voice.

"I don't know what you mean."

"To say you know someone that well. Or think you do. It sounds...strange to me. That's all."

"And that's all you have to say?"

"What else should I say?" She remained perfectly calm as she leaned her head closer to the window. "It's going to make things difficult for you. I'm sorry for that. But it's funny—and you'll probably hate me for saying this—I find this heat absolutely wonderful. Everyone talks about it as if it's some kind of burden but I don't see it that way. Even the sweltering kind. I don't know why I should have thought of it. Maybe it's because I still dream of the cold. But this woman. She thinks she knows you?"

There was so much to Malke he had forgotten—by choice or not—but never this. Never the pointed remarks peppered in and among the distractions. *This woman.*

"Her name is Eva," he said.

"Yes, but I don't want us to refer to her that way, Yitzi. I can't fault you for having let it happen but that wouldn't be fair to me. You see that, don't you?"

Did he? Such a cumbersome thing, fairness: the Pandora's box of misery for the Jew. It seemed to him they were smarter than that. Events were inhuman, beyond reason—and they came in cycles with almost mocking regularity. Wasn't it enough to live through the pain of the moment? But to ask, is this fair—why suffer the slap twice? It was like the man—the fool, Pasco said—who, once betrayed by a brother, rages when the brother can't recognize his fault: "But it's not fair that you don't see how you wronged me..." Does the brother ever care? Never.

"No," Goldah said almost in spite of himself. "I'm afraid I don't see that." He continued to drive, unwilling now to turn his head and meet the unrelenting blue of her eyes, no doubt staring though him…

They're never warm, her eyes, though they seem to look at him with great affection—certainly affection. And he convinces himself it's because of the strain inside Terezín, the need to put on a brave face, to "impress our friends of the Red Cross, otherwise…" Otherwise. How it tests the limits of even her resiliency inside these walls, although he might recall this absence of feeling even from the start. But who has the energy to think that far back now?

He stares across at her, across the little table with its canvas umbrella and chipped top, and marvels at how well she keeps herself inside the camp. People are always remarking on her beauty. And why not? She says it will cause problems one day, but he refuses to let her talk that way.

They can already feel the cold that will descend upon them within the next few weeks, short sleeves letting the sun play on goose-pimpled arms. Somewhere above them, guns are also trained on them. To make sure they sit, to make sure they behave, to make sure they laugh. Yes, today they sit in the folding wooden chairs that teeter on the stone and dirt and have a glass of tea. It might be only for show, but why question that? The tea is hot, the roll is actually made of bread, and he finds himself laughing as Franz—their Franz, Franz Z., late of the National Theater in Prague—sits with them and offers up a hushed, perfectly rendered SS bureaucrat as tour guide of Terezín.

"And these are our Jews," says Franz. "No, no—don't touch! Hands in pockets. You see how plump they are, how happy to sit at a café and pass the time. That one there is a trombone, no, no, not a real trombone—oh, you men of the Red Cross are so comical, so insightful!—but a man who *plays* the trombone in a fine ensemble that the Jews themselves have put together with our aid and encouragement. We're always encouraging our Jews to create a place where they can be happy. And, after all, isn't that what we want for them? And this one here—this is a writer. Yes, we have writers. The Jews are always so smart—writers and artists—perhaps too smart. No, no, I'm joking with you. A Jew can never be too smart! Trust me. Otherwise how could we have them sitting here waiting for death...No, no, no, not for death. Of course not! Another joke. What a fiction. And from a writer. Tell us, writer—yes, you can speak—tell us how it is that you've found your greatest inspiration here in the wonderful gift that is Theresienstadt, how it is that only here you feel you've finally found a place where you can be appreciated? Tell us."

"You're a shit, Franz."

"Ah, the pearls, the jewels that come from his tongue. Wasn't I right to say he's found his inspiration? And even better tomorrow when you'll be gone, gentlemen, and he'll have no smell of baking bread in his nostrils or the warmth of an extra blanket on his bed to distract him—then you'd see the true genius of this man."

"The genius of this man," Lotte says, "is that he rarely speaks, which is more than I can say for you. You might learn to take a page from him."

"'Take a page,'" says Franz. "From a writer. Wonderful. That's why I love her because she's so much cleverer than I am."

"It's not so hard," she says.

Malke is staring beyond them to the entrance of the courtyard, where a few coats of plaster and paint have been slapped on to liven things up. The photographers have arrived with their escorts.

"Order another plate of rolls and more tea," she says. "They'll have no choice but to bring them now." She's finding great restraint today, Goldah thinks, and focus. It's something of a blessing.

He calls the girl over; she, too, sees the photographers and heads off for the food.

Across the courtyard the commandant strides in the uniform of a first lieutenant, with men dressed in suits who share looks of deep appreciation, nodding, nodding, as the commandant speaks, gesturing to the surrounding buildings, a quiet laugh—he's laughing and the men in the suits nod again—while the photographers stare about, stopping every so often to snap a shot, one of them with a large moving camera that he carries across his shoulder as he looks for a spot to place his tripod so as to capture the café and the buildings and the Jews at their ease.

The rolls and the tea arrive. Everyone has been told not to stare, not to look at the strange assortment of men approaching, but to chat—they've been told to chat about simple, everyday things: a child's misbehavior, the pleasantness of the weather, their happiness to be among other Jews. Malke keeps her eyes on the table.

No one is surprised when the men draw near to Malke's table. A girl that pretty and with bright blue eyes, seated across from Franz's long oval face and jowls and high forehead, still—inconceivably—with a bit of a double chin, the perfect picture of the *raffinierte* Jew.

"Good afternoon," the commandant says, dipping his head below the umbrella. He can't quite bring himself to say "ladies, gentlemen," but only Goldah recognizes the omission, as the commandant continues. "You're having a pleasant time today?"

"We are, Commandant," says Lotte. Goldah knows her hand is pressed tightly onto Franz's knee beneath the table.

"These are a few of the gentlemen from the Red Cross, eager to see our city," says the commandant. "I've been telling them we're expecting some colder weather, don't you agree?"

"Yes, Commandant, I think you're right."

"And you're the actor, aren't you? I've seen you. Very funny." He turns to the other men. "This is"—Franz no doubt feels Lotte's grip tighten and he gives his name—"he's been in a number of the productions we have here."

"Yes, Commandant," says Franz. "You're very kind to remember."

A man from the Red Cross says, "And are you preparing something new these days?"

Franz is already embracing his character. "A show with the children. It's quite something."

"A pleasant break from their schoolwork," says the commandant. "We give them sport, swimming, theater. I believe we're seeing their performance tonight."

School in the camp is forbidden. This week, in preparation for the visit, all the orphans have been sent east to make more room. As for swimming, the students from Roudnice, who built the commandant's swimming pool, remember only the beatings and the two who drowned in the process.

"Yes," says Franz. "We keep them very busy."

"And you, charming lady," the commandant says to Malke, his eyes wider, a momentary flush in his cheeks, "no doubt you must also be in the theater."

Goldah sees the hesitation in her eyes, not from fear—never from fear—but he has no idea how she'll respond, and he says, "She's to be my wife."

The commandant turns to him. He would have liked to have talked more with the lovely young woman but must now, out of a German decorum, speak with her man. "How lucky for you," he says. "Another wedding in Theresienstadt."

"Yes, Commandant," says Goldah. "When the weather turns. When it's warm again."

"How pleasant. Congratulations."

"Thank you."

There's nothing more for the commandant here. The group moves on and Franz waits to say, " 'When the weather turns.' You're an idiot. I thought you're the one who doesn't talk."

"I was inspired by the place."

Lotte ignores them both and says to Malke, "So is this really news? Are you engaged and didn't tell us?"

Malke is staring across at Goldah. Her focus has returned. "I don't know. Are we?"

Goldah takes a sip of his tea. It's cold. This time they haven't even bothered to see all the way through on the ruse. "Yes," he says. "Why not?"

———

The thrum of the cicadas made the pauses between them seem less fractured as they stood on the Jeslers' porch, a single bird somewhere above cawing in equally empty conversation. Goldah was still holding her purse. He thought she might ask to see him tomorrow but she said she was tired and, if he wanted more time, she would understand. She might have placed her hand on his arm or it might just have been the taking of the purse; neither of them read too much into it.

"Did you ever think we'd be standing in a place like this?" Malke said.

There were so many ways to answer that question but Goldah simply shook his head; she wasn't expecting more: She had given up on his silences long ago. She let herself in and ten minutes later he was back at his rooms. He opened the door and stumbled over something at his feet before finding the light. Looking down, he saw the envelope with no address, not even a name. He always attributed something mysterious, even sinister to packages that arrived this way, but here the mystery quickly became a dull pain at his temples as he felt the small ring and two keys tucked inside the paper. He had given them to Eva less than a week ago. He opened the envelope, hoping to find a note, but the inside was no more forgiving than the flap.

He stood there imagining her just the other side of the door: the moment she had pushed the envelope under; the next when she had felt the ache to retrieve it. Had he let self-pity guide him he would have tossed the keys onto the table with a false finality. But he didn't.

———

At four o'clock the next afternoon Bill Thomas sat on a stool at the far end of the bar at the Crystal. He'd called to say he'd read through Goldah's second piece and was jealous, desperately jealous, and insisted he buy him a drink. Goldah imagined there was no reason to question the motive—of course there was a reason—but he needed something to distract himself. After all, hadn't promises been made?

"It's damned unfair," said Thomas, nursing a bourbon; Goldah was fine with seltzer. "Not that it's Nabokov—I'm not going to embarrass either of us by saying that—but you have to admit it's a little criminal to be this good in a second language. Please tell me it's only two."

"If that makes things easier," said Goldah.

"Christ. How many?"

"Comfortably... five."

"*Five?* Well isn't that just wonderful. So what is it: German, English—"

"Czech, French, and Slovak. But this is journalism. It's different. It's never more than a thousand words at a time. What can go so terribly wrong?"

Thomas finished his drink and motioned for another. "Plenty. Trust me. Weiss must be pinching himself for luck every morning."

"I doubt that."

Thomas nodded knowingly. "You dumped the girl, did you? Don't worry. He won't care. She can get over it, but this... this sells papers. This gets noticed."

The bartender uncorked the bottle and poured another for Thomas.

"And one for this gentleman here," Thomas said. "At least keep it in front of you. Seltzer makes me nervous."

The barman waited. Goldah nodded, then drank. He had gotten used to the sweetness.

"A newsman who knows his Nabokov," Goldah said. "I think I'm impressed."

"That's the dream, isn't it?"

"What—to write a novel? I thought it was the *San Francisco Chronicle?*"

"I said the dream. The *Chronicle*'s the reality. It may be a little while on that but—"

"I wouldn't have taken you for a romantic."

"I'm not. And it's not because I have something to say. That's a fool's errand. I just like the idea of eight months without having to talk to a soul and getting paid for it."

It seemed to Goldah that this had all the trappings of a burgeoning friendship, especially when pitted against everything else. Friendship, he recalled, allowed for a greater degree of honesty. More than love or duty ever could, if only Malke could understand that. The truth, it seemed, was a small price to pay in order to foster the friendship.

"You've been looking into my cousin," Goldah said. Thomas was too good at what he did to show a reaction. Goldah continued, "I've known it for quite some time. Something about the docks. That's the reason I had Weiss send my piece down to your office in the first place."

Thomas took another sip. He spun his glass for a moment. "I guess I should offer to buy you a drink more often, shouldn't I?" He waited and said, "I knew why you'd come down. I'd read the piece before you came. You may write exquisitely in thirty-seven languages but deceit in spoken English has a rhythm all its own. Pretty hard to master. But I give you full marks for trying."

Thomas's brand of intuition was rare, his ease with it rarer still. Goldah decided not to be surprised. "It was that obvious?"

"I've been at this a while."

"So was I." Goldah heard his own *was* with more clarity than he cared to admit and realized how far he'd pushed that past away: A few paragraphs printed in a newspaper hardly made it real again. He said, "I don't know anything about what Abe is up to. And even if I did—"

"Even if you did you wouldn't tell me and I wouldn't ask and we'd be better off. I know. The nice thing is you *don't* know anything, and your cousin Jesler isn't what I'm after, not really. That's not to say he isn't doing something a little rough around the edges. Money under the table isn't kosher even if it's a Jew who's passing it along. But that's not what interests me. Corruption at a port, that's not news. It's the people he's trying to avoid up north, the union boys. And the man who keeps them in the dark. *That's* who I'm interested in. But I can't promise I can keep Jesler out of it. I thought you'd want to know."

"All because I write so well."

Thomas finished his drink. "We both know how rare it is to find someone down here who"—he chose his words carefully—"appreciates the world beyond this place. I'd rather not lose that for now."

For now, thought Goldah.

"Oh, and you're wrong, by the way," said Thomas. "It's not the flow of guns into Palestine that'll be the problem for your friends. It's Abdullah in Transjordan. He'll try to play both sides. Just a thought."

Thomas was full of surprises. He drummed his hands on the bar and stood. "Tell Jesler to keep Hirsch at a distance."

Thomas left a few coins for the drinks and headed for the door. Goldah tossed back the rest of his own and caught sight of himself in the mirror behind the bar. He noticed how his face had changed in the last few months, fuller and with a darker complexion. It seemed to him as if he was looking at a film he had once seen, though now faded and obscured. He wondered for a moment: Have I really become so easy to read? Maybe that was what had made Eva possible.

PART THREE

12

GOLDAH WAITED in the Jeslers' parlor with Abe. Abe had found his own grandfather's tallis and bag, which now lay perched on Goldah's lap, a few of the fringes peeking out from the crushed-velvet flap. Goldah sat, unaware that he was twisting the little strings around his finger.

"She seemed concerned about the seating," Jesler said.

"Pardon?"

"We don't separate the men from the women," Jesler said.

"Yes, I know. She'll be fine."

"Maybe she can sit in the middle of the girls, do it that way. And we'll sit with Herb and Joe. Unless you think it'd be better to have her with you?"

Goldah set the bag on the cushion next to him. He crossed his legs. Even the way he was sitting felt borrowed. "She'll do what makes her comfortable. We'll be fine."

In the car she sat behind him with Pearl, who offered a few last-minute suggestions on the angle of Malke's hat. Goldah watched in the mirror as the hat edged lower and lower on Malke's face until the shadow seemed to cover the offending cheek entirely.

Jesler parked the car on a side street and they headed toward the crowd making its way through the synagogue doors. The big park—empty on a Monday morning—was just on the other side of the road and seemed far more wide open than Goldah had ever seen it. He toyed with the idea of making a dash for it—the lure of all those impeccably mown lawns—but the picture of a Jew at full sprint on Rosh Hashanah seemed only slightly more off-putting than the prospect of what lay ahead.

Instead he joined the gauntlet of *"Gut yontifs"* and *"Shanah tovahs"*—the necessary nods to the new year—each passing without moment, although he did see a few widened eyes and whispers as he and Malke moved inside and along the aisle to their seats: A last little sin, he thought, before these days of repentance.

The shul was simple, row after row of pews, a small bimah at the front with a wooden ark to hold one or two Torahs. If Goldah had ever imagined a rustic Judaism, one born of the American frontier spirit, it was here in the sanctuary of Agudath Achim that he found it. Somehow his own appearance within its walls felt less jarring given all that was so foreign around him.

They sat, Malke took his hand, and for a moment Goldah's mind seized: It was such a small gesture on her part but it lay beyond his comprehension. She had told him again and again how much she was dreading sitting together—for the first time in so many years inside a real shul on Rosh Hashanah—and how they would be throwing away everything they knew because, here, this was how people prayed. He said it was such a small thing to let go of—how much more had they already left behind—but she seemed inconsolable. And yet she was holding his hand and Goldah had no idea why.

"Do you need to leave?" he said.

"Leave? No. Why?"

"You're all right, then?"

She took a prayer book from the little shelf on the back of the bench in front of them and held it tightly in her free hand. She said, "You remember that beautiful *machzor* my father had, the one with the leather binding and the gilt-edged pages?" He did. She released his hand and, opening the book, stood with the rest of the congregation and said, "So do I. I'm fine."

When they emerged to the street some three hours later Goldah felt relief, not for himself but for her: All that mattered was that she had made it through without incident. There had been one or two moments of concern—the rabbi's need to mention "the bravest among us," every face turning to them with great admiration and feeling—but it had mercifully passed to the real focus of the day, the heroes of the Haganah and the Irgun: "Like our own minutemen," the rabbi had intoned, "seeking the right to shape their own destiny...*vesechezena enenu*...the children of Israel reclaiming their home, two thousand years in the waiting, but at what a cost...at what a cost." Goldah had feared another turning of the heads but the rabbi had saved them with a firm "Amen" and a return to the liturgical routine that had been keeping Malke occupied.

Now, out on the sidewalk, Jesler pulled his cigarettes from his jacket and said, grudgingly, "It'll take us over an hour to get there, at least. Why can't we just go down to the river and do it like usual?"

"Not on *yontif*, Abe," said Pearl, nodding at his cigarettes.

Jesler slipped the pack back inside his pocket. "I like tossing my sins away as much as the next man—believe me—but the pavilion's a long way to go. What's wrong with the river? We've always done it down at the river."

Herb said, "Hell, you can do *tashlich* into a bucket of water, if you want."

"Two thousand years," said Pearl. "That's what the rabbi said. If this is the year Jerusalem becomes ours again, why not make a show of it? Why not cast away two thousand years of sin? I like it, Abe. I like that we're doing something special. Out to the ocean. Why not?"

"Because it might just be a bit premature, that's all. And, as I recall, we're a little touchy on jumping the gun as Jews, aren't we?"

"Well I don't see it that way and neither does the rabbi." She turned to Malke. "Did you enjoy the service, dear?"

"The service," said Malke, aware that, once again, she stood at the center of attention. "Yes."

"And the seating was all right?"

She nodded. It looked as if she might remain silent but instead she said, "It was such a small thing to change in order to be with family."

Pearl beamed. "I just love this girl, Ike." She reached for Malke's hat. "But you should have it just a bit lower on the side, dear. Here, let me show you."

———

Across town Art Weiss was hanging up the telephone in his study and heading back to the dining room for lunch. He was wondering how he might play out this latest development in front of Eva.

"Who was it?" said Mrs. Weiss, as she handed a plate of potatoes to her daughter.

Weiss sat. "It's the damnedest thing."

"Arthur, please. Julian's at the table."

The boy was sitting next to his mother, dapper in his holiday clothes and smiling. He was fair-skinned and had Eva's facial features—a sweet boy, thought Weiss—although

at times he was prone to a look of deep and somber concentration. The doctor had told them not to ask what he
might be thinking about during these moments, and it was
everything Eva could do to keep her word. His hair had
been parted to within an inch of its life this morning, cour-
tesy of his grandmother, the thin strip remarkable for its
absence of any gouging or blood. Mrs. Weiss favored a set
of silver-plated combs and brushes, the likes of which, in
the wrong hands, could mete out a form of torture not seen
since the days of the Second Crusade. Mrs. Weiss did *not*
have the right hands.

"Sorry there, Jules," said Weiss. "Grandpa forgot himself
for a moment."

"That's okay, Grandpa."

Weiss winked.

Mrs. Weiss said, "So was it Jock Snider?"

"Who?" said Weiss, as he reached for a plate.

"Jock Snider," she repeated.

Eva spoke for the first time. "Who's Jock Snider?"

Her mother lifted a plate toward her and said, "Would you
care for some carrots, dear?"

"No thank you, Mother."

Mrs. Weiss took some for herself. "Jock's an old friend of
your father's—from up north. For some reason over the last
few years he's been finding himself calling on the holidays.
Jock's Jewish, of course, but he calls nonetheless and your
father has to remind him. Like clockwork. So was it Jock?"

"No, dear," said Weiss. "It was the Atlanta *Constitution*."
Leaning in closer to the boy, he said, "A rather important
newspaper." Weiss picked up his knife and fork and started in
on his chicken. "They're interested in reprinting Mr. Goldah's
latest piece. Of course they didn't know it was a holiday."

"Mr. Goldah?" said Mrs. Weiss. Even the mention of his name brought a nice edge to her tone. Weiss ignored it and said to Eva, "I'm sorry, sweetheart, but the man's a fine writer."

Mrs. Weiss said, "Did you tell them it was a holiday?"

Weiss continued to watch as Eva kept her eyes fixed on her plate; he regretted having mentioned it at all. "Did I tell them?" he said. "Well naturally, dear. Of course I told them. I would have been remiss not to inform the Atlanta *Constitution* and the *Washington Post*—who've also called about the piece—that they should be far more sensitive to the Jewish High Holidays. I would have done so in Aramaic but you know how few of them speak it these days." He caught the first hint of a smile on Eva's lips.

Mrs. Weiss refused to look at her husband even as she gave in to a small grin of her own. "Now you're just making fun, aren't you?"

"Yes, I believe I am."

Eva said, "Is the piece really that good?"

Weiss tried not to sound too consoling. "It might be for the best, getting that kind of notice. He'd be hard-pressed not to accept a position if they offer one." He saw a moment of the pain she was feeling and it very nearly broke his heart. "But you never know what a man will do. Yes, it's that good."

Eva said, "Well, I'm happy for him then."

"I know you are." Again Weiss leaned into Julian. "And that's what makes your mother the most remarkable young woman I know."

"And Granny," said Julian, "is the most remarkable old woman you know."

Weiss held his laughter in check. "Why yes, Jules. That's right. Granny is the *very* old woman I know." The telephone rang, Weiss set down his cutlery and said, "And *that* will be Jock Snider."

———

The drive out to Tybee had a caravan feel to it, twenty or so cars winding their way past the small islands. The group had caught the approach of a fishing boat at one of the drawbridges, which allowed several carloads to step out and enjoy the midafternoon sun. The water was pale here and seemed to cradle the light in a slow wave of cordgrass and reeds.

Malke said she preferred to wait inside the car. Pearl decided to wait with her while Jesler said he wanted to show Ike something up at the bridge.

Jesler led the way. "She knows I'm stealing a smoke," he said, "but as long as she doesn't see it, she'll let us both pretend." They moved down into the tall grass and Jesler tried to sound offhand. "So...you like Raymond, Ike, don't you? He's got something to him?"

Goldah needed a moment to keep up. "He does. Yes."

"Hard to miss, I guess. The hand...it's not—well, he's not letting it get the better of him. That takes a certain kind of man. Mary Royal's father was the same way. You never knew him but he was just like that. Terrible loss in the war. I suppose that's why she takes to Raymond."

Goldah tried to recall the last time he had heard a black man referred to as an equal since he had arrived in America. He couldn't. Strange how one could become numb to the absence of a word and then shocked by its sudden reappearance. He remembered his own confusion at hearing himself referred to as a man for the first time after so many years in the camp, by a young Russian who had brought him a blanket. At least then Goldah had recognized it as a faint recollection, somehow right and fitting. He wondered if Raymond ever would.

Goldah said, "I'm not sure he has much of a choice, does he?"

"We all have choices."

"Only if they're ours to make."

Jesler took a long pull as he moved them along. He tried a nod. "I suppose that's true." The smoke speared through his nose and he said again with greater conviction, "That's true."

They came to the water's edge where the bridge loomed above. Jesler flicked his cigarette into the water and pointed up. "Just there. It's the old relay line out to Tybee. You see it? They used it during Prohibition. Government inspectors. They'd roll up and the boys would raise the bridge and tell the inspectors a boat was coming through. One of them would then sneak down here and send the signal out to the island, warn them so they could hide the booze. Inspectors never found so much as a bottle of beer, all because of that little box up there."

"Clever," said Goldah without much interest.

"Maybe...or maybe they were just breaking the law." Jesler seemed to be thinking something through. The bridge began to grind into gear and he said, "I guess we should head to the car."

They started back and Goldah—sensing Jesler's need to hear it—said, "Maybe some laws need to be broken."

Jesler was trying to step around a thick patch of mud. His shoes had caught. "I guess that might be true, too."

They drove for another twenty minutes before they found parking was almost impossible out by the pier. Jesler was puzzled and thought maybe there was a party or something, but he spotted a space all the same and they started out for the pavilion. The air was cooler above the beach and Goldah felt as if someone had shaken the place awake and mislaid his memory of it like a dream. He looked out and longed for the haze and the heat and the afternoon he had spent with Eva.

The group was almost to the end of the pier when Jesler said, "Well I'll be damned." The mystery of the cars had been solved: a gathering of forty or so people stood by the far rail, all gazing out at the water. "That's Blumstein," Jesler said, "and those are the Lippmans."

Goldah recognized the shock of Weiss's white hair and, at his side, a little boy who must have been Julian. Several in the gathering began to look back at the approaching horde, talking among themselves as they did. Soon everyone was facing one another and close enough to speak. Only then did Goldah see Eva standing next to her mother. He thought she might catch his eye but no, she was looking at Malke: There seemed to be something so final in that. Even so—and maybe in spite of himself—Goldah couldn't help but find something comical in the standoff: Two groups of Jews staring each other down over the chance to throw their sins into the ocean. He wondered what this might be looking like to a passerby but, of course, no one would have been foolish enough to give it a second glance: a murder of crows, a pride of lions, and here at last, a collision of Jews. He might have laughed if not for . . .

"We've come to do *tashlich*," said the rabbi from the shul.

"So have we," a sharp voice rose from the temple crowd, though not quite courageous enough to step out and be seen. "Plenty of water down on the beach."

The rabbi from the temple stepped out as well. "It seems as if we've both had the same idea this year."

"Yes, it would seem so."

"We'll be done in a few minutes, if you care to wait."

The prospect of standing in line behind the temple Jews sent a momentary buzz throughout the shul gathering.

"No need," said the rabbi from the shul, matching the other's pious if patronizing restraint. "As you've pointed out, there are plenty of places that will suffice."

The temple rabbi held his ground in silence and Goldah heard himself say, "Aren't the prayers the same for both? Couldn't we just do them together, all the sins at once?"

Goldah was used to people staring at him, albeit not quite like this, but at that moment he didn't care, not when he saw an instance of warmth cross Eva's eyes.

"What a generous thought, Mr. Goldah," said the rabbi from the shul, "but I'm sure our friends at the temple have already begun the ritual and we wouldn't want to force them to begin it again." He turned to his own flock. "A chance to walk in the sand like the children of Israel before us. What could be more appropriate this year than that?" He raised his hands and motioned for those at the back to lead them on.

Goldah watched as Eva turned to the water. If not for Malke he would have joined her and taken her hand. Then again, if not for Malke, he would have been with her already. Instead, he felt Malke's hand on his arm—a need to explain what had just happened—before they followed the others back along the pier.

Down on the beach, everyone quickly took off their shoes: The men rolled up their pants and pulled off their socks, while the women did their best to slip out of their knee-high hose without too much complaining. There was a great deal of leaning and grasping and even some laughter before they all began to trudge their way out to a suitable spot not far from the pier. Keeping back of the waves, the men retrieved their *kippahs* and tallisim as the women brought out the pieces of bread they had been carrying in wax paper, sequestered until now in the deep recesses of their purses. Bread for sins, thought Goldah: Only the ducks and seagulls would be seeing the efficacy in that.

The rabbi led them through the prayers, stopping as everyone tried in vain to hurl his or her bread far enough out into the water so that the tide wouldn't bring it back. A few of the younger men managed some excellent throws but most found themselves darting between the waves to retrieve the soggy pieces that lay lifeless on the sand.

"I know which sin that is, Herb Fleischmann," someone yelled, "and I can promise you, you're never going to get rid of it."

"Maybe I don't want to," Herb yelled back, deftly avoiding one wave only to be caught by another.

"You better," yelled Fannie. "Does anyone know if they can dry-clean a tallis?"

The whole thing was absurd—absurd and wonderful—and a far cry from the stupidity up on the pier. Even Goldah was feeling relieved. He had tossed his own bread far enough out to keep himself dry, which allowed him a moment to glance up at the temple crowd. They had finished and were milling about. He saw a few of the children racing in all directions, a necessary release after the quiet observance of yet one more Rosh Hashanah prayer: What sins had they committed, he wondered, to merit that? He tried to find Eva but she was keeping herself back.

"I want to throw a piece," he heard Malke say. The giddiness in her voice caught him by surprise. "And if it doesn't go far enough, Yitzi, I want you to go and get it and do it for me. Will you do that, Yitzi? Will you do that for me?"

He tried to sound encouraging. "Of course."

"Pearl," she shouted over. "May I have a piece? I want to throw it."

Pearl was laughing at Jesler, who was darting tiptoe along the edge of the water, more carefree than Goldah had ever seen him. For a large man he was remarkably spry, although it was anyone's guess when he might topple over.

Pearl shouted at him through her laughter, "Careful, Abe. Careful. You look a sight. Now watch Malke. She's going to try one. You go get it if it doesn't go in."

"I'll get it," said Goldah, rolling his pants higher above his knees. "They're my sins as well."

Pearl's face was pure joy as she handed Malke the bread. "A big throw, dear. Put everything behind it."

Malke stepped forward and with a sudden earnestness sent the small piece of bread arcing high into the air. It took everyone by surprise—the force, the trajectory—and when it landed well beyond the break in the tide, she jumped in the air with absolute pleasure to the cheers of those around her.

It was then that Goldah caught sight of the small body leaving the pier, even before he heard the scream: the tumbling of a child's arms and legs, flattening itself backward before it smacked effortlessly into the water and disappeared below.

———

The water burns even though Goldah sees the gauge beyond the tub hovering at just above six degrees Celsius. They have inserted a tube into his rectum and this, too, shows a temperature that is holding at just below thirty degrees. They are waiting for him to lose consciousness. The men who have called themselves doctors write on clipboards and, from time to time, prod his shoulders, which remain out of the water. If Goldah can strain his eyes downward, he can see his veins more acutely than he has ever seen them before. They look more green than blue, which he cannot understand, and he thinks this is when his eyes have begun to lose their accuracy.

Goldah knows he will die within the next twenty minutes. They have told him this. He watches the slow movement of the second hand on the clock above the table where, only minutes before, they had tied him down so as to insert the tube. They have told him that another twenty minutes is when his body temperature will dip below four degrees and his heart will cease to pump. They explain that the burning will become a warm sensation a few minutes before that. They would like for him to try and stay alive beyond the twenty minutes and, if he is able, they will begin the warming process. It is slow, and there is just as great a chance that he will die because of the shock to his system. They tell him all of this so that he might utter a word or two to let them know when he feels significant changes in either his limbs, his hearing, or his eyesight. They cannot assess these changes without indications from him.

They make it clear that these requests are perfectly reasonable because he will most likely die anyway and then they will need to find another test subject, no doubt one he knows, in order to gather the information they need. He alone will be responsible for the pain and the death of this other because he will have chosen to deny them a few simple responses.

He says, "Burning less."

They look at the clock and the watches on their wrists. They write on their clipboards.

At eighteen minutes he hears a dull sound—like whale song, he thinks—although he has never heard it himself, a mewling that rises and dips, and fills his head like a muffled scream, though it is gentler than that. He sees the men, their movements jagged now, slow then fast, and Goldah struggles to say something.

"Knife" passes his lips. He has tried to say something else, *death* perhaps, but his mind cannot think that far back, and he sees the clock has stopped and he feels the warmth they have told him will come, their movements once again rushed then quiet. He waits for consciousness to slip away but instead feels himself retching and knows he is somehow alive.

"Thirty-one minutes," he hears. "Remarkable."

It is three hours later and he lies on the table. They have brought him back to life. And because of where he is and who he is he can think only to thank them.

He tries to tell this to Pasco the next day in the hospital but there is still a burning in his throat and his jaw feels weighted and uneven. He wonders if it will always be this way. He cannot find a way to speak.

"You were the last," Pasco tells him in a low voice. "It's what I've been hearing. They can show your results as proof that a man can survive that kind of freezing. They're very pleased with themselves. They say your organs are functioning the way they should, except maybe the kidneys, but how well were the kidneys working beforehand anyway? You're the first Jew they've been happy to see live."

Goldah has been allowed to stay in the hospital, not with those destined for selection but with those who can still work. He is one of the prized patients. He has no idea how he has gotten here.

"They might have killed you anyway," says Pasco, "but it's better for them if you're still living. Lucky for you, lucky for me. I heard it all from Frister—the one who was the doctor in Lodz.

He washes out the tub. He was here when they did all the tests the first time, more than two years ago. He said you didn't lose your bowels, which is strange he said—even back then everyone lost his bowels—but not you, so maybe that's why you made it through. Good, hot shit piping through your insides to keep you warm—no, I know you can't answer. It's all right."

Pasco looks back to the door for just a moment, then leans over as he coughs and reaches into the heel of his shoe. He returns with a cube of sugar hidden in his hand—unheard of—and slips it quickly into Goldah's mouth.

"Who knows if it does any good but better to taste that than something else if you don't wake up. So make sure you wake up."

Goldah wonders how it is that Pasco can be talking to him, how he has been allowed inside the hospital. He wonders if, in fact, Pasco is even here but he tastes the sweetness in his mouth nonetheless.

"If you make it out they'll find something better for you. No question. Something easy, maybe up in the labs with me. What a treat for you. Fewer beatings. And they'll give you extras to keep you alive because they need their proof."

Goldah doesn't see the burn marks and bandages across Pasco's chest and arm. Pasco has saved a scientist in a chemical fire. He has been permitted a few days to regain his strength. Only later will Goldah understand their good fortune to have been in the hospital together.

"No washing for you," Pasco says with a quiet laugh, "not for a while, not even with stolen water, am I right?"

Goldah knows Pasco wants to a see a smile; Pasco has been trying so hard. Goldah does what he can with his eyes.

"Sleep and dream of the desert," says Pasco. "What else should a Jew dream of?"

Goldah felt the water closing in all around him, warm and dense; his arms strained against the current. He had tossed away his jacket and tie on the beach—Eva's screams had shredded the sky above—but his pants were now weighted as he tried to push through. Diving deeper in he felt his ears compress, the water darken with weeds, as wild tendrils brushed against his arms like thick strands of hair. He grasped at them, frantic to feel skin and bone beneath, but the current was stripping them away even as he reached out. He was drifting—he knew it—lungs burning, desperation and hope draining from him with every stroke. He had never called out to God in the past, never once, not even at the edge of his own death—not to beg, not to thank—but now he thought: You must answer. Who are You if this is the moment You choose to remain silent?

Goldah swept his arm out, then again, and felt the cloth across his fingers like breath itself. He clenched at the shirt in his hand, the small body close in now, weightless, drawing it into him as he pushed them both to the surface, their heads breaking through as one. Goldah gasped for air and shouted "Here!" only to see the face of the boy bobbing at his side. From somewhere, other hands appeared, pulling them forward until Goldah felt the sand beneath him, the boy torn from his grip. Goldah's own heaves now lay shrouded in shadow from those standing around him.

He heard a dull ringing in his ears as he sucked in for breath. He had no understanding of why the minutes passed as they did—for lack of air, for the shock, for the relief—but they came to him in a strange haze, heightened, as if he were watching himself live through them. It made his own movements jagged and disconnected, the sun too low in the sky to keep anything in focus.

He was standing somehow, pushing his way through the men who had gathered around him. He saw another man kneeling over the boy.

"Ike."

Goldah felt a hand on his shoulder. He had heard his name. He turned to see Jesler holding him back.

"Ike."

Goldah tried to speak but he couldn't: Where was Pearl—where was Malke in all this?

"The doctor needs his room, son. There's nothing else you can do. Nothing. Just stay back."

Goldah was again staring at the boy, both of them unmoving, the small arms stretched out above the head, the face lifeless until, with a sudden jerk, the boy coughed and coughed again. A stream of water spilled from his mouth, and the doctor brought him up.

Goldah found himself wrapped in a bear hug with Jesler.

"Good God, Ike. You brought him back. You did. *Baruch Hashem.*"

There were other hands now on his back as Goldah released himself from Jesler's embrace. He saw Eva stumble to the sand and pull her boy in. The doctor stood, shaking his head, and Goldah thought he heard, "Not even a scratch..."

Goldah watched as Eva cradled Julian's body in her arms, pressing her head to his, weeping, and letting her dress become soaked through from the water. Goldah felt Jesler place something rough on his shoulders.

"Pull it around you, Ike," he said. "You need to avoid a chill."

Goldah let the jacket fall as he moved toward her. The Weisses were already at her side, a lifeguard with them. All three were kneeling down and doing what they could to try to dry the boy and Eva.

Goldah found himself standing over them; he was still hearing the ringing in his ears. Mrs. Weiss was the first to look up, her eyes red and her hair windswept. She was trying to say something but all she could do was nod and cry. Goldah tried to speak as well but Weiss was somehow standing with him, fighting back his own tears as he put a hand out to Goldah.

"Thank you, Mr. Goldah. Thank you." Goldah felt the grip in his hand; he felt it tighten. "I'm not sure I know who you are but I do know how lucky we are to have you here."

The hand released and Eva was looking up at him, her gaze filled with a deep joy—a deeper sadness behind it—and all he wanted was to reach for her, but Jesler was once again at his side, wishing them all well and moving Goldah off, back toward the women.

"We had a little light-headedness," said Jesler. "Maybe more than that...Pearl did. And Miss Posner—she needed her medication...There was some shouting. Nothing too much...It was best to move her off. She's all right now... Herb's keeping her in check. Just over here."

Goldah saw them, sitting on the sand like driftwood, all at odd angles and leaning into each other: Pearl was smoking silently with Fannie and Selma; Malke stared absently out at the water; Herb and Joe stood just behind.

When Goldah drew up, Malke barely turned her head.

"I'd never seen a beach like this until today." She spoke in a distant voice; he wondered if she knew she was speaking Czech. "And now I've seen it. I suppose I'll always remember today for that, won't I?"

Pearl finished her cigarette; she kept her eyes on it as she crushed the stub deep into the sand. "He's all right then, the boy?" Her words carried no weight. "And Mrs. De la Parra, the Weisses?"

"The boy's fine," said Jesler. "They're all fine."

"How relieved they must be." Only then did Pearl look up; her eyes were no clearer than Goldah's own. "And you, Ike—so very brave. Our brave, brave Ike."

Goldah felt his knees buckle; Jesler was there to keep him upright. Malke shouted out to no one, and Jesler said, "We need to get them home. Anything else can wait."

13

THE GIRLS STAYED in bed during services the next morning. The doctor had stopped by last night and again today: A shock like that could be dangerous for Miss Posner, he said. Not that he wanted to be making a habit of it but, just in case, he gave Pearl a sedative as well. As for the ringing in Goldah's ears, if it had stopped . . . well, no reason he couldn't join Jesler at shul. Goldah's motives for staying away from the house were not quite so spiritual.

Thankfully, and to everyone's great relief, lunch passed without fanfare: The girls continued to sleep. Mary Royal had come in earlier than usual so as to keep an eye on things, and Jesler asked if maybe Raymond could come along, too. Just in case.

Jesler now sat at the dining-room table, sliding the last of his apple pie onto his fork and using his thumb as a guide. He had been trying to keep things light. "I wouldn't pay too much attention to any of it, Ike. It was maybe half a minute before she calmed herself down. People are just concerned, that's all. They want to make sure she's okay."

Several in the congregation had suggested that the sight of a lifeless boy must have triggered something in poor Miss Posner. They could only imagine. But how heroic Mr. Goldah had been.

"Took some of the spotlight off you," Jesler said. "I know how you appreciate that."

"Yes..."

"Well...I'm guessing you'll want to go over and see the boy, Mrs. De la Parra." Jesler wasn't expecting an answer; still, a nod would have been nice. "You saved him, Ike. You saved Weiss's grandson. They'll want to thank you for that." Nodding for them both and standing, he said, "Anyway, I'm going to go up and check on the girls. I'm sure they'll sleep. You come back when you want."

Jesler moved out into the hall and listened until he heard Goldah's chair slide back. Jesler then headed toward the kitchen and waited for the sound of the front door latching behind him before he pushed through.

Inside he found Raymond and Mary Royal sitting at the small table with two pieces of half-eaten pie in front of them.

"No, no—it's okay," he said, "don't get up. The girls are asleep. But I'll be needing—" He stopped himself. "I was wondering if I could see you in my study, Raymond?"

Raymond shot a glance at Mary Royal. "Yes, suh, Mr. Jesler."

"Good. You can give me about five minutes."

Jesler didn't need the time. He took it anyway and stood by his desk, thinking he might pour himself a glass, but why go down that road? Better to come at this clearheaded.

Four minutes into his vigil Jesler heard the knock, then watched as Raymond stepped inside. Jesler had laid out several pieces of paper across the desk. He now moved to the window and asked Raymond to take a seat.

"I wrote that all out last night," Jesler said. "I'll be taking it to my lawyer to go through this week. You should have a look." He saw the hesitation and waited for Raymond to pick up the first sheet. "Bottom line, it's four percent," he said. "Four percent on everything. That seems reasonable to me and maybe, depending on how things go, we can talk about that down the line...I don't know. But one thing I *do* know, you can't go telling anyone about this, Raymond. No one. Maybe Mary Royal, Calvin—I'm not even sure on that front. Word gets out that a Negro has any kind of stake...that would just kill the business. You understand? Cohan, Hirsch...anyone wanting to buy a pair of shoes...Kill it. I'm putting that in writing. I've also got a paragraph that says you've got to go easy on the money...how you spend it, at least at the start. Put it away, save it up. No flash. I can help you with some of that, if you want...and I don't know if it's even legal for me to tell you how to spend your own money but we've got to be smart on this. I'm guessing that's something for the lawyers to make right...I'm assuming you've got your own Negro lawyer to take a look at this? In any case, that's all he'd be doing—taking a look. That's just the way it has to be. You understand?"

Raymond continued to stare at the page. He hadn't read a word and now set it on the desk. He tried taking in a long breath before he said, "I ain't never going to say this to you again, Mr. Jesler, but any chance I could trouble you for a glass a whiskey?"

Jesler poured out two and handed the larger to Raymond. Jesler didn't bother to take his own.

"Thank you, suh." Raymond took a sip.

"I don't want you thinking this is because of the hand," Jesler said. "Or that fellow at the paper. I can't have you thinking that." He spoke plainly, not to plead but to put this behind them. "And I can't have myself thinking it, either. I'm sorry for that but that's not what this is about. There's just a time to make good on things and this is that time."

"Yes, suh."

"I guess what I'm saying... I'm saying I'm doing this for the man I think you are and the man I imagine I'm supposed to be. And that's that."

Raymond took another sip. He set the glass on the desk. "Yes, suh. I can see that, Mr. Jesler. Miss Pearl know?"

Pearl... Jesler hadn't even thought about that.

He felt a sudden rush at the prospect of what he was doing: He had written everything out so quickly last night and with such purpose. And maybe he had let the moment get the better of him, but he told himself it wasn't just last night or this morning or even this instant now, seeing this young man gazing into a future he could hardly understand. There was nothing rash in what he was doing. It had come to him and it had made sense of so many other things, and how rare those moments are, he thought, if in fact they come at all. That he was feeling a bit of caution, well...

"I'm still thinking on that."

"Yes, suh." Raymond took a moment for himself. "Mary'll be good on the money. She'll be smart."

"I imagine she will." Jesler saw Raymond beginning to work things through. Jesler said, "You need to know, son, the money... it doesn't change things. Trust me on that. It makes a few things easier, but the rest..."

A silence settled around them: It had nothing to do with the weight or the promise of the moment; it was simply that neither of them could think of anything more to say.

Finally Raymond stood and extended his good hand.

"I guess I should be offering you this, Mr. Jesler."

Jesler gazed across at the thick black fingers, the strength in them—the veins and the tendons—and he knew how they would always dwarf the meaty paleness of his own. He stepped over and took the hand.

Weiss answered the door and Goldah thought: Of course they'd be here. It probably saved him the awkwardness of seeing Eva alone.

"Well look who's here—wonderful," Weiss said. "I was hoping we might catch you if you came by. Come on in. Julian's upstairs, ostensibly sleeping." Weiss was smart enough to announce Goldah's arrival from the hall: "Look who we've been lucky enough to have drop by." At the archway to the living room he said, "The man of the hour. I've told him Julian's upstairs."

Eva was sitting next to her mother. A handful of others stood or sat in perfect groupings across the chairs and settee and, save for the Weisses, Goldah didn't recognize a soul. One woman, older than the rest, held her teacup at just above her waist.

Without warning the room launched into a stream of introductions, followed by a chorus of deep appreciation for his bravery. But it was the woman with the teacup—still seated—who had the good sense to say they should all be getting home. Only then did she stand and slowly make her way toward Goldah, while Weiss escorted the rest down the hall.

"Mr. Goldah," she said with an equally unhurried if quavering warmth, "my name is Peggy De la Parra. I'm Julian's grandmother and Charles's mother...Eva's mother-in-law. I'm sorry we haven't had the opportunity to meet before this."

Goldah tried to mask his shock. He took her hand. "What a pleasure," he said. "I'm...so sorry for your loss."

"Yes," she said, the word hovering between them for a moment. "So much tragedy but so much hope—if we let ourselves see it." She placed her other hand on his and—leaning closer in—said, "I choose to see it, Mr. Goldah. As would have my late husband and my son." She pulled back and patted his hand. "I understand yesterday was the first time you met our little Jules. Quite an introduction."

"Yes."

"He's unbreakable, that boy, although I think this might have been his closest scrape yet. Thank goodness you're such a fine swimmer." She squeezed his hand and turned to Eva. "Mr. Goldah is far more handsome than in his photograph, Eva. You were quite right." She turned again to Goldah. "I don't mean to embarrass you, but...well, there you are." She squeezed his hand one last time and released him just as Weiss was back from the door. "Walk me to the door, Arthur. Marion, you must teach that grandson of yours not to be so reckless. And when you do I'll convince him otherwise and then everything should work itself out just fine."

"Whatever you say, Peggy," said Mrs. Weiss; Goldah had never heard her sound quite so genuine. "You get yourself home safely, dear. And happy new year."

Eva stepped over and embraced Mrs. De la Parra.

"You'll notice, Mr. Goldah," Mrs. De la Parra said, "this is a very beautiful and fine young woman I'm hugging, and that's all I have to say." She let go and took Weiss's arm. "Happy new year, all. Give that boy upstairs a kiss for me."

Weiss helped her down the hall, which left Goldah alone to fend for himself. He imagined there might have been a way to get to one of the chairs but, at the moment, human movement seemed beyond him. Surprisingly it was Mrs. Weiss who came to his rescue.

"Would you care for some tea, Mr. Goldah?"

He did, although it took him a moment to answer yes. Mrs. Weiss called for Bessie and Goldah waited for Eva to sit before he found the courage to move himself to the chair farthest from them. All three waited in this mannered silence before Bessie appeared with a glass and brought it to Goldah.

Even in the short time he had known her, Goldah had felt a certain ease with Bessie around. She was young and very pretty, but it was her candor—perhaps even impertinence—that seemed to relax him, relax them all. It was as if the De la Parras, so secure in their place, could allow her a greater humanity, and that had always been refreshing to him. Goldah was feeling none of that ease from her today.

"I'll take another, as well, Bessie," said Weiss, back from the door and sitting next to him. "With a little extra syrup." Bessie headed out and Weiss said, "Well, here we are. Peggy's a treat, isn't she?"

"Yes," Goldah said almost too eagerly. "She is." He had nearly finished his glass.

"First woman to drive a car in Savannah," said Weiss. "Made quite a stir. She even tried to get her pilot's license at one point. You remember that, Marion? Her husband, Walter, he was a funny one . . . He said he'd always had enough trouble keeping her feet on the ground so he put the kibosh on that one right away. I think she wore an Amelia Earhart scarf around town after that, but then Isadora Duncan died and, well, that was the end of that. A great lady and she just keeps rolling along. She's got two older boys . . . where are they?"

"Atlanta," said Mrs. Weiss.

"That's right. And the girl?"

"Helen is in California, Arthur."

Weiss raised his eyebrows. "Miss Helen De la Parra, artiste of the west. We've gotten packages with jewelry and pottery and, one time, a painting, I think. Don't ask me what of. I believe there was a marriage in there at some point. I remember being invited to something."

Bessie came in with the tea.

"Bessie," Weiss said, taking his glass, "did Miss Helen De la Parra ever get married?"

"Yes, suh, Mr. Weiss. She marry a Dr. Robert Epstein, a heart doctor, in Redondo Beach, California, August a 1938. You give them two silver candlesticks and two more when the first baby come."

"That sounds right," said Weiss. "Bessie's mother, Clara, has been with us since . . . when is it?"

"Nineteen twenty-three, Mr. Weiss. July."

"My goodness. That's a long time. Nineteen twenty-three. And Bessie's been with Eva ever since she got married."

"Yes, suh."

"I think we'd be lost without them."

"You'd do just fine, Mr. Weiss."

"Yes . . . This is Mr. Goldah, Bessie."

She said coolly, "Yes, suh, I know Mr. Goldah. For a time we was seeing quite a bit a him. Not so much no more. Isn't that right, Mr. Goldah?"

Goldah thought the whole room was enjoying the scrutiny. "Yes. Not for a while."

Bessie said, "Well, I think that's a shame. Anything else you'll be needing, Mr. Weiss?"

"No," he said. "I think we're fine."

Bessie stepped out and Goldah quickly said, "The prognosis is good on Julian?"

"Oh, the boy's fine," Weiss said. "Resilient at this age. Bit of a scare—"

"Arthur," said Mrs. Weiss, "I believe Mr. Goldah was asking Eva."

Whatever Goldah might have been expecting, he never imagined to find his surest ally in Mrs. Weiss.

"Oh," said Weiss. "Of course...Yes."

Eva said, "He's doing fine. I'm not sure he knows any better."

"That's good," said Goldah.

"It is, yes...I did thank you, didn't I?" She seemed almost apologetic. "I'm a little foggy on yesterday."

Mrs. Weiss was suddenly on her feet; she set her glass on the table. "Daddy and I need to get going, dear. I'm sure you and Mr. Goldah have a good deal to talk about."

Weiss was mid-sip and quickly brought himself forward. He was not alone in his surprise. "Going?...Oh, that's right...Yes. We need to be going."

All four were now on their feet.

"Well," said Weiss, leaning in for a hug from Eva. "Give him a big kiss from me when he gets up. Tell him he very nearly took ten years off Grandpa's life."

"Yes," Mrs. Weiss said, "I'm sure he'll find that very amusing, Arthur. Goodbye, sweetheart. Kisses from Granny."

Weiss said to Goldah, "By the way, I need to talk to you about your latest piece. A couple of big papers are interested. Might be quite an opportunity for you."

"Arthur," Mrs. Weiss said with a look thirty years in the making, "we need to go."

Weiss said quietly, "We'll talk about it at the office."

Goldah expected a curt nod from Mrs. Weiss but instead she said no less directly, "I was wrong, Mr. Goldah. I was wrong and I apologize."

Goldah stood, slightly stunned.

Mrs. Weiss continued, "I believe I said you were a broken man and that was a terribly heartless thing for me to say. I was simply frightened for my daughter—more frightened than you can understand—and such things trump anyone's feelings, no matter who they might be or what they might have gone through."

"Mother, I'm sure Ike—"

"Let me finish, dear. Then you can tell me what Mr. Goldah is thinking." She spoke again to him. "I'm not looking for your forgiveness—my husband and daughter can attest to that. And I'm not saying this because of your supreme act of courage yesterday, for which I shall be eternally grateful. I'm saying it because I now see you deserve to be with someone of equal quality. I don't dare to imagine what you share with that young woman we witnessed on the beach yesterday but I do know that that poor creature is a shattered person—"

"Mother, please."

"Eva, dear—I can't possibly seem more ghoulish in Mr. Goldah's eyes than I already do so, as I say, let me finish." She turned to him. "You must think me quite an overbearing person, and I am. I don't have the genteel graces that so many of my friends possess. I choose not to hide behind kindness and perhaps that's a callous thing to say as well. I speak my mind because I feel a great deal. Some might say it's quite remarkable that I've managed to raise such a sincere and genuinely warm young woman...and I will not have you thinking for one moment that her father had one iota of influence over that...but you must know that her capacity in that regard is due in full measure to her own quality, which I admire with more wonder than you or she will ever know. And if she feels as deeply for you as she does, then I will now add to your burden by freeing you from any concerns you might have about my reaction to what you choose to do, as principled as that choice might be. If I were my dear friend Peggy I would now take your hand and hold it with great affection, but I am not Peggy. I will simply say that whatever you think you owe to your past, whatever pity it stirs within you, cannot be more worthy than the future you would have with my daughter." She took her purse.

"I should tell you, Mr. Goldah, that later today my husband and my daughter will be yelling at me for this. Or they'll be thanking me. Either way, it will be entirely up to you."

She leaned in and kissed him on the cheek—an unnatural gesture to be sure but one she managed all the same.

"That was my exit, Arthur. You need to come and take my arm so we can go."

————

"She played Ophelia in the tenth grade."

Eva stood with Goldah in the hall and listened as her parents' car pulled out on the street.

"She calls it her great triumph," she said, "although today's performance might deserve an honorable mention, don't you think? My father played Laertes, which was a bit strange as they were dating at the time, but Mother says it helped her with the mad scene. I've never fully understood why."

Goldah thought: Even now she has such strength, frantic strength. But it made his own silence seem all the more frail by comparison.

He said, "She kissed me, I think?"

Eva managed a smile. "Yes—I think that's what that was."

"May I hold you?"

He had caught her unawares. Remarkably she kept her smile. "What would be the point?"

He took a step toward her and she said, "You should see Julian. I think it would be good for him to get up. He needs to thank you, as well."

"It's not necessary...Yes. If you think that would be all right?"

At the top of the landing they heard a sudden scampering of feet just the other side of one of the doors, the telltale squeal of box springs as the boy dove back into bed. Eva

245

kept her ear pressed to the door, waiting until she thought the silence might be too much for Julian. She then slowly pushed the door open and stepped inside.

The boy was lying on his back, his head tilted to the wall, eyes closed and his small chest breathing heavily from the exertion.

"All right," she said, "I know you're awake. I never said you had to stay in bed. I want you to say hello to someone."

The eyes remained shut; the boy was playing his moment to the full.

"Julesy," said Eva, "this is Mr. Goldah. He's the gentleman who pulled you from the water."

The boy instantly turned his head and opened his eyes. He stared for a few moments. "Hello," he said.

Goldah tilted his head so as to match the angle of the boy's. "Hello."

Julian seemed puzzled though intrigued by Goldah's strange posture, so much so that he began to move his head deeper into the pillow to see how far Goldah might go. When the boy began to enlist his shoulders in the effort, Eva said, "Come and shake Mr. Goldah's hand, Jules."

The boy straightened up—as did Goldah—and slid himself down to the floor. He was in a cotton bathrobe tied neatly at the waist, which he wore over his pajamas. He inched his feet into his slippers, rubbed them briskly against the carpet, and then bounded to his mother's side. With equal animation he extended his hand. Goldah leaned down and took it.

Julian said, "Thank you, Mr. Goldah, for jumping in and saving me."

"It was my pleasure. I'm glad you're all right."

"I should probably take some swimming lessons. Would you teach me?"

"I . . . don't know . . . maybe."

"Really? You think so?" The little hand released with a sudden enthusiasm. "Did you hear that, Mother? Mr. Goldah said he might teach me to swim."

"I thought we had Grandpa signed up for that?"

"Oh, yeah, Grandpa. Well, maybe we could all do it together?"

Eva said, "Are you hungry, Jules? I know Bessie's got something down in the kitchen. Pie and lemonade. You can go if you want."

"All of us?"

"In a minute."

He put his hand out again. "Good to meet you, Mr. Goldah. Thanks for getting me. I almost gave my grandpa a heart attack."

He was hurtling down the steps before Goldah could answer.

"Careful," Eva shouted after him but it was Bessie's "Don't need no wild animals tearing through this house" that bellowed from downstairs and brought Julian into line.

Alone with Eva, Goldah said, "He's a fine little boy. And very well behaved."

"Today—yes."

He reached out and took her hand.

She said easily, "I'm not sure I want you doing that." He tried to let go but she held it all the same. Flipping the hand over, she began to examine it, rubbing her thumb across the black stains she now discovered between his second and third fingers. "You've been writing."

"Yes."

"They should get you a typewriter if they want your pieces. I'll tell my father."

"I prefer a pen. I always have."

247

"Then they need to get you a better pen."

He pulled her in close; he hadn't thought to do it but his arm came around her back and held her there.

She said, "It's not very fair, is it, a distant kind of hope? I've lived through that once. I'm afraid I can't do it again."

How was it, he wondered, that he could forget this part of her, even for a moment? How selfish of him to think she ever could. He thought: If only I had the power to erase the last two weeks. It wouldn't change the past or the future—he knew that, of course—only the way he looked at them. That was the malleability of memories: They lived in pockets of the mind, vivid or dulled depending on the lens one chose to see them through. Happiness, as it turned out, had nothing to do with suppressing or relishing or even coming to terms with the unchangeable. Happiness had only to do with a shifting of that lens, something forever out of his control. Somehow, up until two weeks ago, he had learned to see so much through her. Now that was gone, and he felt a deep shame for having refocused hers once again through the death of her husband.

She pulled away and said, "I won't ask if she makes things easier, or if you find some kind of comfort in...I don't know." He heard a hint of her mother and knew he deserved it. "I can't really care about that."

"Yes," he said.

"I'm not sure I even know what that would mean. But I do know I make things easier for you in the only way that matters because that's what you do for me...You see that, don't you? And I'm sorry—but I can't just let this happen."

Had he said he loved her at this moment it would have meant nothing. They both knew how much he did. Why point up how small a role it played in all of this?

"You're right, of course," he said.

"Am I?"

"Yes."

"But it doesn't make a difference, does it?" She seemed so tired of talking about it. "She won't stop being a part of what you were in all those terrible places. She can't. And if you abandon her now you'll never forgive yourself for doing it. Worse, I'll be the one to have let you see it through. And what good is that?"

14

CALVIN SAT with his hands on the kitchen table, palms down, fingers flat and wide. He was gazing at the gaps between his knuckles as he listened. He knew the boy needed to get it out all at once. No reason to have him catch a look that might temper his excitement.

"Well?" Raymond said when he figured he had said enough. He set his backside against the edge of the counter and looked over at Mary Royal. She was standing quietly by the wall, hardly moving. Raymond waited for Calvin to look up, but Calvin kept his eyes fixed on the table.

"Well," Calvin repeated, "there it is. Getting lawyers in on it, too."

"Yes, suh."

Calvin noticed the beginnings of a hangnail on one of his fingers; he tried to rub it away with his thumb. "How about you, Mary? What you thinking?"

"Me? Whatever Raymond wants to do, he should do."

Calvin nodded to himself, still looking at the finger. "'Whatever Raymond wants.' I guess that makes sense." He chewed at the nail and rubbed it again. "Even if you the one that got the ball rolling in the first place—no, I don't mean nothing by it. Just seems to me the two a you need to be making a decision, not just Raymond here. Must've been some kind a courage to talk to him."

Calvin's calm was having a sobering effect, more so his strange inattention. Raymond seemed confused by it and looked over at Mary Royal again. She said nothing.

Raymond said, "Mr. Jesler done most a the talking."

"That sounds about right," said Calvin.

"He said he wanted to be a better man."

"Did he? Those are fine words." Calvin left it at that and Raymond said, "I do something wrong? I needed to be talking to you before I done it?"

"No, son."

"Then why ain't you happy about it?"

"I'm happy."

"Don't seem it."

"I'm a little old to be doing a jig on the table, if that's what you waiting on."

Mary Royal said, "He don't mean that, Pawpaw—"

"I know what he means."

Raymond heard the edge in Calvin's voice as if it were his own and said, "Ain't no reason to get sharp on Mary."

"I ain't getting sharp."

"Then why you acting like this? I'm sorry it ain't you he talked to, but that's just the way it is."

Calvin placed his hands back on the table—flat and wide—and he breathed out with a quiet laugh. It took them all by surprise and he looked over at Raymond.

"You think I'm jealous on you, son? Is that it?"

"No, suh—"

"You a war hero—a man getting on with things when most would a just set out and given themselves up. You under-stand that?"

"Yes, suh, but then why ain't you taking my hand and shaking it and telling me congratulations?"

"Because you ain't seeing it all the way through, that's why." Calvin let the two of them share another glance. "I know what you done is strong, believe me. The way you tell it—down in Yamacraw—Mr. Jesler knows what kind a man he got with you. And I think more a him now than I ever done. But you forgetting one thing. You forgetting Jacob... That's right. That boy's one a his own, and Jacob's too smart not to start seeing what's going on here. I don't care how good a man Mr. Jesler is. No man's that good when it comes to protecting his own. And that's just the way it is."

Calvin hadn't wanted to say it, bring a young man down like that. He expected to see the air go out of Raymond's chest—a man had to know the truths he couldn't escape—except Raymond didn't let the air out.

"I guess you're right," Raymond said. He spoke in a voice Calvin had never heard from him before—quiet and certain and somehow faraway. "Mr. Jesler's going to need to figure that out. Same way he figured this out. Ain't that right, Mary?"

Calvin followed the boy's gaze to the girl's and saw in that moment how things had moved beyond him, even before he had sat down at the table.

Raymond wasn't asking for his approval or his praise. He wasn't even asking for his blessing. He was simply hoping that Calvin could trust Jesler at his word. Calvin felt his fingers like brittle bones on the wood and he thought: Now what's the chance a me doing that?

———

Friday afternoon found Goldah reading through a stack of notes in Weiss's office. Weiss sat the other side of the desk

253

adjusting his lamp, while Bill Thomas stood by the window, finishing a cigarette and trying to catch what little air the fan had to offer. Goldah felt Thomas's anticipation like a hand on his shoulder as he leaned forward and set the last of the notes on the desk.

"It's nothing definitive," Weiss said, "but I thought you should know. There's very little to tie Jesler to it, if anything. Still, the implication will be there."

Thomas said too quickly, "I'm after bigger fish with this. I've told you both that."

"Yes," said Weiss, "but Savannah's a small place, Mr. Thomas. The big fish have a tendency to bring the little ones along with them."

Goldah appreciated Weiss's reasonableness, more so the glass of water he'd insisted on pouring. A glass of whiskey would have said so much more. Goldah said, "You wouldn't print without proof?"

"Of course not, and right now there's no link between Jesler and this fellow in Atlanta. But I do have to ask—you've never heard Jesler mention Meyer Hirsch, have you?"

Goldah knew Weiss was only doing his job. Still . . .

"And if I had?" asked Goldah. It was only a moment's defiance. "No, I haven't. I don't have much to do with the store these days. There might have been something going on at the store. I'm not stupid. But the depth of it . . . I can't imagine Abe would be tied in with these kinds of people."

Thomas said, "He probably doesn't know what kind of people they really are."

"So what is it you want from me?" Goldah asked.

The question caught Weiss by surprise. "Nothing," he said. "I'm simply telling you this as a favor—as a man who writes for this newspaper—so you can let Jesler know."

"Even though there's nothing to tie him to this?"

"Not yet," said Thomas.

"And you're certain of that, seeing as this is such a favor you're both doing for me."

Goldah might have regretted his tone but it had Weiss backtracking.

"Look...the story isn't Jesler. We understand that. Honestly, I'm not convinced we even *have* a story, however enthusiastic Mr. Thomas might be. We're going to run it as a gradual build, an article or two per week starting next Friday. Nothing too explosive. Something along the lines of"—he thought a moment—"the role the unions play in Georgia, the links they have up north, how things work in the various professions...electricians, truckers, the port. All very general. That being said, we'll have to see where it goes. You know as well as I do how these things work. There's never any predicting what might come up."

"So you're anticipating it leading to Jesler?"

"I'm anticipating nothing," Weiss said more emphatically. "Without proof of a connection there'll be no need to go down that road." He shot a look at Thomas. "Isn't that right, Mr. Thomas? And my feeling, once we start mentioning Atlanta, the *Constitution* will jump in and lend the whole thing some speed."

"So who's your source?" Goldah had to ask even if he had no hope of getting an answer. Weiss and Thomas remained silent. "No, of course not...You ask about Hirsch but I go in blind when I talk with Jesler. This is quite a favor you've done me."

Weiss said, "You know I can't ask Mr. Thomas to reveal a source."

Goldah had played that card himself so many times. It was unnerving to be on the other side. And then he said, "The redhead." Goldah spoke without hesitation, as if a single word could clarify everything. "The boy at the store. Jacob. He's the one who's been feeding you the information, hasn't he?"

Thomas didn't say a word but Goldah knew. Could a four-teen-year-old boy truly understand an act of betrayal? Goldah said, "Why on earth would he do that?"

"I have no idea," said Thomas. There was no reason to hide it now. "I think maybe at the start he thought if he exposed what was happening at the docks he'd be able to get Cohan off of Jesler's back."

"That makes no sense," said Goldah. "He would have been taking Jesler down with him."

"Agreed. I don't think the kid saw things that far down the road. I think he thought he was helping Jesler."

"And somehow you chose not to mention this to me the other night."

"Would you have told me if the situation was reversed?"

Goldah knew it was a fair question. "And did you confirm any of this or did you just take the word of a fourteen-year-old?"

"He's not like any fourteen-year-old I've ever met."

"So no confirmation." Goldah looked at Weiss. "I'm having trouble understanding how you allowed this."

"I didn't know about it at the time."

"'At the time.'" Goldah did nothing to hide his contempt. "But you have no trouble using the information *now*, do you?"

"There *is* no information," said Weiss, "despite what Mr. Thomas thinks the boy knows. Whatever he's said about Cohan—we already knew. It's the possible connection to the man in Atlanta, this Hirsch, that changes things. But we don't have that connection." Again he looked at Thomas. "I'm right in saying that, Mr. Thomas, aren't I?"

Goldah said, "So the boy didn't give you Hirsch."

Thomas hesitated. "No, he didn't. There is no connection, yet."

Weiss spoke to Goldah: "On the other hand, if the boy were to have any hard evidence—"

"Which he doesn't," said Goldah.

"Not at this time—no."

"Which means *at this time* you have no reason to get in touch with the boy unless he comes to you. I'm right in thinking that, yes?"

"Yes," said Weiss, eager to put this to bed. "Absolutely right."

Goldah turned again to Thomas. He was suddenly struck by something Thomas had said earlier. "'At the start,'" Goldah said. "What did you mean by that?"

Thomas tried to dismiss it. "It doesn't change anything."

"What did you mean?"

Thomas tapped a cigarette from his pack. "The kid's been talking about the young Negro...the one who got hurt. He thinks he's involved with Cohan." Thomas lit up.

Goldah couldn't quite believe what he had just heard. "That's not possible," he said.

"I know that," said Thomas. "But the kid's convinced everything out at the docks started when you arrived."

It was now Weiss's moment to stare incredulously. "What in the world are you saying, Mr. Thomas?"

Goldah saved him the trouble of answering. "He's saying Jacob feels threatened. The boy thinks he's getting squeezed out of his future in the business, so he's casting Mr. Thomas's net a bit wider to Raymond and me." Goldah looked over at Thomas. "And that doesn't have you questioning everything else the boy has said?"

"Everything?" said Thomas. "What kind of journalist would I be if it did? This latest stuff—it's ridiculous, of course, a

Negro and a camp survivor in bed with Harry Cohan or this Hirsch in Atlanta. But the rest? The kid's gotten that right at every turn. And if he gives me the link to Hirsch, why should I care why he's doing it? On a story like this, I can guarantee you no one at the Prague desk of the *Herald Tribune* would have cared one way or the other, would they?"

———

Hirsch and Cohan—faceless names—lay on Goldah's mind hours later as he stood atop the ladder among the shelves at the store. He had been finding this the quietest time to come in, the place empty and cool and with nothing more to think about than the mindless repetition of restocking boxes. Tonight, though, that was different. This time he had come to think. There had to be a way.

He was so preoccupied that he failed to hear the back door opening or the footsteps along the cement floor, and he certainly wasn't prepared for the "Hey there, Mr. Ike," which cut through the quiet air of his concentration. Had Goldah been cupping more than a single box under his arm, the whole stack might have fallen on Raymond's head, but as it was, Goldah was holding just the one and now juggled it to his chest before reining it in.

"Guess you didn't hear me," Raymond said. "If you need a minute, you go on and take it."

"That's very kind of you."

"Looks like some kind a monkey tricks you got yourself going there, swinging back and forth, slipping them boxes in. Nice and smooth. You got to teach me that sometime."

"I've still got one box up here. My aim is pretty good."

Raymond laughed and said, "What you doing here, Mr. Ike? No reason to be taking on extra work."

Goldah slid the last one in and started down. "You've been thinking all the boxes have magically found their way up onto the shelves over the last few weeks—is that it?"

"Ain't been thinking about it at all. If the boxes get up, they get up. Just thought Jacob was doing it."

"Sorry to disappoint." Goldah stepped off the ladder. "So what brings you down?" He reached for the glass of water he'd set on the ground and realized his sleeve was still rolled up. Quietly, Goldah let it down and chose not to see Raymond staring at his forearm. Goldah said, "I thought Friday night was shrimp and ribs out at the place in Pooler for you and Mary Royal?" Goldah drank.

"You been paying attention, Mr. Ike. No, we'll head out in a little bit. Just thought I'd come down, take a look. Quiet here with no one around this time a night."

"It is."

One of the bulbs overhead flickered and Raymond said, "I can take that glass for you, Mr. Ike. Wash it out."

"That's all right. I still have a few more stacks to go."

"I can help with them boxes, too, if you want."

"No—no reason to get your shirt damp. Anyway, I like doing it on my own."

"Okay...Oh, and Mary'll probably want to know—Miss Posner doing better? She had quite a scare."

Goldah always appreciated Raymond's sense of things, more so the way he showed it. "She's fine."

"And I guess Miss Eva thanking her lucky stars for you."

Goldah waited before answering. "I should probably get back to this."

"Yes, suh."

Raymond looked to go and Goldah said, "Why'd you really come down tonight?"

Raymond thought a moment, shrugged. "Guess some-one needs to be keeping an eye on the place seeing how Mr. Jesler's mind's been elsewhere. Make sure everything's okay. No trouble, really. Maybe I just like the quiet, too."

The sound of a car passing in the alley broke through and Goldah said, "Abe didn't send you, then . . . to check up on me?"

Raymond's confusion lasted only a few seconds. "Mr. Abe knows you down here?"

"I don't think so—no."

"Well then he don't, 'cause I come down on my own."

Goldah nodded. Best to let it go.

"You okay, Mr. Ike?"

Goldah set his glass on the floor. "You're a good man, Ray-mond. I'm glad Abe realizes what he has with you."

Raymond's concern became something more pointed. "Mr. Abe say something to you?"

"To me? About what?"

"About me and my place here?"

Goldah heard the change in tone. It seemed a strange question. "He appreciates you very much, if that's what you mean."

"He told you that?"

"He did, yes."

"'Cause he said we wasn't going to be talking to no one about my percent."

Goldah realized he had overstepped. He had no idea what Raymond was talking about. Hirsch and Cohan flooded back and Goldah nodded and said, "I imagine he did," hoping it would be enough.

Raymond took another moment before saying, "Makes sense, I guess, you being family and such. You got a stake in the business, too." He nodded in a way that seemed more to convince himself than Goldah. "You best get back to your boxes. I got to get myself over to Mary's. You have a good night, Mr. Ike."

Goldah listened for the door, then hoisted himself back up onto the ladder with a new set of boxes in tow, all the while unaware that Jacob, tonight quiet on his cot, lay staring coldly into the darkness.

15

IT WAS ANOTHER DAY before Goldah was summoned. He rang twice, then knocked before Jesler came to the door. At first Abe looked puzzled—distracted by something, a cold sheen across his brow and cheeks—until, with a sudden recollection, he snapped himself into focus.

"Oh...sure. Here you are."

Jesler had telephoned this morning, but it was Malke who was calling out to him.

Jesler ran a hand across his slick forehead and ushered Goldah in. Halfway down the hallway, he took hold of Goldah's arm and stopped him. The look in his eyes was equally jarring. Jesler said, "I know you're here to see her...I don't want to get in the way of anything and I suppose this might sound a little crazy, but you haven't mentioned Hirsch to anyone, have you? I mean...I can't see how you would have, but just in case I wanted to ask. If you had...in passing or something?"

Goldah kept his gaze level, careful not to show even a hint of recognition. He owed Jesler that much. "No, Abe, I don't recognize the name. You've never mentioned a Hirsch to me. Is everything all right?"

Goldah watched as the eyes ticked through some unseen list before the head gave way to a reassuring nod. "No—sure. That's right. You don't know him. How could you?" Jesler let go of Goldah's arm. "That's all right. Okay. You go on up. She's in her bedroom."

"Is everything all right?"

The moisture on Jesler's face seemed to gather in his eyes—the expression confused, lost, then broken. Ever so slightly Jesler shook his head and a faint shade of life returned. "I don't know," he said quietly.

"It's okay, Abe. Everything will be okay."

An unnerving calm swept over Jesler. He tried a smile and patted a hand on Goldah's shoulder. "You go on up. She's waiting. Hard to say what for but . . . Take care of yourself, Ike. That's the most important thing." For some reason Jesler nodded again before moving off. Goldah had no choice but to head for the steps.

Upstairs, her voice was faint through the door, stronger with a second stab at it.

"Come in."

Goldah pushed through. The room was dark. "I'm here, by the desk," she said, though Goldah struggled to find her. "I prefer it without the lamp. You can sit on the bed."

He waited for her outline to grow clearer. A few shards of sunlight broke through the drapes and he sat.

"You see," she said. "Isn't this more pleasant?"

Goldah felt as if he had lived through this summoning before, not with Malke but with his father: childhood essays submitted for approval, hours waiting outside a door in anticipation of the verdict—final and absolute. Goldah could recall nothing of kindness from those sessions by the desk, no indication of pride or love, only a search for the truth, the frustration and the humiliation scrawled across each line in his father's pen, and shredding what little of himself he had put on the page. Goldah had always received top marks for his writing, but he had never once considered the work his own. To still live with that sense of deceit...

"Much more pleasant," he said. "How are you feeling?"

"They've let me sleep a good deal. The medicine has been good for that. A bit woozy." He thought she might be drinking something at the desk but he couldn't be certain. She said, "I can't stay here anymore, Yitzi."

"No, of course not." He had been anticipating this. "We'll find you some rooms."

"No. I can't stay *here*...in this place...with these people. Any of these people. I feel the shame too much."

"I know," he said. "It will pass. No one sees what happened on the beach as anything other than what it was. You had a reaction. How couldn't you?"

"What are you talking about?" Her tone was suddenly more strident. "I don't care what these people think."

Goldah tried to gauge her expression but the shadows were falling across her face. He said, "I don't understand."

"Yes you do. Of course you do. You know exactly what I mean. The shame. For being here. For being here at all. They can't understand that. They never will."

She was taking them back to the camp, but he knew full well it was Eva who was causing her shame.

She said, "Don't tell me it isn't there with you every moment. The things we did...the things no one should know you're capable of doing...and yet here we are, and you think a bit of shouting at the water has anything to do with that? Don't sit there so quietly and think I don't know."

"And what is it you think you know?"

"Plenty, Yitzi, I know plenty. Trust me." She leaned forward and her eyes caught the light; he saw how empty and unwavering they had become.

265

He said, "Why don't we talk about finding you some rooms of your own?"

"Would that be easier for you? Would that make this place real, have them all thinking you're just as real? But of course you're not, and I'm the only one who knows it."

She had always taken aim at him with a willingness to wound, but this...he could feel the depth of her hatred.

He said, "You're upset. I've put you...us...in a difficult position. I'm sorry for that."

"I'm not upset, Yitzi. I simply know what we both live with."

"And if I see it differently?"

"Because of this woman? You think because of her?"

"Why not?"

"'Why not?'" He heard the disdain in her voice. "Should I laugh? Where was this man before the war...before the *Lager*? Does he exist even now? When the guards came, when they moved through the bunks one by one, girls screaming until they had given everything of themselves, even as the guards would beat them to death afterward. The guards couldn't let anyone know how they had defiled themselves with a little Jewess...the shame of it. But I never screamed. Not once. I chose not to and my beatings were easier. And when they made me pregnant, I found someone to kill the baby inside me because you couldn't have the guards finding that. There was always someone to kill a baby in the blockhouse...always someone who knew. The women laid me on the ground and held me down and covered my mouth so I wouldn't give myself away with my own screams. And when they were done, this face...it was a blessing because the guards saw what I had become and they no longer wanted me. *Then* they beat me...my cheek, my nose...shattered them because they had so liked my

266

face before and now it was gone. And if ever I said any-thing...A blessing, the palsy. We all had such blessings, didn't we? And now you have this woman."

She spoke without life, the words cold, and only then did Goldah see the wet creases along her cheeks.

He said, "You want me to say I regret living through it? I won't."

"Good—why should I want that? I don't. It's only the moments when I chose to survive—the hundreds and hun-dreds of them when I couldn't let myself die—that I regret, not the surviving. The instinct to live...It's a terrible thing, isn't it, unless you give in to it among those who understand how truly terrible it is. In there, in the *Lager*...no one cared to be forgiven for living. No one saw it as life. But here...It's not their pity I can't stand, Yitzi. It's their innocence. These are the ones who would have screamed and died and been freed from it all. They can't know the shame and it's too much for me to see them every day."

Goldah felt nothing at hearing her story. This was his lin-gering horror. To feel nothing for such things. And if this atroc-ity could stir nothing in him...was all feeling just a shadow?

"No," he said aloud, hardly aware that he had spoken.

"So you do see?"

He had lost himself in the shifting light on the floor, a scat-tering of narrow spikes, each one tapering to the darkness by the door. Even they, it seemed, could find no escape.

"What?" he said.

"I can't stay here."

"I know. And where will you go?"

"*You?*" For the first time she spoke with surprise. "Is that what you think? No, Yitzi—it's where will *we* go." Her face came full from the shadows. "Even if you love this woman, it won't change a thing. You'd see your shame in her every day. Can you imagine that, the loneliness of it? I'm saving you from that by taking you away."

"You think Palestine will be any different?"

"No one there will see us this way. No one will have lived this easy life of a Jew. *We* won't see ourselves this way and we'll live again. Here...here we have no chance at life, not the way we knew it. Is your love worth so much more to you than that?"

Jesler had been through the desk drawers, the filing cabinets, even the safe by the back wall. Nothing in any of them mentioned Hirsch by name, save for a page here and there that made vague reference to an import/export company out of Baltimore called Hoover and Son. It was Hirsch's coy nod to the storefront operation in Atlanta. Hirsch had been very clear on its necessity: "If someone should ask, and God forbid, Abe, I'm not saying anyone would, but if someone should—someone with a badge or a cheap suit or smelling of Pinaud and Barbicide, you know the type—you need something...something official-looking to wave in a face. Baltimore? Please. Who's schlepping all the way up to Baltimore? They look, you're fine, end of story." The pages were untouched; nothing had gone missing.

How, then, had Thomas mentioned Hirsch by name over the phone?

He moved back to the drawers—along with his third glass of whiskey—and anxiously started sifting through a stack of receipts when he saw Jacob standing the other side of the desk. Jesler didn't know how long the boy had been there or what he might have overheard—Jesler had been mumbling to himself—but Jacob continued to stand there.

"Hey," Jesler said, trying to sound offhand. "I'm in the middle of something here. You can see that, can't you?" He moved down to the second drawer. "I told you yesterday, we'll get to whatever it is once I sort this through. Okay? If it's about the pay"—Jesler began to flip through the pages of last week's Jacksonville run—"I said I can do a nickel, maybe a dime more an hour…we can talk about it, but right now…why don't you go and grab yourself a Coke and I'll see you later." Jesler set the stack haphazardly on the desk. He started in on the central drawer and noticed the state the boy was in: hair mussed, T-shirt stained and dingy. Jesler said, "You get yourself in a fight or something?"

Jacob arched his slim shoulders. He meant to show defiance but the awkwardness of the gesture came across as the too-eager pose of a raw recruit awaiting orders. He said coldly, "When'd you start giving Raymond a percent?"

Venom, in the voice of one so young, carries less menace than histrionics. Had Jesler been a little more clearheaded he might have recalled the way genuine hatred manifests itself in a deeper, more resonant timbre. Instead, all he felt was his own frenzy melting away in the face of it. He said, "What are you talking about?"

"You know what I'm talking about. Raymond's in on some deal and I ain't a part of it."

Jesler stared across at the boy—at the pale skin and the probing eyes—and saw the pieces slowly fall into place: How they lined up was of no consequence; he knew Raymond would never have said anything. Neither would Ike. Who else could it be? Jesler thought: The boy—it's been the boy all along who's brought me to this. He expected his own voice to erupt in anger but his words came calmly when he spoke: "It's not 'ain't,' son. It's 'I'm *not* a part of it.' We've got to get that right. You need to keep working on it."

"I said I know Raymond's getting a percent. I said I know that."

"Yes, I heard you. We still need to work on the language. Who'd you tell, son?"

Jacob refused to buckle. "Tell about what?"

"Let's not play it that way, okay? No reason to waste either of our time. About whatever it is you think you know... Raymond, the docks, Atlanta." Jesler saw the shoulders inch ever so slightly downward; he knew this was well beyond the boy's grasp. "You make a choice like that you've got to live with what comes from it. You talked to the newspaperman, didn't you? You told him things you thought you knew. It's all right. I just need to know what you said. You want a glass of water? You need to sit down?" The boy was angling his shoulders back but his chest had begun to shake. "When did you talk to him, son?"

Jacob stared straight ahead.

Jesler said, "That newspaperman's got ideas of what's going on here and he needs someone to tell him he's got it right, even if that someone doesn't know all of it. Which you don't. But that was to protect you. It's always been to protect you."

Jacob had never looked quite so young as he did now. Whatever hardness he had crafted from a man's expression faded into the gentle features of a boy—the eyebrows too delicate to sustain a glare, the jaw too smooth to express contempt.

Jesler said, "Your percent, son...that comes when you're sixteen. It's how I set it up last year when I worked it through with the lawyer, but that's not something you needed to know about." He saw the instant of shock and remorse register in the boy's face, the tears beginning to form; to his credit, Jacob refused to break down. "I don't have a son of my own and...well...I'm not likely to have one unless Mrs. Jesler knows something I don't. You see what I'm saying? As for Raymond, he's a grown man and maybe I wasn't always thinking about him and his future, but that's not a concern of yours. It's all right, son. My mind's been elsewhere so I guess I didn't see it. And maybe I'm a little relieved to find it's been you."

Jesler stood and moved around the desk. Jacob was trying so hard to keep himself upright. Maybe it would have been better, thought Jesler, to have railed away at him, raised a hand. Anger has a way of keeping up defenses, but comfort...

"I know what you know," said Jesler, "and I know what you think you know, and there's a difference. But son..." He let the boy lean into his chest. He held him there and let him weep. "You're going to need to tell me what you told him."

———————

Eva ducked into Pinkussohn's pharmacy to pick up a prescription for her mother. She had given herself an endless list of these little tasks, anything to keep her mind from ticking through the permutations that seemed always to leave her drifting and alone. Not alone, of course—she would always have Jules—but the waiting for her husband, Charles, had carried something noble with it, an idea of sacrifice or the will of God or whatever other comforts people had thrown her way. But here...this was simply a slow grinding down of hope until, with a little sputter, she knew Ike would come to her and say how sorry he was, but...

Eva was so focused on not running into anyone she might know that she nearly missed Mrs. Jesler and the Posner woman sitting at a table by the window. They were having coffee, and a few cookies were on a plate between them. They looked happy. Eva knew she could slip by unnoticed, but she thought: Why not put an end to it now, save herself that miserable goodbye from Ike? How much easier on everyone.

She stepped over and said, "Hello there, Mrs. Jesler. Miss Posner. Do you mind if I sit for a few moments?"

Pearl had no choice but to be gracious. Malke's face made it more difficult to gauge her expression.

Eva said in German, "I'm so sorry we haven't had a chance to meet before this, Miss Posner." She turned to Pearl. "Is it all right if I speak to Miss Posner in her native tongue? I don't mean to be rude."

Pearl was only too glad to be kept at a distance. "Of course...I didn't know you spoke...yes of course. I'll order us some more coffees." Pearl called over the waitress and Eva said to Malke, "I see you're feeling much better. That's good."

"You speak German," Malke said without a hint of appreciation.

"I studied it at college. I wanted to help with the war effort if I could."

"How very ambitious of you. Do you speak German with Yitzi, then...with Ike?"

"No. We haven't done that. I think he enjoys working on his English."

"Yes."

"You'll forgive me, Miss Posner, if I speak plainly. I don't imagine either of us has much small talk for the other."

"No. I don't think we do."

The coffees arrived. Pearl quickly moved to the bowl of sugar, the cream, another cookie.

Eva said, "I wasn't aware of your connection to Ike before you arrived. I don't mean to say that he kept it from me—"

"He thought I was dead," said Malke. "Yes, I understand that."

272

Eva hadn't expected this bluntness; somehow it made things easier. "I also don't want you to think that what happened between Ike and myself was in any way frivolous. A number of people were quite against it when it began."

"Yes, I've heard that."

"We're very different communities here."

"I suppose you might see it that way, yes."

"It goes back a good deal of time."

"Does it? Do you want me to say then that you were both very brave to pursue it? How very brave of you."

Candor had quickly moved to something quite different. Only Eva's decency kept her seated. "Not at all," she said with quiet restraint. "It was hardly brave compared to what the two of you have been through."

"Please . . . please don't do that, miss. You think what you're saying is compassionate but it's really pity or worse. I don't mind at all . . . truly, I don't. Pity has never been a problem for me. Perhaps Yitzi finds it comforting. I don't. But I wouldn't want you to convince yourself later that pity was the reason things went as they did."

Eva found herself fighting off a moment's dizziness. She had come over only to make things easier for Ike—how, she hadn't thought through—but now that instinct had passed. When she spoke, it was for herself alone.

"I don't pity you, Miss Posner, I admire you, although I'm sure you'll tell me how that offends you as well. But it's not you I care about. I simply need to know that what you're doing is for him and not to convince yourself that his choices make yours seem like the right ones. That would be truly pitiful. No, let me finish. To love him as I do is to be willing to lose him as long as I know there's something inside you that I will never be able to give him. Something he himself can't understand

273

now, but that you, because of your love for him, know to be true and will show him one day. *That*, and that alone, is the reason things will go as they go."

If Eva saw a crack in Miss Posner's otherwise flawless stare she chose to ignore it. She felt a first flush in her own cheeks but refused to give in. Instead she turned to Pearl with an airy smile and said, "How kind of you to let us introduce ourselves, Mrs. Jesler." And, placing her hand atop Pearl's, she added, "And how kind of you to have shared your Ike with me, even for so small a time as we had. I've always wanted to thank you for that."

She saw Pearl's eyes begin to well up and Eva stood, her own now burning even as she blinked away the pain.

"A pleasure to meet you, Miss Posner. Mrs. Jesler."

Outside, it was everything she could do not to collapse to the pavement. Eva thought: What a heartless, heartless woman. And how heartless of me to think it.

———

Thomas was at his desk when Goldah pushed through the swinging doors. It was late: He knew he'd find him alone.

Thomas didn't look up; instead he continued to scan the sheet in his typewriter. "Hey, Ike. Look, I'm sorry about the way this whole thing has worked out."

"You have a minute?"

Thomas marked something on the page, sat back, and tossed his pencil onto the desk. "It's not what I wanted, you have to know that, but Weiss is giving it the green light. And what do you care? The *Post* wants you up in Washington next week for an interview. You're on your way."

Goldah stepped over and placed a large envelope on the desk. "I brought you this."

Thomas hesitated, then picked it up and pretended to weigh it in his hand. "Am I supposed to guess?"

"You could open it."

"I'm sorry about the kid, too. I really am. But he came to me."

"Why don't you open the envelope."

"You really can't see any of this from my side, can you?" Goldah said nothing. Thomas let out a long breath, then peeled back the flap and pulled out the pages. Taking a quick glance at the top sheet, he said, "What is this?"

"They're yours. You wrote them."

Confusion didn't suit Thomas's face. "I don't follow," he said.

"You were right about Abdullah in Transjordan. Much more interesting than guns. It makes for some powerful reading."

Thomas stared vacantly across the desk before turning to the pages.

Goldah quickly saw the reaction he had been hoping for: uncertainty to surprise, curiosity to deep interest. He let Thomas get through the first of them before saying, "You see what I mean?" Thomas flipped through to the next and Goldah said, "It goes on from there. You eventually get to some very interesting ideas about the Sinai Peninsula and the Egyptians, but you'll have to hold off on those for another month or so. You've got seven pieces there, all told. I'm not sure I agree with any of them—in fact, I know I don't—but for an American gentile, I think it makes sense. I myself would have followed the guns, but then again, I'm not you."

Thomas looked up. Admiration now colored his disbelief. "How did you do this?"

"You write well. It makes it easier to capture a voice when that's the case. I did get your voice, didn't I?"

"This is—"

275

"Yes—it is. And, I'm sure you've guessed I've done it so you'll drop everything to do with Hirsch and Cohan."

Thomas was still reading. "Yeah, I get that."

"Tell Weiss you were after the truth and forgot the facts. Put it that way."

Thomas looked up. "And you're just handing these to me," he said. "You realize you won't be able to write about this yourself, at least not from the angle you want. You're torpedo-ing your entire gun-supply argument. I mean you're letting *me* torpedo it, if that makes any sense."

"I do. Yes."

"And I'm assuming each one of these keeps piling it on."

Goldah saw the calculations ticking away behind Thomas's eyes, the words *gift horse* spinning past them, the fear that he was being duped or outmatched, all of it set squarely against the prospect of what this might mean for him. The hardest part for Thomas, of course, was giving himself over to a mind more sophisticated than his own. Or maybe it was his integrity. That's why his hesitation held firm.

Thomas said, "And you'll let it go just like that? No piece on the partition plan two weeks from now or on who gets how much of the Negev?"

"Just like that," said Goldah.

"They won't like this up in Washington."

"I don't believe they will."

"It'll be some time before they give you another chance."

"I understand that."

Goldah knew what Thomas was thinking: I'm not seeing it all the way through, but I am, I am...It was the unfathomable thought that someone could ever throw himself under the bus like this.

Goldah said, "They'll have what they want. A fresh new voice on the Middle East, one with some insight behind it. I wouldn't be doing this otherwise. That voice just won't be mine. Maybe even better not coming from a Jew."

"And all so some tiny dock story doesn't go to press?"

Goldah said, "The first of these pieces—maybe the first two—you'll have to publish with Weiss."

"And if I say no?"

"For some tiny dock story?" If Goldah wasn't so intent on getting this done he might have admired Thomas for this last pang of conscience.

Thomas said, "Weiss won't go for it."

"Of course he will. He likes the notoriety. Another *Morning News* feather in his cap. It won't matter who's handing it to him."

Thomas said, almost protectively, "Are you sure you want to do this?"

Goldah stood. He said nothing. It was enough to bring an end to the calculations. Thomas set the papers on the desk. "It's not so tiny, is it," he said, "the story? I'm on to something bigger here, aren't I?"

Goldah owed him that much at least. "Honestly? I don't know. But I'm not willing to take the chance."

"And does Jesler know what you're doing for him?"

"That's never the point."

Thomas sat with that for a few moments. "So where did you learn to write like this?"

"Mimicry isn't that hard."

"No, I mean like this. All of it. Those first pieces you published with Weiss."

Goldah had no interest in going down this road. "You keep at it," he said. "You get better. Are we good, then?"

"No—that's not it. This doesn't just develop over time. Trust me, I know. Where?"

Goldah waited and then heard himself say, "My father."

"He was a teacher?"

"An editor. A novelist. He wanted to be Joseph Roth." Goldah let himself smile, if only for a moment. "*The Radetzky March*. That sort of thing."

"Did he ever write it?"

"He did, yes." Goldah recalled a line or two. "A beautiful piece of writing. Prague before the first war. My father was a great prose stylist, the best I've ever read."

"Did he get it published?"

"He didn't. No."

Thomas gave a too-knowing nod. "The plight of the novelist. The dream dashed."

"It was burned. They burned the manuscript."

Only then did Thomas see the ground onto which he had stepped; he knew to stop asking.

Goldah said, "I watched him die, my father. He stood there, freezing in the cold and looking at me while he waited for a bullet. They didn't allow him to speak. I'm not sure what he would have said."

Thomas said nothing, and Goldah added, "We're good, then?"

Thomas nodded and Goldah turned to go.

It was a lie, he thought. His father had spoken. He had taken Roth's own words as his last: "My novel will be good, I think, more perfect than my life." One last desperate plea for the truth and then the shot. Even now Goldah didn't know whether his father had spoken in defiance or delusion. Whichever it was, he had meant the words for his son alone, a final nod to the bond they had never shared.

16

GOLDAH SAT at the table in his small living room and let his eyes wander to the single shelf of books he had managed to amass: a thin hardback of Rilke, Döblin's *Berlin Alexanderplatz*, and a terrible translation of Hasek, all of which had come piecemeal from a bookshop in New York's Greenwich Village: He wondered what his father would have made of them. They had each arrived wrapped in thick brown paper, with a short note from a Mr. Aberbach, the proprietor, thanking Goldah for his fine taste and encouraging him to choose his next from the list of soon-to-be acquired volumes. Mr. Aberbach wrote in a stylized German that bordered on the obsequious and allowed them both to think that such a world, distant as it was, might still exist. For Goldah its only remnants now sat on this shelf, alongside a series of Zane Grey titles and a few from Dashiell Hammett. The last in line was a well-kept first edition of Chandler's *The Big Sleep*. These had been gifts from Eva, chosen from her husband's favorites. Goldah wasn't much inspired by the Grey but he did like the hard, honest quality of the others. He thought: People don't really talk that way but wouldn't it be nice if they did? He heard the knock at the door and opened it. Eva stepped inside.

She had brought a box from Gottlieb's and set it on the table. She said, "I'll make us some tea. The hot kind, I know."

He followed her to the small kitchen, where she smiled when she saw the kettle over a low flame. He said, "It just needs to come to a boil."

She turned the flame up and said, "Always one step ahead."

"I never am. You know that."

She brought a hand to her eye and smoothed away a tear. "I'm afraid I'm getting ahead of myself, as well. We can do this quickly, if you want. I'm glad you called."

He said, "We can sit."

"It's almost boiling."

He hadn't expected it this way, standing in a doorway, her purse on her arm. How she managed her smile nearly broke him. He said, "She wants to go to Palestine."

Eva's shock lasted only a moment. "My goodness," she said. "That's certainly a long way to go."

"You don't really debate things with Malke once she's made up her mind."

"No," Eva said, "she certainly does speak plainly." Her eyes flashed and she said, "I ran into her...with Mrs. Jesler. Downtown. I felt it was right that I should introduce myself."

"And you came out unscathed?"

The smile still held, like a shattered mast suspended by its rigging. She said, "Do you need her?" Her eyes had grown red and she blinked the tears away. "I won't ask if you love her. I wouldn't want to know that. But if you need her, if she brings you something..." She opened her purse and pulled out a handkerchief. She shook her head and dabbed at her eyes. "I'm so sorry for this. I really am." He stepped toward her and she reached for the kettle. She said, "I think it should be all right now." The pot waited on the counter. "The leaves are inside?" He nodded and she poured. "We'll let it sit for a few minutes." She set the kettle back on the stove.

He said, "She's gotten it wrong, you know. She says she's come to save me."

This cut deeper than he expected. "Did she? I didn't know you were in need of saving."

"I'm not. I never have been. That's the strangest thing about what people see now." He never thought to tell her this; perhaps he had been foolish to believe he couldn't. "Those of us who came through it didn't need saving. We never did. We had saved ourselves in whatever ways we could long before anyone found us."

He saw her face as he had never seen it—masked and unknowable—waiting for him to step closer or to pull herself away if he should. He had no idea what she might do.

He said, "It's what I was before the camps that kept me alive inside of them, all those years learning to become numb, detached, watching from a distance. It's what allowed me to live beyond them, until now. You don't let me stand apart. Malke would, and she knows it, even if she can't admit it."

Uncertainty slipped across her face, a shadow of the loss that lay behind her eyes. When she stepped across to him and held him—pressing her cheek to his chest—he couldn't fathom how she was doing it, or why.

She said, "I don't let you. You're right. I never would."

He found himself wrapping his arms around her. Whatever words he imagined he could never say rose up from his chest only to be lost to the sharp ring of the telephone. It jolted them both and he felt her arms tighten. They stood there as it rang and rang until, finally, Eva said, "She won't hang up. You need to get it."

She let him go and he picked up.

"Ike?"

It was Jesler.

Goldah said, "This isn't a good time, Abe."

"You need to get over here. It's...You just need to get over here now."

———

Jesler had the door open before they were up the porch steps. His surprise at seeing Eva passed quickly as he ushered them inside. He said, "I'm guessing you know what this is about. I called the Kerns and the Fleischmanns. Pearl just needed the girls around."

They came to the parlor. The men were standing uncomfortably by the window, while Pearl sat between Fannie and Selma. She held a handkerchief in her lap, her eyes raw from crying. She stood wearily and went to Goldah, nestling herself into him for an embrace. Remarkably she reached out to Eva and squeezed her hand. Pearl said, "I'm so glad you're here, dear. I really am."

Goldah was about to ask the unthinkable when Jesler said, "We found it this morning. On the mantel." He was holding an envelope. "This one was addressed to us." He nodded toward the mantel. "That one's for you. She wasn't here when we found them."

Goldah saw his name written in Malke's hand on the second envelope. Jesler handed him the first. "You should probably read this one," he said, "but I don't know."

Goldah pulled the sheet from inside and began to read.

Dear Pearl and Abe,

I want to thank you for opening your house and for the charm you made in your welcome. You are people with great heart and feeling and I have great happiness to know you. Yitzhak Goldah ist sehr fortunate to have you as his family.

When I first come to your house I have such bad memory, things I do not know, things which are empty, but when I see the boy on the beach I begin to see other memorys. Then I know I am perhaps not the maiden Malke Posner, the betrothd to Yitzhak. I know this Malke Posner. She is dead in the Lager at the time I see a small boy who is killd. They die together. I remember this. I cannot know why I am thinking I am Malke Posner since this time. My mind has many troubles. I am asking you to forgive.

I want now to go to Palestine. I will explain this with the government office in Virginia. They are keeping my papers since the time I enter America. They will understand. I will go to Milton and Sophie Lubeck for help. I wish you not to worry. I am strong. I will go to Palestine.

I am also writing to Yitzhak Goldah. Please give him the letter.

You are gracious and I will never forget.

With heartlike greetings...

She had left no signature. Goldah read through it twice, stopping on the two words in German she had let slip through. Malke had always had trouble with "very"—such a simple thing, but she could never remember it. He knew she hadn't been aware...or perhaps she had.

Jesler said, "Have you ever heard of such a thing? I mean, after everything...in the recovery camps or—"

"No," said Goldah, then, "Once...perhaps. I don't know."

Pearl said, "That poor girl doesn't even know who she is. She could have stayed with us. She really could."

Goldah handed the letter to Eva. He stepped over and took the second envelope.

Jesler said, "Even you thought it was her, didn't you, Ike? I mean—"

"Yes," said Goldah, "I did." He opened the flap. The letter was in Czech. He read:

Yitzi,

They wouldn't understand so this way was easier. And, please, don't let them get in touch with the Lubecks or anyone official. Tell them you'll be the one to look into it. Then do nothing and be done with it—if for no other reason than I'd like to keep my name as it is.

You always said I was unpredictable, reckless. You thought you were charming saying it. You weren't. And you were wrong. You're wrong now if you think it. This is how it has to be, not because you feel for her or don't feel for me, even if you do feel something for me. (I don't think I could have endured you telling me that.) No, it's how I feel that matters. You might not believe this but I do love you. I always have. Very much. And I'm telling you this not out of malice or to cause you pain but because it breaks my heart.

Yes, it breaks my heart to know how much she loves you and how I would never be able to convince you I could give you even half as much. Can you imagine what it is to see that?

This feeling is so terrible in ways you cannot know, yet, even then, it tells me something I had forgotten, something far more important than any of this. It tells me I am no longer in that place.

I am no longer there.

If I can feel my heart breaking in this wretched way then somehow I have come back. You would say this is what any woman tells herself so she can know she is alive. I can hear you saying it even now but it makes no difference to me. To have this pain is to have hope. What a ghastly thing to say but, I suppose, that must be the final gift from the Lager. Pain as a blessing, as a promise. This, as well, is something these innocents could never understand.

In this way, you have given me back my life, unknowingly. I now save yours, and I do it willingly. Let yourself see that, Yitzi—for once—otherwise all of this will have been for nothing.

She told him not to worry; she told him she would find her way. She signed it with a small *m* as she always had, and Goldah heard Jesler behind him.

"Are you okay, Ike?"

Goldah nodded. He folded the letter and placed it in his pocket. Eva moved to him and handed him her handkerchief. He hadn't realized he needed it.

Jesler said, "Did she tell you about the real Miss Posner?"

Goldah was looking at Eva. She showed no relief, no joy, no concern. Hers was a look only for him, filled with such knowing and devotion that he felt himself for the first time rooted in this place.

"Yes," said Goldah. "She did. A very brave woman."

17

THE LAST HOUR among Congregation Mickve Israel—with its pipe organ and choir and chanted psalms and English—had taken more of a toll on Goldah than he cared to admit. Not that the morning had gotten off to a particularly promising start. Weiss had asked Goldah what he thought of the place and, on instinct, Goldah had said it was a beautiful shul. Instantly, a man seated directly in front of them had turned and said, "This is the temple, sir, not a shul. The temple."

Quite right, thought Goldah. A few minutes later he had been staring up at the ceiling—for what reason he couldn't recall—and noticed the broad crucifix design in thick wooden beams, inlaid across the vaulted arches. Quite right... quite right.

Now, ducking out in need of a break, he moved down the steps to the street and felt the swelter thicken around him with the scent of hydrangeas and gardenias. It was only a slight improvement over the tang of men's cologne that stifled the sanctuary air. Both carried an unwanted sweetness, although the flowers seemed strangely more ripe. It was something Malke would have noticed. So very American, she would have said, even the plant life here has a brashness to it.

Goldah moved across to the park at the center of the square where, mercifully, the trees were keeping the sunlight at bay.

It was as if Malke had never been here. All the questions yesterday—about who she might have been, where she had gone—all those cautious musings on the frailty of the mind, and so much consoling and encouragement, all of them settled with a simple "at least now you know." But hadn't he known before her arrival, or at least thought he had known? Somehow the truth about her death had ceased to be the truth, although for everyone else, the facts were now laid bare: She had died in the camp.

Goldah found himself by a bench, about to sit, when he noticed Calvin sitting at the other end: of all people, Calvin just sitting there, his eyes closed. Goldah was hesitant to disturb him but the coincidence seemed too good to pass up.

He stepped over and the eyes opened, and Calvin looked up. He said, "Hey there, Mr. Ike. You taking a break?"

It was as if he had been expecting him. Goldah said, "Have you been waiting for me?"

"Waiting on you? No, suh."

"You just like it here?"

"I like it fine. Can't stay too long, though. Somebody always coming along saying, 'Boy, what you doing here,' so I pick my moments. But ain't the reason I'm here."

Goldah thought to ask; instead he sat.

Calvin said, "It's the day for atoning, ain't it?"

"It is."

Calvin nodded, then looked out at the square. "I get the day off. Felt maybe I'd think a bit on atonement. This seemed the right place for it."

Goldah said lightly, "And what do you have to atone for, Calvin?"

"Ain't talking about me, Mr. Ike."

Goldah expected Calvin to turn to him but the eyes remained distant.

Calvin said, "I hear Miss Posner ain't in Savannah no more."

"That's right."

"Not really Miss Posner was it, though? That's a tough one."

"It is, yes."

"Easier on you, I guess, with Miss Eva. Hard all the same."

"Yes."

Goldah leaned forward and cupped his hands under the front slat of the bench. It was as if he was preparing to stand but couldn't quite bring himself to make the full effort.

Calvin said, "I like this square, Mr. Ike, I do. I like it real fine. I like how you can see down to the big park and the fountain, but you still here with your bench in the shade."

"It's very nice."

"It's these oaks that done it, winding all over the place." Calvin looked up at them as if he were giving the trees their due. "And all that moss hanging down. That's what makes it Savannah. Moss in all them trees."

"I've heard that, yes."

"Can't take it off them neither cause it's a living thing, the moss. That's a law, even if the tree all withered up. Can't even brush it away. You know that?"

"I didn't. No."

"Well now you do." Calvin's gaze had settled on a single oak across the park. He nodded over to it. "No worries on that one over there, though. You see it? Big one, thick, all them branches empty. No moss dragging it down. Must be where they lynched a man." Calvin looked at it a moment longer, then turned to Goldah. "That's what they say. Moss don't grow on trees with that kind a death on it. I guess that's another kind a law."

Goldah had no answer.

It looked as if Calvin might say something more but, instead, he turned again to the square and the two men sat in silence. When Calvin finally spoke, his voice was low and soft. "It's good what Mr. Jesler done. For Raymond. And I guess he picked the right time a year. Guess he's thinking he's atoning for all his sins. Easy to convince yourself you doing more than what you really doing—doing it for someone else and not yourself—but four percent, that ain't taking care a it, not by a long shot. Maybe I thought Jewish folk would understand that better than most."

Again Goldah said nothing. He realized it wasn't the words he was struggling to find; it was a way to understand his own feelings of impotence. Maybe, then, he had been writing about the wrong things for Weiss all along. And maybe that was something he could remedy.

"They'll understand it," he said.

"That so? Could be you alone in thinking that." Calvin's eyes settled again on the large, barren oak. "But that tree'll be here, be here with all them others long after you and me gone. And maybe most folks won't know about it and maybe they will. Or maybe they'll just want to forget what it is. But you and me, we'll know, Mr. Ike, won't we?"

"We will, yes."

Calvin moved himself out onto the edge of the bench. "Anyway," he said, "it's good how things working out. I'm happy for you. And I'm happy for Raymond, too." He saw a man making his way over and Calvin picked up his hat and stood. "I'll see you down at the store sometime."

Calvin set his hat on his head, tipped it to the man walking by, and headed for the street.

Goldah joined Eva at her parents' for the breaking of the fast. What they were breaking he wasn't quite sure of. The dining-room table was arrayed in heaping plates from one end to the other.

"I used to serve shrimp and grits," Peggy De la Parra said, ensconced on the living-room sofa and insisting that Goldah sit with her. "But Walter, my husband, he said he thought that showed a bit of sass, getting rid of all those sins and then...well. Not that Walter knew a kosher day in his life but I could understand his concern. I always kept a plate of it in the kitchen for my father, who would sneak away. I make a very fine shrimp and grits, and I wasn't going to deny my father that particular treat."

The rest of the guests milled about, a few of the faces now familiar to him, a future friendship or two lurking in the cordial smiles and firm handshakes. He wondered which of these might be rounding out an evening's foursome down the road. Eva had headed off to another part of the house with friends of her parents; she had left him in good hands.

Peggy said, "And I understand there was some confusion about the other young lady. I would have loved the chance to have met her."

Goldah truly believed she would have. He might have told her as much if not for the sudden appearance of the Jeslers in the hallway. They stood close to each other, like two new arrivals in a foreign land, willing but overwhelmed and waiting for an official nod of approval. Pearl held her purse tightly in both hands.

Goldah said, "I'm so sorry, Mrs. De la Parra. My cousins are here and I don't believe they know anyone." He stood. "If you'll excuse me."

"Of course," said Peggy. "And bring them over when you can. I'd love to meet them, as well."

Goldah made his way to them, surprised by Pearl's eager smile. She brought both hands to his face and drew him in for a kiss on the cheek. She said, "So you didn't waste away to nothing. I'm glad to see it."

Goldah decided to spare her the truth.

Jesler said, "Don't look so surprised, Ike. Was it wrong for us to come?"

"Not at all. Of course not. I'm just—"

"So are we," said Jesler, "but Arthur insisted. He said we'd probably be seeing a lot of each other in the future so why not start tonight. I can't say I don't agree with him." Jesler lurched, then reached back for one of the chairs that was lined up against the wall. "Oh dear. A little light-headed," he said. "I'm sorry." He sat.

Pearl was instantly by his side. "I told you you should have had a coffee at three. There's no sin in that, Abe. Goodness. Are you all right? You don't feel warm. What do you need, sweetheart? What do you need?"

"A little tea, maybe."

Goldah said, "I'll go get it."

"No, no, no," Pearl said. "You stay with Abe, in case he needs to be moved. I'll go find it myself. You just stay right here."

Her need to care for Abe trumped any feelings of awkwardness. Pearl bulled her way through the crowd, her radar fixed on pitchers and ice.

Goldah said, "I can get you an aspirin."

Jesler took hold of Goldah's arm and said, "There's no light-headedness, Ike. I just need to talk with you for a moment. Is that all right?" Goldah saw the look of concern. He took a seat and Jesler leaned into him to speak. "All this business with the port...all the...anyway the paper's not going to run it, I know. And I'm certainly in your debt for that, whichever way it is you managed it. Weiss told me there were rumors about something, my name coming up or some such thing, but he said they're completely unfounded, happens all the time." Jesler looked frail for a moment. He wiped his fingers across his upper lip.

Goldah said, "You're sure you're all right?"

"I'm fine. I'm fine. It's just I've...I've gotten myself into something, that's all. It's not the best thing, it's not the worst, but I shouldn't have gotten you involved in it in any way, and I'm..." The fingers now worked the brow. "I'm ashamed I did. And maybe I'm a little ashamed of what I'm doing, but you've got to make your way and I'm trying to figure it out, so if things get a little messy down the road..." He looked up and saw Pearl making her way back. "Anyway," he said more quickly. "I'll figure it out. Don't you worry about it. I just wanted to say how grateful I am." And from the depths of some hidden reserves, Jesler produced a warm and inviting smile, and a hand for the glass that Pearl was swooping in with.

"There's my angel," said Jesler.

"Drink it down, Abe. You look terrible."

"I'm fine. Don't worry. Just need to get something in me. Ike, you take Pearl to see Eva. Pearl has something for her. I'll stay here. I promise not to move."

Pearl said, "I'm not going anywhere."

"Yes you are. I'm fine. Take her, Ike. That'll make me feel loads better."

"You're sure?" said Goldah.

"I'm sure. Now the two of you just go."

Goldah got to his feet and Pearl instantly clung to his arm. Whatever boldness she had shown in getting the tea was gone.

"Don't you go anywhere, Ike," she said. "These aren't my people. I don't know anyone here."

"I don't know them, either."

"Well they certainly seem to know you."

Goldah turned to Jesler. "I'll take care of her." He then placed his hand on Pearl's arm and said, "Now let's go find Eva."

She was in the kitchen with Julian, dabbing at a stain on his shirt.

"It's fine, Jules," Eva said. "Grandma has other glasses and I promise I won't tell her."

Goldah said, "Hello there."

She turned, cloth in hand. "Well, hello. And Mrs. Jesler. You catch me—"

"It's Pearl, dear. Pearl. And here—why don't you let me do that. You have guests."

"You're one of them, Mrs. . . . . Pearl."

Pearl set her purse on the table. "My goodness, it's the simplest thing, unless your young man isn't comfortable with strangers."

Julian stuck out his hand. "My name is Julian De la Parra. I don't believe I've had the pleasure."

Pearl couldn't help but laugh and instantly took his hand. "Well, the pleasure is all mine, Mr. Julian De la Parra. My name is Mrs. Jesler but you may call me Miss Pearl, if you like. And how do we find ourselves in such a predicament?"

Julian said, "The glass was too close to the edge, Miss Pearl. I've been told before I have trouble remembering such things."

"Well, that's something we all have trouble with, isn't it? What a treat for me to meet such a polite young man." Pearl looked over at Eva. "And . . . I was going to give it to your mother, but since you're here." Pearl opened her purse and pulled out a baseball. "Is it all right?"

Eva said, "Oh, you shouldn't have."

"No, it's a pleasure. Please."

"How thoughtful. Jules, what do you say?"

Pearl handed the ball to the boy, and said, "Mr. Jesler and I have had that for quite some time. It's very special to us. Do you see the signature? That's Hank Greenberg. Hankus Pankus. He was a famous ballplayer and Jewish, just like all of us, except he could play baseball. Do you like it?"

Eva said, "Jules, sweetie, what do you say?"

"Wow," said the boy. He then remembered to look up. "Oh, yes, thank you, Miss Pearl. Is it for me to keep?"

"Well who else is it going to be for, except a fine young boy?" said Pearl. "Of course you keep it."

"Wow."

Pearl looked over at Ike. "Now you two go off and do whatever it is you need to do. I'll finish cleaning this up. It's no trouble at all. I'll be just fine, won't I, Mr. De la Parra?"

Julian looked up at his mother. He seemed completely at ease. Even Goldah was struck by the little man's comportment. Eva nodded and Julian said, "That means my mother said it was all right, Miss Pearl."

"Well that's fine, then."

Pearl took the cloth from Eva. She then pulled a chair over and sat and began to examine the stain. "Now let's take a look at that stain. You tell me all about baseball while we clean this up. Go on, you two. Just tell Abe where I am. He's probably already up and about if I know him. Now tell me, Julian—may I call you that—are we in school yet?"

Goldah might have stayed for the entire show but Eva was already leading him back through to the dining room. They

295

saw Jesler and her father talking and laughing, and Goldah assumed they would be heading over but Eva kept moving him to the hallway.

She said, "Everything's taken care of. Jules is staying here tonight. You need to come along with me."

———

They sat by the water's edge, a bit of cheese and bread and two bottles of beer behind them on the blanket. A band was playing up on the pavilion, the music distant yet full. To Goldah's ears it was a lush, incoherent sound that made the quiet patter of the waves all their own.

"Thick as thieves," Eva said. Her head was tilted back and she was staring up at the stars.

"Your father and Abe? Yes, they certainly seemed to be enjoying each other's company."

"Well, that's good."

"I suppose it is." Goldah watched something out on the water, a bird or a fish. He didn't know which.

She said, "You didn't have anything to do with that, did you?"

"The two of them? Does it matter?"

"No. But it was a good thing you did or didn't do."

Goldah saw it again. "You like the Jeslers?"

"Of course."

"It was very sweet, the ball." He sounded as if he might be trying to convince himself.

"It truly was." She turned to him. "Is something the matter?"

He thought a moment, about the way Jesler had talked, the desperation and the gratitude, but for what? Goldah knew he hadn't done it for Abe or for Pearl. He hadn't done it even for Eva. He had done it for himself. Calvin was right: That was always the way. And maybe it was time to do something for someone else.

Goldah shook his head. "They're good people."

"They are."

A sprinkling of surf sprayed up onto his legs and he thought of the first time he had seen this beach, how far it had stretched, the ocean endless against it. He wondered now, as perhaps a child would, if even a single drop of water had ever made it all the way across to some distant shore; better yet if it had found its way back.

Eva said, "Was she kind in the letter?"

"She was."

"It was a decent thing she did. More than decent. I wouldn't even know the word for it."

He took in a long breath; he had grown accustomed to the deep heat in his lungs and he thought of Malke, not as she was but as she had been and would be, in another distant land, this one barren and dry. He said, "I wouldn't have gone."

"You're sure of that?"

"I am."

"You had me wondering... And if she hadn't gone?"

"But she did."

"Yes."

He thought to look at her but instead stared out at the water. "It was such a simple thing. The self I'd made or the one you made of me. One to survive, the other to live. It took me some time to see the difference." Only then did he have the courage to turn to her.

She kissed him and waited for him to bring his arms around her. "We should go in." She was already getting to her feet. "I brought suits, although I think we could chance it in our skivvies." She glanced quickly around and reached for the zipper on her dress.

"Dipping?" he said.

"Not quite."

She stood there, quietly watching him, this time content not to find any words. Reaching down, she pulled him up and waited as he removed his shirt and trousers. She then took his hand and together they dove under, sheltered within these shores and certain to find the surface again.

Author's Note

The story of the Jews in Savannah is, to some degree, the story of Savannah itself. When the port was first founded in 1733, it was seen as a sort of landing spot for English castoffs—what the original charter referred to as "the meanest and most unfortunate of our people." Not surprisingly, a group of Spanish and Portuguese Jews, who had fled to London seven years earlier and who were now members of the Sephardic congregation at Bevis Marks Synagogue (still thriving today), were encouraged to set sail.

The idea of Georgia had first been conceived by a former member of Parliament and a prison-reform activist named James Edward Oglethorpe. Oglethorpe saw the New World as a place that could be guided by the most noble of sentiments—*non sibi sed aliis* (not for self, but for others). The charter thus forbade liquor, large landholdings, and slavery in this new Eden for the "worthy poor."

It was with considerable hope, then, that the Bevis Marks Jews, along with two German Jewish families, boarded the *William and Sarah* and arrived in Savannah in July 1733.

Arrived, yes, but landed, no.

The stories that document the first weeks of the Jews in Savannah are many, but they all involve Oglethorpe (welcoming or hesitant), an outbreak of yellow fever (or malaria), and a doctor by the name of Nunez (or Nunes or Nunis, depending on the source). Whatever the exact details, the basics remain: When the city's only doctor fell victim to the fever, and with the Jews still waiting out in the harbor—urged by some to sail off to wherever wayward Jews were meant to sail—Oglethorpe had no choice but to allow Dr. Nunez to disembark in order to tend to the sick. With Nunez came the remaining forty-one Jews and a Torah that, as it happens, remains the oldest in North America.

Over the next two hundred years, the Jews thrived, fled, and returned. The arrival of the Spanish only a few hundred miles to the south in 1739, during the War of Jenkins' Ear, had many of the first colonists heading north (to Charleston) for fear of being burned as heretics should the Spaniards take Savannah. Meanwhile, as the city evolved into a great port, the antislavery dream quickly gave way to financial expedience. And the Jewish community changed as well. Reformism replaced Levantine Sephardic practices and, with the influx of Poles, Czechs, and Russians, the classic dividing lines between German Enlightenment and Eastern European Orthodox/Conservative Jewry were drawn. Thus, by 1947 the separate camps were well entrenched.

Interestingly enough, there was *one* source of agreement between the Reform and Orthodox communities at the time: their attitudes toward the impending State of Israel. Neither wanted it. It was the Conservative Jews alone who embraced Zionism. The Orthodox rejected it on liturgical grounds—the Jewish people had yet to be redeemed—and the Reform didn't want anything that might undermine their aim at assimilation, since a state for the Jews would only make them stand out. It remains one of the strangest moments of confluence in the American Jewish experience.

Internal struggles aside, the Jewish community as a whole had already become an integral part of Savannah society, situated in the ever-fluid hierarchy of American immigrant culture. They had their own businesses, their own clubs, their own politics—Herman Myers was the first Jewish mayor, elected in 1895—and their own neighborhoods. And yet they were Southerners through and through. How that impacted their relationship with the African-American community is one of the inspirations for this novel.

Today the internal wounds have healed. The three Jewish communities coexist in ways that most other cities would envy, so much so that the Reform and Conservative congregations share a Hebrew school. And everywhere one looks there are reminders of how vital the Jewish community has been to the city: from the shop names along Broughton Street, to the majestic design of the Congregation Mickve Israel synagogue (consecrated in 1878), even to the student center at one of the leading design universities in the world, Savannah College of Art and Design. The building once housed the Orthodox synagogue. Now, if you visit, take a look at its ceiling. You'll see one of the most remarkable Stars of David depicted in the stained-glass window—just one more reminder of the enduring legacy of the Jews in Savannah.

Acknowledgments

I wish to thank Richard Babcock, Susannah Bailin, Yvonne Cárdenas, Judythe Cohen, Marjorie DeWitt, Kathleen DiGrado, Gioia Diliberto, Ariel Felton, Lee Griffith, Nova Jacobs, Morton Janklow, Jeannie Kaminsky, James Lough, Andra Rabb, Jeremy Rabb, Tamar Rabb, Theodore Rabb, Peter Spiegler, Ashley Waldvogel, and the late Ethyl Rosenzweig, Francis Wagger, and Larry Wagger, for all their insights and inspiration.

I would also like to thank the Savannah Jewish Archive and the Georgia Historical Society.

And finally I thank Judith Gurewich for her tenacity, sensitivity, and wit. Her commitment to this book and to the editing process has been nothing less than a marvel.

JONATHAN RABB is an American novelist, essayist, actor, and writer. He is the author of five novels: *The Overseer, The Book of Q,* and The Berlin Trilogy (*Rosa, Shadow and Light,* and *The Second Son*), a critically acclaimed series of historical thrillers set in Berlin and Barcelona between the world wars. *Rosa* won the 2006 Director's Special Prize at Spain's Semana Negra festival, and was named one of *January Magazine*'s Best Books of 2005. Rabb has taught at Columbia University, New York University, and the 92nd Street Y, and is currently a professor in the writing department at the Savannah College of Art and Design.

⚡ OTHER PRESS

You might also enjoy these titles from our list:

THE GLASS ROOM by Simon Mawer
A FINALIST FOR THE MAN BOOKER PRIZE

A stunning portrait of a family trying to impose order and beauty on a world on the brink of chaos at the outbreak of World War II

"Achieves what all great novels must: the creation of an utterly absorbing world the reader can scarcely bear to leave. Exciting, profoundly affecting, and altogether wonderful." —*Daily Mail*

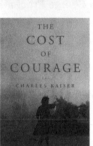

THE COST OF COURAGE by Charles Kaiser
The true story of the three youngest children of a bourgeois Catholic family who worked together in the French Resistance

"A thorough and quite accessible history of Europe's six-year murderous paroxysm... *The Cost of Courage* documents, through the life of an extraordinary family, one of the twentieth century's most fascinating events — the German occupation of the City of Light." —*Wall Street Journal*

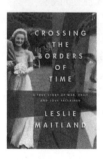

CROSSING THE BORDERS OF TIME
by Leslie Maitland
A dramatic true story of World War II, exile, and love lost — then reclaimed

"*Schindler's List* meets *Casablanca* in this tale of a daughter's epic search for her mother's prewar beau — fifty years later." —*Good Housekeeping*

Also recommended:

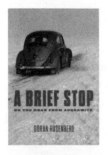

A BRIEF STOP ON THE ROAD FROM AUSCHWITZ by Göran Rosenberg
WINNER OF THE AUGUST PRIZE

A shattering memoir about a father's attempt to survive the aftermath of Auschwitz

"A towering and wondrous work about memory and experience, exquisitely crafted, humane, generous, devastating, yet somehow also hopeful."
—*Financial Times*

THE IMPOSSIBLE EXILE: STEFAN ZWEIG AT THE END OF THE WORLD by George Prochnik

An original study of exile, told through the biography of Austrian writer Stefan Zweig

"Subtle, prodigiously researched, and enduringly human throughout, *The Impossible Exile* is a portrait of a man and of his endless flight." —*The Economist*

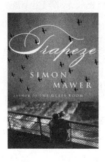

TRAPEZE by Simon Mawer

A propulsive novel of World War II espionage that introduces Marian Sutro, heroine of *Tightrope*

"The book is full of the fascinating minutiae of espionage — aircraft drops, code-cracking, double agents, scrambled radio messages. There's a romance, too…Mawer exhibits a great feeling for suspense, and produces memorable episodes in dark alleyways, deserted cafes, and shadowy corners of Père Lachaise." —*New Yorker*

OTHER PRESS　　　*www.otherpress.com*